ONLOOKERS

In her new book, set against the same background and re-introducing some of the same characters of her last, *The Lost Railway*, Gillian Avery explores very different themes. The novel centres on a mid-Victorian diary kept by a young woman of rare sensibility and powers of expression, living out of the world, intensely aware of the changing seasons and of a small, closed circle of acquaintances.

When the story opens, in the nineteen-eighties, a literary society formed to honour the diarist has commissioned a new edition from a young and rather prickly academic. It soon becomes plain that his editorial problems are by no means confined to the remote period and place that exert such a fascination on the readers of a less tranquil age. In her observation of the local enthusiasts and of the university dons who run the society Gillian Avery achieves scenes and characters with a sharpness that is all the more memorable for its absence of malice.

From the controversies and ruffled feelings of the twentieth century we plunge back into the real life that the diary chronicles. Every diarist is an onlooker. In the subtly bi-focal view we see the process extended, the onlooker onlooked, and can enjoy the comedy of multiple errors.

As always Gillian Avery writes with simplicity and grace and with that rare sense of period and atmosphere that can only be distilled from a combination of knowledge and imagination.

by the same author

THE LOST RAILWAY

ONLOOKERS

Gillian Avery

COLLINS
8 Grafton Street, London W1
1983

William Collins Sons & Co Ltd
London . Glasgow . Sydney . Auckland
Toronto . Johannesburg

British Library CIP data

Avery, Gillian
Onlookers.
I. Title
823'.914[F]   PR6051.V/

First published 1983
© Gillian Avery 1983

ISBN 0 00 222673 1

Set in Linotron Sabon by
Rowland Phototypesetting Ltd
Bury St Edmunds, Suffolk
Made and Printed in Great Britain by
William Collins Sons & Co Ltd Glasgow

To Lyndall Gordon

PART ONE

Chapter 1

SEPTEMBER

The church was surprising; one would not have expected to encounter the French Gothic manner in Radnorshire. Admittedly it is a county of Victorian churches, but all of them put together in the barest, plainest style, since there has always been in that part of the country a dearth both of prosperity and of large landowners who might have been expected to finance something more elaborate. Besides the Welsh, like all Celts, have little concern with the visual arts. Mairwood church might not have looked foreign in north Oxford say, or in a London suburb; here, standing surrounded by hills, the gaunt three-storied farm the only building in sight, it seemed almost freakish.

It was large for one thing (large, that is, for a rural parish that appeared to hold only two dwellings – the farm and the big house a few hundred yards back down the lane). And it was elaborate in design, cruciform with a central tower and a pyramidal spire whose formidable expanses of blue Welsh slate were broken by the steep gables over the tower windows, elegant with their pierced stonework. The staircase turret with its sharp-pitched roof like a dunce's cap gave a decidedly foreign air. There was also an apse, and a rose window in the transept that faced towards the lane.

'Where does the congregation come from?' said Jennifer Hancock. 'There was nowhere we passed within walking distance.'

'They don't. I think you'll find the answer to be precisely that. Look, the Warden's Bentley. I never thought he'd come to a bun-fight like this.'

She turned to look. High, black, with severe sculptured lines, it stood a little apart, an elderly roué among the anonymous rabble of Escorts and Cortinas parked in the lane. But she sensed that Trevor was holding back. 'Come on, we'll be late. Anyway, it may not be his.'

'Of course it is. You seem to forget I studied it and its occupant for five years. The turntable that he had for getting the bloody thing out of the college into Canterbury Lane was slap opposite my window.'

They went up the steps into the churchyard. Ahead of them a line of the late middle-aged moved slowly down the path, husband and wife mostly, but sometimes women together. Each pair would pause at the porch before disappearing within.

'I told you how it would be. Everybody's wearing a suit but you.'

'Or a smart blue blazer with a crest and brass buttons. You'd like to see me in that, I daresay, like your frightful uncles.'

'I don't mind. It's just that I'd have thought proper clothes would have given you more presence.'

'The Warden would have been very disappointed if I'd failed him over this. He always wrote me off as a hopeless tearaway, a north country oaf who deliberately set out to flout all conventions.'

'But you could have worn a tie.'

'Oh stop your nattering. It's too late by three or four hours because you know I haven't got one with me. Look, this must be Edgar Wittering ahead – him of all that correspondence.'

Outside the porch, smooth-faced, neat and balding – it could only be the figure of one of the society's officials. For every couple he had a ready word, a clap on the shoulder, or a handshake.

'That's his wife next to him. What do you bet her name's Mabel?'

'Doris.'

Embossed crimplene in dusky pink, navy blazer, had passed into the shadows ahead. There was now no one between them and the Witterings. Trevor braced himself. He was, Jennifer knew, ill at ease, uncertain of his status. His book might have been momentarily successful, well-noticed, but he was not sure how much he could rely on its reputation to carry him through social situations such as this.

'Trevor Hancock,' he mumbled, stepping forward. 'And my wife Jennifer.'

The shining pink face creased with smiles. 'Mr Hancock! This is a very great pleasure – we were beginning to wonder whether you were going to be able to make it – as you were just that bit doubtful when you wrote. And this is my wife Irene.' He gave the word only two syllables. The large and floral lady beside him nodded with happy though mute amiability. 'Well, Mr Hancock, I think I can safely say that your long journey is going to be well worthwhile. There is splendid news, our President is here after all. When I asked him last year he thought he was so busy that he did not think there was the remotest chance. I accepted this with many regrets and did not raise the point again for I know full well how many calls there are upon him. Then like the bit of blue that suddenly appears in a dull sky and heralds finer weather – I heard last month that he *thought* he might be able to come after all. So I wrote to him at once to ask if he could *really* manage it, and if so, if he would read one of the lessons. And the answer was 'yes' and he is really here. And not only Mr Tosswell but Dr Adeane who is the principal of your own college, am I not right?'

'The Warden.'

'Yes, the Warden of Canterbury College. And in addition to all this we have secured the presence of Miss Gwynneth Rhys-Williams to sing. And the Vicar of St Barnabas, Pimlico, who is to give the address and tell us something of the Tractarian ideals that inspired this beautiful church. You know how, of course, Louise's Edward was much influenced by James Skinner who at one time was Vicar of St Barnabas? We always strive for a connection like that. So all in all it is going to be a very special occasion. Now I won't keep you any longer, but of course we will meet again at the Knulle assembly. There will be more delight there for our President has agreed to read from the Journal. And I think, though of course it would be rash of me to promise, that I *may* be able to persuade him to read from the Louise poems. Several of our members have asked me if I thought he would, and I have told them that it is not for me to say, but that I have the very warmest hopes that Mr Tosswell will allow himself to be persuaded.'

Inside the church there was a shock of surprise, first from the chilliness, then from the dark. It was not that they stepped in from a particularly bright afternoon; on the contrary the sky was heavy with cloud and there had been rain earlier. But the windows with their dense glass let in very little light, so little that the Hancocks paused uncertainly by the door. But not for long. Mr Wittering spoke over their shoulder, in suitably hushed though commanding tones.

'Mrs Pritchard, Mr and Mrs Hancock. Take them to the transept. Irene and I will be coming in very shortly but we just want to make sure there are no more latecomers.'

The transept seemed to be the place of honour. Sitting four or five pews back they could make out in front of well-known white head and beside it the iron-grey curls – a juxtaposition very familiar in Oxford. They exchanged knowing looks.

'Since when has the Warden been a doctor?' Jennifer whispered.

'Of course he isn't.'

'They've put you at High Table. With him and Tossers.'

'And without a tie. That'll please A. A. no end, he loves carrying on about what the young wear these days, or fail to wear.'

The Witterings now edged themselves into the transept, pausing first to whisper deferentially to Tosswell and Adeane and then hovering over various occupants of pews behind. But at last even Mr Wittering was seated.

'You have a service order?' He leaned over between Trevor and Jennifer. Trevor held up the xeroxed sheet.

'Good, good. We could have found you one, of course. I always have plenty of spares – so many like to send them to absent friends. Such a full church, most gratifying. I don't know when I have seen a better turnout, though of course our numbers are increasing all the time.'

The start of the service silenced Mr Wittering, though his voice was at their shoulder as the clergy advanced from the vestry. 'We used the 1662 Prayer Book as you will see. You young people may be all in favour of the later alternatives, but they would be quite out of place here.'

At least, thought Jennifer, it gave them an excuse for their conspicuous unfamiliarity with the Anglican rite. Trevor would have despised this attitude as sycophancy, but she came from a less robust background, and she was aware that she, like the rest of her family, was always struggling genteelly to do the right thing. Beside her, Trevor made little effort to join in the service, but from the pew behind they could hear the voice of Mr Wittering ringing out confidently in the psalms and canticles, and leading the responses. She did not feel under any obligation to attempt to listen to the address; she had acquired from chapel youth an ability to switch off any sermon, however noisy or prolix. She observed the cleric who ascended into the pulpit to be a mannered little man with over-elaborate gestures, and settled back to study the church.

It was evident that whoever had built it had spared no expense. The stone pulpit, carved with reliefs, stood on marble columns, the clustered columns of the chancel arch were of marble too, and the carved foliage of the capitals was the work of no ordinary country mason. The pews they sat in were oak of an elegant austerity. There was nothing visible that the prejudiced might dismiss as unpleasingly Victorian. The glass in the transept opposite was of high quality, the rose window was broken into small roundels in which ruby reds and clear blues predominated. It seemed to depict the Creation; she thought she could detect the finger of the hand of God in the centre, and there were beasts and birds elsewhere.

The descent of the preacher from the pulpit passed her by, but the arrival of Miss Gwynneth Rhys-Williams on the chancel steps did not, for Mr Wittering leaned forward to put them in the picture. 'I have had very good reports. I have not actually heard her myself, but members tell me she is well thought of, and when she wrote to offer her contribution I accepted with alacrity.'

Miss Rhys-Williams, large and much-beaded, sang 'Where'er you walk', and 'Waft her, angels'. She was no Handelian and her voice was unpleasantly breathy. Jennifer with a chapel background had encountered this sort of thing many times, but Trevor came from a family both more godless and more musical; his outrage was palpable.

'So appropriate,' murmured Mr Wittering close by their ear. 'She could not have chosen better.'

Trevor's hand on her thigh clamped Jennifer to her seat at the end. 'For God's sake don't hurry out. I don't want to be tripping over the Tosser and the Warden. Give them a chance to get away first.'

The congregation trickled out. The trample of feet ceased, there was a happy hum of voices outside, emptiness and silence within. Trevor removed his hand. 'Now we look at the church.'

It was even more splendid than could have been guessed from the transept. The chancel walls were inlaid with marble, the sedilia had a carved canopy, there was a stone altar with a fine relief of the crucifixion.

'There's Irene behind you. Keep on looking.'

But Mrs Wittering had come, it seemed, expressly to devote herself to them. Mild-eyed behind the upswept frames of her glasses, whose dressiness seemed to belie her personality, she was yet stern of purpose. They were called on to admire the cedar roof, the stone vaulting in the sanctuary, the gilded pipes of the little organ in the north transept – everything, they were told, of such good quality that even after decades of disuse the fabric was still in good order.

'Is it only used for this service?'

'I think they have a monthly service in the summer season. The people in the farm look after it, they are very devoted. They always do the flower arrangements for us. Some of our members have asked whether they could take it on, we have some very keen flower arrangers. But we don't want any feelings hurt so we leave it as it is.'

14

Mrs Wittering, with an unexpected sense of the dramatic, had kept the best for the last. 'And this is the Louise window.' There was a detectable note of emotion in her voice as she indicated the rose window at the west end. It was larger than either of those in the transepts and perhaps the most magnificent of all, brilliant with blues and sea-greens. The centre roundel showed the Annunciation, a glowing bronze-robed angel beside a Virgin in white and yellow, both with bowed heads, and behind, hills and a hazy smoke-blue sky through which rays of light struck down.

'"The sunbeam strikes throughout the world."'

'Yes,' said Mrs Wittering approvingly. 'I'm glad you spotted that. Edgar would know just where it comes, of course, but that's what I always think of when I see the window. And the sun does break through the clouds just like that when you are up on Radnor Forest. I always think they were so clever the way they managed to suggest cloud in the glass.'

'But why,' said Jennifer boldly, 'the Louise window? Is it dedicated to her?'

If Mrs Wittering was surprised by the ignorance that such a question displayed the mild eyes did not show it. 'The Virgin was drawn from her. Mr Hancock will spot the likeness at once when he sees the photographs. Edgar and I did think that it would be a very good picture to have on the cover of the book – Louise *and* the hills.'

Trevor condescended no reply but stared up at the Virgin. Certainly there was something a little secular about the face, a hint of a smile, and, unusually, the hair that streamed out under the circlet of flowers was tawny-coloured.

'She seems an attractive young woman.'

Mrs Wittering here did allow a faint expression of surprise at such a tritely obvious remark. 'She was very beautiful.'

'And she is buried somewhere near here?' Trevor surveyed the walls.

'No, that tablet over there is to Edward Benbow, her husband, who of course built the church. And near it a plaque to his four sisters who died of scarlet fever when they

were young. And beyond that a tablet to Margaret Talbot –
you will remember the name from the Journal, the daughter
of the Rector of Ludwardine.'

'The brown house-mouse?' said Trevor after an effort.

'Yes. She wrote a number of children's books. One of our
members managed to find one of them and wrote about it in
our Proceedings.'

'What was she doing here?'

'She came to live near here. In one of those cottages on the
Gletton road.'

'Then Louise Fleming is buried in the churchyard? Or
should we call her Louise Benbow?'

'Fleming,' said Mrs Wittering almost sternly. 'The Journal was written before her marriage. No, she is not buried in
this country. She died in Nice.'

'In Nice? I'm sorry, I'm ignorant about Fleming background as yet. I'll be getting it up of course, but for the
moment all I know is the Journal.'

'Dr Adeane mentions it in the introduction.' Mrs Wittering tactfully lowered her eyes to that they should not witness
her interlocutor's shame. 'She spent most of her later years
there. For health reasons.'

'Yet she seemed so robust when she wrote the Journal. All
those mammoth rides and walks over the hills. Like
Dorothy Wordsworth.' He put this in hoping to please. But
Mrs Wittering ignored the attempt at flattery. Or more
probably, accepted the comparison as a cliché.

'Her constitution was not at all strong,' she said severely.
'She had a very poor heredity. And a brother who died of
consumption.'

'We haven't showed up too well.' They were sitting, an
hour later, in the undoubtedly very beautiful garden at
Knulle Court. 'In fact you are probably being reported to
Mr Wittering at this very minute. You shouldn't have talked
about "getting up the Fleming background." It sounds
irreverent and off-hand.'

It was unwise of Jennifer. Trevor was already ruffled by a
feeling of having made a poor showing. She would have
done much better to have tried to soothe his *amour-propre*.

But even after five years' experience of him she was still taken in by his outward attitude of brusque self-sufficiency.

'Damn the Witterings. This frightful creeping what-will-the-neighbours-think – aren't you ever going to grow out of it! Everybody here can think that Louise Fleming is the queen of all diarists and all sweetness and light besides, but there's no reason for me to pander to it too. Or you, for that matter.'

In anger, Trevor was never a respector of place. Wherever he was he behaved exactly as he might by his own kitchen sink. Nor could he be easily subdued. Tact, argument, total silence, none of these would ever deflect him; he habitually went on until his anger blew itself out, oblivious of all auditors except the one with whom he was immediately concerned. He was certainly oblivious of Mr Wittering's approach, though Jennifer was not. She put her hand on his arm and frowned, and then turned to smile in as unaffected a manner as she could muster, wondering how much had been overheard. But Mr Wittering's genial face betrayed nothing.

'Now I am coming to take Mr Hancock away from you. Some of our members have seen reviews of his book and are anxious to meet him, and as always we have a tight schedule and so much to be fitted in. I can allow half an hour more of informality before we get on to the next items on the agenda. Mrs Hancock, would you like to join one of the parties that is going back to Mairwood? We have been given special permission to go inside the house and see the organ. It is the only room that remains structurally as it was and it is a great opportunity.'

'I think that as it is so fine now, and such a beautiful garden . . .'

'Yes, it is tempting to sit in the sun now that it has at last come out. But I knew it would, it has never failed us yet for our day of Remembrance. And I daresay you will have another chance to see the organ when Mr Hancock begins work on his book.'

As Trevor, still flushed with anger, was led away, Jennifer reflected that resolute amiability was obviously a way to silence him. Though it probably wouldn't work if a wife practised it. She sat on, staring about her. It was a lovely place. The seventeenth century stone house was behind her. Here, below the terrace, lawns swept down to the swift shallow river, beyond which, through the fringe of alders, there was a glimpse of sunlit meadow. Groups moved round the garden, some drawn by the river, others admiring the borders, and the clematis which climbed up poles. The heat of the sun was mellow, not oppressive, and even from a distance she could sense the contentment of the members of the Fleming Society; tea might be behind them but there were glories still ahead. Trevor's ill-temper had been an intrusion.

'Mrs Hancock, I'd like you to meet Mrs Gorton from Hereford.' Jennifer who had been blinking drowsily, started up. Mr Wittering was there, with a birdlike little lady whose delicate froth of curls was tinted pale strawberry. 'Now if you will excuse me I must just run away to finalize arrangements with our President. Mrs Gorton is one of our founder members and a most regular attender of all our functions.'

They smiled at each other uneasily. 'Such a beautiful afternoon', said the strawberry curls bravely, 'after this wet summer. But then September does often turn out fine and we've always been so lucky. And such a lovely place. You can see why Louise had that feeling about the Ludd valley. It does seem to be shut off from the world, doesn't it. Did you go to see the organ?'

'No.' She searched for a reason why she had not but could find none. 'Did you?'

'I saw it last year at the concert. One of our members has a daughter who is studying music and she did a lot of work to find out the things that Louise might have played on it. She sang the 'Lost Chord', you know, and some hymns. And played polkas, of course. She had put on Victorian costume, it really was such a pretty sight. It was almost as good as the TV programme. I expect you saw that. Two years ago. Or perhaps it was three. The years slip by so fast I can't count.'

'No, I'm afraid we didn't see it.'

'Oh they did it beautifully. Some of us were rather

worried that they might spoil it, put in things that weren't there. Like they did with Kilvert's Diaries, though that wasn't at all bad when you think what they could have done. Some of the society took part dressed up. They didn't have to say anything, they were just there. Mr Wittering was there, in the church for Louise's wedding. Of course the Journal doesn't go as far as the wedding, but I think they wanted to get in the church, finished. Because there's so much about the building of it that it really would be a shame not to let people see what it was like in the end, wouldn't it. But the people who made the serial had been so careful, they'd used the photographs, you really would have thought you were back in Victorian times. It is your husband who's going to write about the photos, isn't it? I think that's what Mr Wittering said.'

'Yes, though so far he hasn't seen them.'

'Oh, he hasn't seen them.'

'You have, then?'

'Oh yes, we all know them quite well. They were taken by Arthur Proctor who lived here at Knulle Court. The society made slides from them which they show at lectures. And copies have been available to members for quite a long time.' There was now an interrogatory silence; it was up to Jennifer to justify herself – or rather, Trevor.

'It's a project of Stern and Chantrey's,' she began lamely. 'The firm that published the Fleming Journal.'

'Of course.' The little lady clearly did not need to be reminded of that.

'They are also my husband's publishers. He has written a book about diaries and so I suppose they thought he might take on something about this diarist. Publishers get ideas like this.'

'Yes, I suppose they do.' Clearly the ways of publishers were too impossibly tortuous to attempt to disentangle. There was a long pause. 'Some of us had hoped that perhaps Mr Tosswell . . . or Dr Adeane . . . ?'

It was merciful that Trevor was not here; perhaps it would not have been said to him. 'I suppose they thought that they could not take on that amount of work. Mr

Adeane may feel that it is really not his line.' She naturally did not add that it was not Trevor's either, but that at his age and in his position one gratefully snapped up such crumbs as were dropped from the rich man's table.

'But Dr Adeane's introduction to the Journal was so beautifully put, don't you think?'

It was. Antony Adeane carried literary style to a high pinnacle of perfection. Trevor had once remarked savagely that he concealed his interior vacuum with it, as Americans concealed ignorance by jargon. The elegance was never wordy; a classical education had given him a passion for succinct clarity – the lack of which in contemporary prose he habitually and monotonously deplored. Undergraduates remembered his comments on their essays which he would dismember before them, plucking out unnecessary verbiage until it seemed nothing was left. He had also a musical ear, his sentences were beautifully balanced and flowed with a seemingly uncontrived grace.

The introduction to the Fleming Journal had in fact told the reader very little. It described how Henry Tosswell had found the four exercise books tied together with ribbon, in a Hay-on-Wye bookshop in a lot which the young assistant thought, though he was vague, had come from an auction in a Hereford saleroom; how the Louise poems had been written first, and how only after the publication of these had it been realized that the Journal from which the inspiration had been derived was in itself worth publishing. The rest of the introduction had been a delicate tribute to the personality of the writer (Antony Adeane could find himself attracted to women on the printed page), and such facts as there were were mostly taken from the pages of the Journal.

None of this, of course, could Jennifer say; it was clear that the pronouncements of both Tosswell and Adeane were treated as holy writ. But the little lady seemed to decide that perhaps she had been ungracious, that upon such an occasion as this it behoved the Fleming Society, as hosts, to be generous to outsiders, however crass.

'You say that your husband has written a book about diaries.'

'Yes, he did.' Jennifer, nettled by this time, would have liked to be able to indicate that it had made quite an impact in the right circles, had been accorded lengthy and serious discussion in the sort of literary journals that would never reach the Fleming Society.

'What a delightful subject.'

The adjective made it abundantly clear what unbridgable abysses lay between Trevor's writing and what members of the society liked to read. 'He found it very absorbing,' she said guardedly.

'Pepys and Boswell and Kilvert?'

'Not so much those.' (In fact they had been only accorded a dismissive line or two.) 'The book was called *The Inward Eye*. It was about the more introspective writers – Gide and Kierkegaard and Kafka.' Mrs Gorton could be felt to reel under the impact of the aweful foreignness of the names. 'I suppose it's rather a difficult book.' Some of the phrases she had typed for Trevor sprang to her mind – id-rapture and diachronic observation, Kafka's ego-defeat, Kierkegaard's ontological view of the self. She was tempted to spray them over Mrs Gorton and see what would happen.

But Mrs Gorton was unnerved enough. 'I'm afraid I don't read anybody like that. Like Kafka, I mean.' (She had evidently seized on the one name she recognized.) 'Was the Louise Journal published in time for your husband to write about it?'

'He didn't. I'm afraid. Somebody should write a book about the diarists who describe a society – like Pepys and Kilvert – and Louise Fleming, I suppose.'

She had included the last as an afterthought; Mrs Gorton ignored the slight. 'Yes, Dr Adeane could do it so beautifully. It is really a pity he doesn't write more.'

Here was Jennifer's chance. Having listened to Trevor on the subject for five years she could have lectured Mrs Gorton on the Warden's obsessive fastidiousness, his horror of exposing himself to criticism, his extreme reluctance to commit himself on paper. She felt that, married to a former member of the college over which Antony Adeane presided, she had more rights in the matter than the Fleming Society who appeared to treat him as their own particular possession. But she knew that it would be regarded as blasphemy.

'Still,' said Mrs Gorton generously, 'he must have a lot to do running the college. Did Mr Wittering say that it was your husband's own college?'

'He was an undergraduate there and then a research fellow.' (But Jennifer despised herself for the emphasis he had put on those last two words.) 'He teaches at Bradford now.'

'I expect he misses Oxford, doesn't he. I've been there quite a few times. In fact I was there only in May with the Over-Sixties. I asked the porter at Canterbury College to show me the little cottage in the grounds where Mr Tosswell lives. I couldn't go away without seeing that. It seems so right that he should come back to Oxford in the end. Well, I say the end but of course it's more like a beginning – the Louise poems, I mean. And a poet ought to live in Oxford, oughtn't he. The history in all those stones! All those famous people who've walked over them. It must have been sad for your husband to leave.'

It had been, and Trevor, she sensed, always had his head turned over his shoulder, looking back at it. The first year after he left he had spoken of it as though it were still home and he would be returning. Now, though he gave himself out to be a permanent and willing exile, was scornful of its complacent self-absorption, she knew that Oxford had only to lift a finger of encouragement and he would leap on to the next train, to crouch in a cellar and subsist on baked beans, if need be, provided only he was given a foothold there.

But the approach of Trevor himself meant that none of this was ever said. Both women turned their heads with a certain apprehension, Mrs Gorton visibly daunted by the proximity of one who was said to expound the dark mysteries of Kafka, Jennifer wondering whether his black mood had been exacerbated by exposure to members of the society.

'Well,' he said. 'Hard pounding.' It was a phrase, Jennifer knew, only uttered during spells of good humour. Mrs Gorton tactfully disappeared.

22

'Who was that old bird?'

'Just a member. From Hereford. She thinks that A.A. is utterly utter.'

'They all do. But in front of the Tosser they nearly faint with emotion. Our Edgar treats him like some sort of pope, backs away from the presence.'

'It's funny. I haven't seen such respectable people since chapel days. Don't any of them know anything about his past – what most of his poetry is *about*?'

'That's all years ago, they won't have read any of that. And his memoirs are incredibly discreet – nothing in them that might not have happened to Wittering, well, not much anyway. The poems you're talking about would have seemed impenetrably "modern" – they'd have been scared off by the sight of the first line. The things that he's writing now in his dotage, now that he's a reformed character – the Louise poems and that – well, the literary wallahs may think they're a load of crap – soft in the centre – what have you, but Flemingites and their like get shudders of ecstacy, thinking that they are in the van of the modern movement, actually enjoying Tosswell.'

'Have you gone and how-do-you-dooed him? You can't go on skulking and lurking forever.'

'Well I did, Edgar saw to it that I did. I was even allowed to jump the queue. Two queues, one for A.A., one for the Tosser. They were both complimentary, said they'd enjoyed the book.'

So this was why he was in such a good humour. Aloud she said that they had better go and settle themselves, that Mr Wittering was visibly fretting.

The gathering of fifty or so had now grouped themselves in an expectant half circle on the grass, facing the house. On the steps leading up to the terrace stood Mr Wittering, behind him Tosswell, perhaps a little ill at ease, leaning against the stone urn that crowned the parapet. Half a dozen cameras were levelled in his direction, Mr Wittering gallantly shuffling to and fro so as not to obscure the line of vision. Then he held up his hand.

'And now no more. All good things must come to an end –

especially when there are more in store. But before I can turn you over to our President there are a few things that must be said first.'

There were, of course, a great many. The audience shifted from foot to foot, but not, it seemed, because they were bored. Trevor might give gusty sighs, but everybody round him was laughing appreciatively. Even Adeane, elegantly poised on a shooting stick, could be seen with a benevolent smile on the austere profile. Mr Wittering first thanked them all for their presence, and running his eye over the faces below, intoned to the accompaniment of delighted applause an incantation of the places from whence each had come – Leamington Spa, Gloucester, Cheltenham, Birmingham, Hereford, Cardiff . . . 'It's like a conjuring trick,' said the lady next to Jennifer rapturously. 'He always does it and he never gets anyone wrong.'

Then tribute was paid to the goodness of Captain and Mrs Pike in allowing Knulle Court to be used once again for the gathering (the associations of Louise with it of course made it a double delight), to the excellence of the tea and the stalwart service of those who filled the cup that cheered, to Father Beaconsfield for his illuminating address, to the talent of Miss Gwynneth Rhys-Williams (and he felt he should read out some of the notices she had received in the *Bude and Stratton Post*, the *East Grinstead Courier* and the *Wallasey Evening Mail*), to the ever-faithful Wyvern Coach Services who had as usual transported the Worcestershire contingent (a model of reliability in days when this quality was all too often lacking), and above all of course to the very great pleasure their President was giving them by sparing time from his multifarious duties and important commitments to come here this afternoon. Since he knew that members were always interested in what Mr Tosswell had been engaged upon, he proposed finally, with their President's permission of course, to give just a short account of his engagements during the summer: opening speech to the International Poetry Congress in Tokyo in June, lunch at Buckingham Palace the same month, unveiling of the tablet to W. H. Auden in the Poet's Corner in Westminster Abbey,

24

interview on BBC television with Bernard Levin in July, poetry readings in York, Cheltenham and Bath, reading of the Louise poems on BBC radio 3 the same month; August he was allowed to spend as vacation (laughter and much applause), early September at Little Gidding with Sir Hugo Rouncey – many members would know by this time that Mr Tosswell was helping with Sir Hugo's eagerly awaited setting to music of the Louise poems. And Saturday, September 20th, a very important engagement with the Fleming Society.

Henry Tosswell during all this was behaving, it had to be conceded, with commendable lack of self-consciousness. Standing at the top of the steps he looked perhaps a little apprehensive, but he succeeded in neither smirking nor scowling during the Wittering extravagances. He had dressed for the occasion. In Oxford his frayed jeans, sandals, open-necked shirt were a cliché. But for the benefit of the Fleming Society he had put himself into a suit. It appeared to be one that he had had for long enough to grow out of. It was short in the leg, and from time to time he would uneasily try to pull down the sleeves to cover more of his shirt cuffs. His was an extraordinary face, Jennifer thought staring up at it as she had never been able to do in Oxford days. While Adeane looked all of a piece, a distinguished sixty-year old, Tosswell was an unnerving blend. She was reminded of that Bergman film where a rider uncovers the face of a cowled figure by the wayside, and reveals a skull. From behind, Tosswell might be thought a young man with that mop of curls, straight back, eager stride. When he turned the face was as ravaged and furrowed as a centenarian. And yet for all that the eyes and the smile were youthful.

And he had a beautiful speaking voice, she had to concede that when at last Mr Wittering gave place to him and he came down the steps to begin the reading. There was nothing of the fruity delivery of the elderly actor, nor the pious voice that she remembered being accorded to 'literature' at school. He had chosen the episode of the Christmas *tableaux vivants*, and he read with enjoyment, expertly distinguishing between the various participants. The audience who had been for the most part reverently hushed during the performance, only the boldest presuming to laugh, applauded ecstatically at the end.

'I always wish he would give us those last pages, where Edward proposes to Louise,' said the lady next to Jennifer. 'But I've never heard him read it. Perhaps he thinks it's too sacred. Oh but he does do it beautifully, I could go on listening forever.'

'Marvellous act the Tosser puts on, I must say,' said Trevor as they drove away down the Gletton road.

'You mean his reading?'

'Oh that, of course. But it's the great man slumming that it's worth watching. The smile and the affable word for people who bore him rigid.'

He spoke with considerable heat, and Jennifer knew why. He had been expecting, though this had naturally never been expressed, that the Oxford members of the party would combine to hold themselves apart, the Athenian courtiers watching the prancing of the mechanicals. But this had never happened. Trevor had had to form his own Athenian court; Tosswell and Adeane had gambolled contentedly with the provincials. He felt betrayed, that they should have supported him.

'They almost seemed to enjoy it,' she said carefully.

'It's the sophisticated upper class way of going native. For an afternoon you affect a sort of prelapsarian innocence, and then you go back to the Oxford life feeling delightfully purged and superior to everybody else because you have mixed with the great outside world. That's A.A. With the Tosser you have to add the fact that he still hasn't got over the excitement of being respectable again. It gives him the same sort of kick that someone in the Fleming Society might get from a peep at Montmartre. He really is a reformed character, you know. He glories in it. He's in chapel every evening. A.A. goes because he admires seventeenth century prose and orderliness and fine singing, but with the Tosser it's the joy of being a sheep again. And he adores being treated like one by the Flemingites.'

'A.A. can't like being called "doctor".'

'God, that's funny. And when I referred to him as "Mr" our Edgar put me right pretty smartly, I can tell you. I could see a think-bubble coming out of his head "that young man is jealous and disrespectful".'

'He doesn't know you're one.'

'Presumably not. And he certainly doesn't know that A. A. thinks that graduate degrees are ridiculous pretentious nonsense, a vulgar American habit, and that's what's wrong with ME, plus the fact that I read English, a non-subject that the properly educated should absorb in their sparetime – snuff up by osmosis.'

Ten miles further on he returned to the attack. 'My God, how do they come to be that shape?'

'Tosswell and the Warden? I was wondering if that was the suit he wore to Buckingham Palace. I suppose that at the poetry readings they would like him in his jeans.'

'No . . . the Fleming women. They bear no relation to any female curves the anatomist knows. You can't see how it works. It's all one sphere with a bolster strapped on above.'

'I suppose all the bulges get smoothed out by corsets and pushed into other places.'

'And all those pink and blue curls. They must spend their lives and their husbands' pensions at hairdressers.'

'You once said, when we were still in Oxford, that you were sick to death of unkempt dons' wives with their knees still muddy from the allotment, out shopping for wholefoods with their unwashed hair blowing all over their faces.'

'Well, I take it all back now. Give me nature in the raw rather than these prinked up elderly dolly birds.'

'If you'd looked more carefully you'd have seen plenty of others. The Irene type, bulgy and floral. Or the spinsters in hairy tweeds and brogues. To say nothing of military men with natty little moustaches.'

'Oh for heaven's sake don't niggle about detail. Basically they're all the same type, the *Reader's Digest*, country house guided tour sightseer. Onlookers, that's what they are, experiencing everything vicariously. Outsiders, looking in. They don't want real life, they want to see it on telly, go for cruises and package holidays and have it pointed out to them by a courier. Do you notice that they all talk about "Louise", coyly implying that she is an intimate friend? It gives me the same horrors as people talking about "Jane". And of course it's the same sort of person who does. They all love this diary, it tells them just what they want to know about the Victorians. And leaves out the things they'd rather not know. It makes them feel that they are peeping in at a dolls house. That's what one old crone actually told me – cross my heart. It was the same one who asked me if I approved of structuralism. I asked her where she'd heard of that and she said there had been quite a bit about it in the *Daily Telegraph*, though she hadn't really read what they said. I don't know whether I'll ever be able to go through with this. I'm sick to death of the whole thing already, and I haven't even started yet. Think of all the correspondence with old Wittering. If he can write four foolscap sheets on three separate occasions, just to fix up with me about this beanfeast, think what he's going to do when I get started on the photographs.'

'Perhaps you'll be able to get through without him.'

'Not a hope in hell. He's the repository of the faith, the guardian of the sacred flame, the person who knows all the ins and outs of the Fleming characters. I can't move a step without Wittering. Aaron Stern told me that in the beginning, and every single member I was presented to told me exactly the same. "A mine of information", "A walking encyclopaedia". So I've got to toe the line and keep polite because if I lose his goodwill I'm scuppered. I'd never have taken it on if I'd known it was going to be like this, I can tell you.'

A statement which both of them knew was untrue.

Chapter 2

APRIL

'There's no need to take all this trouble,' said Trevor possibly for the seventh time. 'You're not entertaining the Warden.'

'It'd be simpler if I was. I'd just give him some olives and a Camembert.'

'Which of course sprout on every tree in Wales. The staple diet of the natives.'

'It's this oven that mystifies me,' said Jennifer gloomily, crouching on the worn linoleum. 'The dial on the outside seems to bear no relation to what's happening inside. Even if I could see it – how *could* people build a kitchen right into the hill behind? It wouldn't be so bad if I was giving them lamb or beef, you could pretend that those should be eaten half-raw. But pork is *dangerous*.'

'Why did you get it then?'

'Because it seemed the safest. Safest in terms of eatableness.'

'What I can't understand is why in a countryside that seems to be bursting with cattle and sheep you can't get any meat that's fit to eat. The animals *look* all right.'

'They kill their beef too young, when it's overgrown veal and they don't hang it properly. Or else it's cow beef. I suppose they don't hang the lamb properly either. But I can't understand why the only chickens are frozen ones.'

'Country people only like junk food.'

'That's true enough. If you go into that shop in Ludwardine you'll see all the women buying spam and swissroll and tinned peas for dinner. And the odd can of baked beans. Look, this meat is still giving out red juice – when are the Witterings actually coming?'

'I don't know when they're coming. I said "lunch" and

that means 1 o'clock to most people. Though you've got to allow them time to find the cottage, and you know how long it took us on the first day. Why don't you hack bits off the joint and grill them? That's what Mr Micawber suggested when David Copperfield was in the same sort of tizzy as you.'

'I just feel I could do with a kind presence like Mr Micawber.'

'Then wait till Edgar comes, he'll probably fill the bill. Look, you do think that this is the time and place to tell him about Maurice Benbow?'

This had already been thrashed out so thoroughly that the topic had no flesh left on it. To Jennifer, embroiled with a meal that showed no signs of ever being ready for the table, it seemed totally unnecessary to introduce it now. But she bit back an irritable reply; if Trevor was put out of humour he was quite capable of noisily sulking throughout the lunch party.

'I thought you had decided that you were going to tell him today.'

Trevor, as she knew he would, rehearsed the stale patter of the last few weeks. 'He won't like it. But it's got to be said. And anyway I'm not the instrument of the Fleming Society. Even if I were I wouldn't be prepared to keep up all this fiction that she's queen and goddess and if she was alive today they wouldn't have killed Kennedy and taken a shot at the Pope. To say nothing of Hiroshima.'

'Mr Wittering would expect you to tell him. You can't withold vital information. Cripes, there's a car outside. It must be them. Go and see to them for heaven's sake. And do try to be nice to them, they haven't done you any harm.'

As she shoved chunks of oozing pork under the grill, that like the rest of the stove seemed implacably set on maintaining food in a state of raw inedibility, she listened to the conversation outside.

'So you found us then. It's more than we were able to do. We were cruising up and down the Gletton road for half an hour before we found someone to direct us.'

'No difficulty, no difficulty. I knew at once where it must

be when you said Cwm Hir. This is the quarry foreman's cottage. There used to be quite a little colony of quarry workers here, but I suppose most of the cottages weren't as substantial as this and fell down. A pity now that folk are scouring these counties for holiday houses. Did you say that this one is your own?'

'No fear, we haven't moved into that income bracket yet, it's as much as we can do to keep the roof on our Bradford terrace house. We've rented it for a month, for me to get up the Radnorshire scene. It was described in the ad as a holiday cottage which will explain the furnishings you'll find inside, and the inadequacies of the cooking arrangements which my wife is wrestling with at this minute. I've always noticed that people who let holiday cottages have sadistic streaks where kitchens are involved.'

'Now I wonder if I would know the landlord. I know so many people round here.'

'It belongs to a fellow called Williams who lives at Llandrindod. (That gay cosmopolitan spa as the handbook calls it – on the strength of the putting green and the boating lake, I believe.) At least, I think it's Williams, though I'm never sure whether it might not be Jones or Davis, which made it awkward the other night when I had to ring up to say that water was pouring through the bedroom ceiling.'

'It all used to belong to the Duggans. "Quarry" Duggan, you remember? He owned this quarry and several others and built himself a large house here not very far from this one. It's gone, long ago, there's never been a trace of it in my time. And when I was a boy living in Gletton we used to wander all over the place so you can be sure that if there was a ruin we'd have known about it. The local story was that the Quarry Duggans' son so disliked the place that he blew it up after dad had died, to extend the quarry workings. But even the quarry has come to an end now. Have you discovered where Mr Reedy lived?'

'The Mr Quiverful? The downtrodden curate with all the children? No, I'm afraid I'm not much of a hand at that sort of sleuthing.'

'I daresay you've passed it many a time. It stands just opposite the turning to Knulle.'

'Oh that eyesore in the purplish brick with the bay windows. Yes, I suppose it looks as though it had been put up for some worthy purpose.'

'Quarry Duggan had it put up for him. He built a little mission chapel for the quarryworkers and employed Mr Reedy to look after it. He was by way of being a philanthrophist, though you can see from the Journal that the local gentry didn't care for him much.'

'I'm afraid I haven't really got to grips with the Journal yet,' said Trevor later as they sat in the living room drinking a sweetish South African sherry out of chipped tumblers. They had sat there in the Parker Knoll chairs for a long time, listening to the clatter from the dark little kitchen beyond, pots being flung into a stone sink, saucepans being scraped, the opening and shutting of the oven door — sounds frenetic yet dispiritingly unproductive. He spoke with a hint of truculence as though anticipating criticism; he was aware that he had signally failed to keep his end up in the conversation, which had flitted rapidly over places, personalities and genealogies of some of the obscurer Fleming characters. 'Of course I've read it, but I certainly can't be said to have got a command of the detail yet.'

'Edgar has lived with it for a long time now.' It was perhaps the first time that Irene Wittering had spoken after the usual polite murmurings when she had accepted the sherry. But her silence was in no way an aggressive one. It seemed clear that as long as there was someone else ready to talk she was happy to sit tranquilly and listen. 'The diaries came just at the right time, the year that he retired.'

'Yes, Irene's right of course. It couldn't have been better timed. I'd got this business in Hereford (it was a run-down little place when I bought it, but it was the biggest gents' outfitters in the city when I left). And really the world seemed to have come to an end when I didn't have to go along to Widemarsh street every day. If I didn't have to get up to go to work, well, there didn't seem any point in getting up at all. Some people sink themselves in gardening, and

32

that's all right, but there's always the winter. And then the Louise Journal came out and Irene saw a write-up in the *Hereford Times* and went and got it for me for Christmas. The best Christmas present I've ever had in my life. You might say it changed our lives from that very day.'

'And that same Boxing Day we had to drive out to look at Mairwood church.'

'Yes, Irene didn't know what she'd started that Christmas. You might say it took at once – we spent the next few months going round looking at all the places in the Journal.'

'And in between he made a huge map of that part of Radnorshire. It covered half the lounge wall, and we stuck flags in the places we'd been to.'

'Most of them I'd known as a boy. (I think I told you I lived at Gletton for the first 20 years of my life – in fact I learned the trade at Rodd's in the High Street; fifteen shillings a week I got in those days, ten shillings went to my mother and five left for myself and I managed to do more with those five shillings than I could with five hundred pounds now.) And I knew Ludwardine too because I had an uncle who had a hill farm up that end of the valley so I'd spent a lot of holidays tramping over the forest. But it was nearly all new to Irene, and I must say she's done well picking it all up.'

'It gave me something to do when the children had all left home.'

'I couldn't have managed without her, we get so many enquiries and visits from folk who want to know things about the Ludd valley – it usually ends up with us taking them on a guided tour. And then we get pulled into things quite outside. Like the campaign a few years back to keep Radnorshire Radnorshire and not Powys along with Brecon.'

'You don't seem to have been very successful there,' said Trevor with an irritable eye on the kitchen door, trying to calculate whether another round of sherry was desirable.

'No, of course we knew it was as good as a lost cause when we took it up, but it seemed a good thing to let our views be felt. Some of our members were very strong about it. They felt Radnorshire had a lot of history and traditions, and what with Louise and Kilvert to speak up for it the name ought to be preserved. Even in those days we had a good few members.'

'When was the society formed?' Trevor had taken a furtive look at the sherry and had realized that the bottle would not run to another round. All right if they were using sherry glasses, but a centimetre of it looked insulting at the bottom of a tumbler.

'It was quite soon after the Journal came out – the following year, in fact. It all started up after a meeting of the Kilvert Society, funnily enough. Irene and I belonged in those days though we've had to give it up now. Until there are more than 24 hours in the day there just isn't time. There was a group of us there who said "why not Louise too?" So we took a stall at a book fair in Hereford a few weeks later and signed on about 50 members – I was quite astonished at the enthusiasm. Of course by that time the book clubs had taken it up and it was selling almost like *Diary of an Edwardian Lady*. Then came the television serial, and that had a mention of us and after that members came pouring in. And as it's been shown in Australia and America and Canada we get enquiries from there too. Yes, the correspondence is – well, I won't call it a burden because I love it – but quite a consideration. And there's the Proceedings. I did send you copies of the Proceedings?'

'You certainly did.' The pile of xeroxed sheets, going right back to the first number, had been kicked round Trevor's study and monotonously cursed from the day of their arrival.

'You'll find some useful stuff there I daresay. We've had some very scholarly things in it as well as the chit-chat that people do like. I try to keep a balance. Somebody wrote quite a learned piece about the Ludd valley railway (which ruined a lot of the local people including Richard Boys Talbot of Ludwardine Court). It doesn't get mentioned much in the Journal, but it's all in the area and that's what counts. And on the books that Louise mentions, like Mrs

Ewing's works. One of our members who's a librarian wrote a nice little piece about her.'

The kitchen door was pulled open. Trevor shot to his feet. 'Lunch! I'm afraid I'll have to take your sherry tumblers to the sink, the cottage doesn't run to more than four glasses. It's just Yugoslav Riesling, which is all the Gletton Co-op could provide. Plenty of the hard stuff, I could have got about six different brands of vodka, so it's not that they're teetotal.'

'We once went to Bulgaria,' said Irene Wittering serenely. 'But we haven't ever been to Yugoslavia.'

'That sounds very exotic,' said Jennifer. 'Will you have roast potatoes? And cauliflower? I'm sorry about the apple sauce, there's no greengrocer in Gletton so I had to get tinned stuff.'

'Thank you, that's lovely. No, I wouldn't say Bulgaria seemed very foreign. We'd really wanted to go to the Scilly isles but we left it too late. The hotel we stayed at was called Sunny Beach and the food was just like England. We don't go away now in the summer.' She spoke with recognizable relief. 'It's our busiest time.'

Trevor came back from the kitchen with the rinsed tumblers. 'What are the people like round this area now? From the Journal it seems there were quite a lot of nobs once – I mean two of the clergy alone were baronets. Of course we've only been here a few days, but I can't say I've seen much sign of landed gentry.'

'No, the houses have all gone – well, there are the Pikes at Knulle Court of course. Mairwood House has been divided into flats, Gletton Abbey is a retirement home for old folks (our eldest daughter is urging us to put our name down for that and it would seem an ideal place). Ludwardine Court was burnt down many years ago – no, there's really no one left like the Benbows were, and certainly nobody with enough money to build a church.'

'I saw his portrait – Sir Edward Benbow's.' Trevor was now approaching dangerous ground and was visibly bracing himself. '(Do you want some salt? I'm afraid it doesn't pour so you'll have to take the top off. The atmosphere here is as damp as I'm told Hong Kong is.) Yes, I wrote to Maurice Benbow. You warned me that I probably wouldn't get any reply. But in fact he did write and suggested I should go down to Bournemouth.'

'Now that was a piece of good fortune,' said Mr Wittering cordially. If Trevor had been expecting resentment he was disappointed. 'He doesn't often rouse himself. He must have been having a spell of good health – how lucky that it coincided with your letter. So you went down of course.'

'So I went down.'

'And how did you find him?'

'Well, strange.'

'Yes, he is a strange personality. His mother was all in all to him, and apparently after her death he lost his main-spring.'

'What was his father like?'

'Of course I never knew him, he'd died years before my time. He was Louise's younger son, the elder one died when he was a student at Oxford, just like Louise's own brother. Thre was an inherited tendency to consumption, as you may know. But from what Maurice said on the only occasion that I met him I fancy that his father was an irascible sort of man – rather like Louise tells us Edward's own father – Sir Samuel the brewer – had been. And that drew Maurice close to his own mother. And you saw all the other pictures?'

'Yes, the four little Benbow girls – Edward's sisters.'

'The four blossoms,' murmured Mrs Wittering.

Mr Wittering looked at her affectionately. 'Irene can't look at that poem of Mr Tosswell's without the tears coming. And on the occasion that Mr Tosswell gave it at one of his readings I had to hand over my handkerchief, her crying got beyond those little bits of lace ladies carry in their handbags.'

'I saw them all, I suppose. The portrait of Sir Samuel who certainly looked a terror (didn't he die in a fit of rage?). The pastel of the diarist herself. Sir Edward as a little boy. And the one of him in middle age with the church in the background – a very striking face, very handsome in an austere way. Maurice Benbow was anxious that I shouldn't miss anything. I must say they looked pretty odd stuck hugger-mugger on the walls of that cramped little flat.'

'Yes, a very different setting from Mairwood House – though Maurice would not have known that so very well, of course.'

'He spoke of Mairwood.'

'Oh yes, he went there. But his grandfather died in 1925, when Maurice was only eight, and his father as you know was a serving soldier and never lived there. So the place was sold.'

'Maurice spoke of his grandmother.'

'Whom so sadly he never met. Such a tragedy – to have this living member of the family, who might have been expected to have such memories and . . .'

'But Maurice did say something.'

'Yes?' Mr Wittering drew his knife and fork together neatly and looked at Trevor; his manner was politely attentive, but lacking, it seemed, in any great curiosity.

'He said that his grandmother had had to retreat to the south of France because of some scandal; that there was a rumour of another man.' Trevor confronted Mr Wittering with a look of defiance, his chin thrust forward. Jennifer knew the look well, it was his native Yorkshire way of awaiting a fight. Just so would his mining forebears have prepared for a bout with naked fists and clogs.

'Yes,' said Mr Wittering mildly. 'It was only to be expected that he would tell you that.'

Trevor was toppled. Then he spoke like an indignant small boy. 'But he told me that this was the very first time it had ever come into the open.'

'Yes, he told me that too.' Mr Wittering tactfully withdrew his eyes from Trevor's all too apparent discomfiture, and stared down at the formica top of the table. 'The fact is generally known in the society though there is a tacit agreement that it should not be aired in public. There are, as you probably have observed for yourself, quite a number of romantically minded older folk among our members who like to think that broken marriages have only come about recently. Not that Louise's marriage was ever really broken.

You could say that they just lived separately after 1890. The BBC saw the point when they made the film of Louise – that the Journal ends at the moment when it seems that Louise and Edward are going to live happily ever after, and that the film would please many more people if it finished there too, and didn't go into any unpleasant details.'

'Edgar went up to London specially to persuade the producer,' said Mrs Wittering. 'He thought that letters alone couldn't make the point.'

'Yes, I suppose it was my arguments that prevailed. Not that there were any unpleasant details known – but there is just no knowing what might have been invented. No, I think we can take it that though in the diary all seems very happy, Edward and Louise were not really suited. Though it is probably best to take what Maurice says with a pinch of salt. He got the story from his mother who seems to have taken against her Benbow in-laws. Still, perhaps Edward should never have married at all, just devoted himself to his church works. Louise was so lively and high-spirited, she would have felt crushed.'

'And there was her mother-in-law, old Lady Benbow,' interposed Jennifer. She found herself instinctively moving in to cover Trevor, to give him time to pull himself up from the fall he had taken. He had presented her during those interminable discussions with an infinity of ways in which Mr Wittering might be expected to react, but this response had never occurred to him, or to her. 'She was such a fusser – and I suppose she went on living with them after the marriage.'

'And the poor girl would have felt her waistline was being watched all the time to see if there was a new blossom lurking below.' Trevor, it seemed, had made a recovery. 'Even if Lady Benbow didn't go as far, as I understand mothers-in-law have done in the past, to scrutinize the personal linen.'

'Need you have said that,' said Jennifer an hour or so later, 'about the waistline and the linen?'

'Sometimes I just have to prick balloons.'

'I didn't think they needed deflating.'

'Anything that gases need deflating – you can take that as axiomatic.'

'They were very kind. I thought it was touching the way he gave you all those notes about Fleming personalities and said it was for you to write them into literary form because he just didn't have the way with a pen.'

Chapter 3

APRIL

They were spending the whole of the Easter vacation at Cwm Hir, with the idea of Trevor making himself familiar with the countryside before he began writing. At first they went about it in a fairly haphazard way, driving a few miles in a different direction each day and getting out of the car and walking. The investigation of Ludwardine they put off for a week or so, telling themselves that it could be done when the weather stopped them walking on the hills.

'Aren't we ever going to do more than have a drink in the Talbot Arms?'

'We'll "do" Ludwardine today,' said Trevor with resolution. 'From A to Z. And you can write to Mr Wittering and tell him that I'm a good boy and you're pleased with my progress.'

They started with the monument. It stood at the end of the village, so that they had driven past it often enough, cursing it as a traffic hazard and trying to round it without being annihilated by the traffic that pounded through the village – the cars with their caravans on the way to the coast, the stock vans, the roadstone lorries, and the juggernauts that kept mid-Wales generally supplied with the necessities of life – from potato crisps and meat pies to Yamaha motor bikes.

'There is, in case you don't know, an establishment in Llandrindod that calls itself the Auto Palace,' said Trevor. 'It's got more plateglass than anyone else in the town. They actually say so in one of their advertisements. Those up there are presumably destined to grace its shop windows.' They were standing on one side of Ludwardine's High Street, waiting for a chance to get across to the monument, but the deafening roar of the car conveyors that were passing made it difficult to hear him.

'It looks like the Albert Memorial done on the cheap,' he said a few minutes later, staring up at the extraordinary assembly of statues in canopied niches, buttresses and pinnacles. 'To the proud memory of Richard Boys Talbot 1825–77. Radnorshire's noblest son. Visionary, philanthropist and friend. Well, what do you know! He isn't in the diary, at any rate, whoever he might have been.'

'It's before the diary, long before.'

'Yes, but she put in so much that happened before her time, and you have to admit that there are a lot of local legends and history. You'd have thought she would have mentioned Radnorshire's noblest son.'

He brought this up when they called at the rectory a few minutes later. It was a new, square little house of shiny red brick in the lane that also held the school. The rector, a sandy-haired young man who sat with a leg over the arm of his chair, had seemed agreeably pleased to see them, whoever they might be. His wife, he said, was down at Gletton where she did part-time teaching at the local comprehensive school. He had made them a cup of Nescafe and turned on the electric fire in the study.

'Radnorshire's noblest son – yes, it's quaint, isn't it. There really isn't any memory of him here now. He brought the railway to Ludwardine, and lost all his own money, and most of the local landowners' cash too in so doing. And the railway's gone a long time ago. The person who knew most about it all was Tommy Thomson, the doctor here, but he died last year. And you say he's not in the diary? Well, it's not for me to comment on that; I've yet to read it.' He smiled with what appeared to be complacency.

'Is this a question of principle?'

'Oh no, I'd hardly call it that. Lack of time, really. I don't come from this area, in fact this is my first year in a rural parish – I was in Swansea before. I might have read it if I was a native.'

'Swansea was my home town,' said Jennifer. 'At least, I was born there.'

'Really? I used to play Rugger for Swansea Old Boys – until the bishop said that too many of his curates were getting damaged every Saturday, and put an end to it. (If you think there's no discipline left in the church these days, remember that.) No, a country parish is a very different cup of tea from a town one, I can tell you.'

'A better cup?'

He shrugged. 'Well, the air's cleaner, you could say that. And you breathe enough of it. There are five parishes in this group – Ludwardine itself, Llanfihangel about four miles up the Rhayader road, Mairwood three miles down the Gletton road, Cwm Hir, and Knulle. On Sundays I'm on the trot for twelve solid hours and if something goes wrong – the car won't start or some ancient mariner keeps me talking at the church door – then the whole pack of cards falls down.'

'Five – that's a lot.'

'The bishop only let on about two. I discovered about Cwm Hir when I arrived, and then the Mairwood and Knulle chap went off his nut and Muggins is the only man who'll take them on. And it isn't as if there's any affinity between the places. Llanfihangel is half way up Radnor Forest; Cwm Hir, Knulle and Mairwood are in the lusher bit of the Ludd valley – the mountain sheep and the valley sheep you could say. Anyway, they simply don't mix, never have and never will. We even have to have two harvest suppers, at Llanfihangel and Knulle.'

'Which does Ludwardine support?'

'Ludwardine feels itself to belong to the hills, so they all trot up the valley to the Forest Inn to do their feasting.'

'You're right, it does feel quite different. We even notice that the sheep are different in the fields down the end we're staying. Up on the hills they leap away from you like startled stags; in the valley fields they stand and stare. And Mairwood, you'd never get a church like that west of Ludwardine.'

'Oh *Mairwood*. Yes, that's one of my crosses.'

'You don't go all the way with the Fleming Society then?'

'Well . . . I take it you are members?'

'Over my dead body.'

'Then I'll say that I treat them with considerable reserve. They're all townspeople of course – well, I don't hold that against them, I started off as one myself – so they have sentimental views about the country. It all ties in with kindness to animals, trips to view country houses, anti-pollution and keeping the footpaths open, which your real native couldn't care less about. And they get no end of a kick at trooping out once a year to the back of beyond and having an old-style evensong at a country church. People that I bet never go near their own parish church will drive a hundred miles or more to this one. Of course it is nice to see the church filled (though I wasn't there last year to see that extraordinary sight) but I'm not really sure that it's worth all the fuss and commotion and correspondence that goes on to get it that way. I reckon I have six jobs – Ludwardine, Llanfihangel, Cwm Hir, Mairwood and Knulle – and the Fleming Society. The correspondence! It comes to a hefty sum in postage stamps – and the telephone calls! (I don't pay for those, of course. But I bet it steps up the subscription.)'

'This is Mr Wittering?'

'It is Mr Wittering. And then he likes me to organize an annual Louise Fleming essay competition or diary competition or some such with the school children. And currently there's all the business about putting up a plaque at Mairwood to commemorate the marriage. There was a missive only this morning. Here. "The wording has been decided . . .", blah blah blah. "To be cut in Portland stone by Pollocks the Hereford monumental masons and picked out in royal blue. Plans have been prepared and a faculty applied for. But we must not anticipate, perhaps it will be refused . . .", and so on, and so on. Of course it will be refused, the diocesan board won't like royal blue, even in a church that only has one service a month a quarter of the year. But if it is refused would we like instead a flower stand (with engraved shield giving details) or a hymn board or a small set of shelves for prayerbooks? I ask you, no wonder poor old Bob Page went off his head.'

'Because of Mr Wittering?'

'Well, not entirely, it has to be admitted. The size of the

place for one thing. I remember him saying to me tearfully the first time I met him – and just before he got taken off to Talgarth – "it's the size of a cathedral!" Poor old fellow – though I often think of that when we are tearing our hair to know where to turn for funds for the fabric. The roof will have to be done soon, that's for sure. And there's the Fleming Society rabbiting on about a flower stand. There are only fifty people in the parish all told, and of those five (three adults, two children) are the only ones you'd call regular. Of course there are summer visitors; they like to come to a church in the middle of fields – we can thank the Fleming Society for that. But really the only long-term solution would be to declare the church redundant and try to sell it – like they did with Mansel Gamage in Herefordshire. But the Fleming Society made a tremendous outcry when I suggested it and the diocese got cold feet.'

'But sell it for what? What could anybody do with a large Victorian church in the middle of nowhere?'

'Search me. I freely admit that what concerns me is that it should be closed. That would cure one of my headaches.'

'Did Edward Benbow's dreams ever come to anything? The school and the choir and the pensioners?'

'Is that what he dreamt about?'

'You'll have to read the Journal to get a full account of his aspirations, but he seems to have been just as much of a visionary as your Boys Talbot here. He wanted to have a religious community, daily services with fine music, a resident choir school and a congregation of old age pensioners who would live – oh I don't know – in superior almshouses, I suppose.'

'I hadn't heard all that, though I realized that Benbow must have been a man of pretty lavish ideas – I mean, that inlaid marble! And did you realize the roof was made of cedarwood?'

'Mrs Wittering told us.'

'Yes, I daresay she would. Poor Benbow – if he could hear the music now, such as it is. There is a honky-tonk piano, you probably were aware of it if you were at last September's service. Mrs Howes of the Home Farm (they've been

44

there for generations) battles away with it. And the singing is mostly me. The organ packed in years ago, it's probably dense with dead mice. No, there never were any almshouses that I know of. There was a school, you can see that on the Gletton road near the Mairwood gates. It closed long before I came and the children go to Ludwardine, the older ones to Gletton. The church must have cost a packet, he probably didn't have anything left over for the rest.'

'What sort of impression do you have of him?'

'Of Benbow? I've never stopped to think. I just grapple with the problems he's left me with. Tommy Thomson was the person for that – the doctor I told you about. He was absolutely fascinated by people, dead or living. He could be very wrongheaded about them, I never knew a man more prejudiced, but he was interested even in the ones he hated. You could always go and call on Josie, his widow, I suppose.'

'But you don't exactly recommend it.'

'I wouldn't go so far as to say that. She's moody and awkward, a misfit here really. And she and I don't see eye to eye. She reckons I spend too much time with the young, but I say that when there's only one man to do six men's jobs then it's reasonable to put one's money on the rising generation, even if it means that the oldies don't get all the attention they think they deserve. In the old days – the diary days – there was just Ludwardine to be looked after, and the rector was a gentleman of leisure who sported a curate to do all his work for him. I daresay there was time to make tender enquiries about their rheumatics then.'

At the Stores the shopkeeper had thought that Mrs Thomson was probably at home, that she didn't go out much these days, and so they had pushed open the tall white gate inscribed 'The Grove'. The bottom hinges had come away, the gate had almost to be lifted before one could squeeze through it. Inside, a sea of grass waved over what had once been a garden. Distinction between flowerbeds and lawn had long ago disappeared, and in any case both were threatened by the saplings which reared themselves everywhere. Huge sycamores, a forest of rhododendrons, cut the property off from the village, dulled the sound of the traffic in the High Street and darkened such open ground as there was. It looked as though trees were marching on the house.

'Goodness, poor Mrs Mortimer,' said Jennifer staring around her. 'Didn't the diary describe her as a fanatical gardener? At least, I hope she kept it better than this.'

They looked at the house undecided. There seemed to be no obvious front door. A conservatory with much of its glass missing ran along the whole of this side, the house door within was open. Trevor put one foot inside, and then, seeing a bell push tackled it. Far away in the depths of the house there was a jangling.

'Who is it?' shouted a voice.

'It's only us,' said Trevor, off his guard.

'You fool!' whispered Jennifer. 'Of all bloody silly things to say!'

'Well, there's a limit to what you can shout into the void. What do you expect me to do? Give her my curriculum vitae?'

'We were looking for Mrs Thomson,' Jennifer called. 'The rector told us to come.'

'That's no answer.'

'Well, at least it tells her we're respectable.'

'Respectable! That's all you ever think of. Can't you ever move away from Chapel coffee mornings?'

A figure appeared in the shadows at the bottom of the hall, and then moved towards them. She had black hair – too black for nature, surely – but not much of it, a scanty fuzz of tight curls, and she was dressed in the high fashion of Hampstead some ten years before, a Liberty skirt down to the ground in a jungle print of flames and browns, beads and bangles. In a countryside whose women favoured synthetics and pallid colours her appearance was unexpected. She had a cigarette in one hand and looked at them with undisguised hostility.

'What has the rector sent you about?'

'It's a long story, I'm afraid. But basically it's in connection with a book I've undertaken to write.'

46

'Oh books, I like books. You'd better come in.'

They were taken into a room towards the back of the house. Every wall was covered with books; the shelves sagged under them. She waved in their direction. 'I go out and buy car-loads of them at Hay. I'm addicted to books, like I am to smoking. It's the only thing that keeps me sane. Funny, all the time Tom was alive I said that if ever I was a widow I'd get out and away as soon as the funeral was over. In those days I used to be off to London two or three times a year just to stop my brain atrophying altogether. And now that he actually has died I find I can't do anything, I'm just stuck, and I suppose I'll stay stuck until the end of my days. Well, what book are you writing? Sit down and I'll get us some sherry.'

'Thank you,' said Trevor a few minutes later. 'That's kind of you. So, here's to the breakaway from Ludwardine.'

'That'll be the day. But it won't come. Not now.'

'Oh, you never know. Well . . . the book is, as I suppose you might guess, about the diarist Louise Fleming. It's a picture book really; people don't seem to be able to read these days. So there's to be a lot of Victorian photographs taken by one of your local lads, with me supplying 20,000 words or so of text. About the diarist and the background generally. I suppose it's needed, as Adeane managed to say pretty well nothing with the utmost elegance in the introduction to the diary.'

'Why should I have guessed it was about her? Anyway, I didn't.'

'You have heard of her though?'

'She is one of my obsessions. Anyone in Ludwardine will tell you I have plenty of those.' Mrs Thomson had lit a fresh cigarette with desperate, hungry movements. She was, now that they could see her in full light, older than her style of dressing had originally suggested. The face was sallow and wrinkled, the face of a difficult, probably tiresome woman; she had deep-sunk brown eyes that stared at them with intensity.

'I don't think the rector knew she was an obsession, he

just thought you might know something about some of the characters.'

'No, he wouldn't realize that. We barely communicate. He disapproves of me. He's so simple himself he thinks everybody else should be the same, and that fresh air and bashing around on games fields can cure anything. And he knows I disapprove of him – all that nonsense about "the young people" – football, discos, theatricals, barbecues, he never stops. But not a glimpse of them in church, oh no, that's left for the old people that he hasn't got time for. Though I don't want to give you the impression that I identify with the old folk. I may be one, but I hate them. And I don't go to church either. I gave that up years ago.'

'Why is Louise Fleming an obsession?' It seemed wisest to stick to the issues least fraught with emotion.

'Well, to begin with, she's a good writer.'

'No, I suppose she isn't a bad writer. I can see my wife looks alarmed. All right, Jen, I'm not going to prostrate myself at her shrine, but I don't mind saying that in her small way, and considering how short the journal is (it covers not much more than a year), she's not at all bad. Though nothing like the society have blown her up to be, of course. She had a feeling for time and place and people, for instance, in the same way as Kilvert. She leaves out a lot, there's no hint of the grim rural poverty that Kilvert noticed; Ludwardine is cosy like Cranford. Which is why the society loves her so dearly, those golden days of yore. But sometimes she observes people rather better than Kilvert (and amazingly precociously when you think she was only 17). She can be more detached and critical. But the Fleming Society has got hold of the wrong end of the stick. So has Tosswell for that matter. (You know he's used the journal as a source book for poems? The Fleming Society think rapturously of analogies between Miss Fleming and Dorothy Wordsworth, Tosswell and William, but the fact is that now the old fires have died down he's desperately casting around for second-hand emotion.) But Wittering and co. see the whole thing as an idyll, they never seem to notice the underlying melancholy.'

48

Nor did Mrs Thomson appear to have noticed much of what Trevor had said. 'Kilvert,' she said broodingly. 'She's not really like Kilvert.'

He was nettled. He had treated her as a peer, an intelligent woman, and had expanded accordingly – clearly to no purpose whatever. 'I didn't say she was. I only pointed out one instance of similarity.'

She ignored him. 'She doesn't artlessly let herself go like Kilvert. He unconsciously bares himself, she's far more careful. I don't mean that she's discreet; she can be nicely catty about people, almost bitchy sometimes. But those soppy daydreamings that Kilvert went in for, that make him so touching really – do you remember how he lies in bed and composes the speech that he imagines delivering at the wedding breakfast after he has married his Daisy? And he's so affected by it that he weeps? Well, Louise doesn't go in for anything like that. She's dignified all the time she's falling for Edward – none of those ghastly girlish outpourings that I and everybody else put into our diaries. She does it the way all of us would like to have thought we could behave. There she is at first spirited but basically docile – Emma and Mr Knightley if you like – then gradually realizing that it isn't just a guardian/ward relationship and beautifully overcoming her awe of him, though to the end she wonders whether she isn't unworthy of him. And then all those rambles over the hills together when you are left to infer that they were pouring out their hearts to each other, only nothing intimate is ever really recorded. Kilvert would have made a fool of himself blurting it all out and we would have thought "poor sod" – because courting and sex are just comic in real life except to the two concerned. But she's much too artful for that, and too fastidious. She's even artful enough to show herself sometimes in a bad light – like the time when she disgraces herself by fidgeting in that meeting of the school managers, and getting herself ticked off by her Edward. Or playing dance music on Good Friday. That is why,' said Mrs Thomson, staring at them sombrely, 'I say Louise Fleming didn't write that diary.' She made this announcement in flat unexcited tones, as though it were a statement of no particular interest, that did not really merit discussion.

There was a silence. Then Jennifer spoke. 'You mean you think it's a forgery?'

'Well, not a forgery. Doesn't that mean you want to deceive someone? I think it's a sort of private fantasy, written by someone who was just an onlooker. A woman, of course. I'm a woman myself and I know what the sex can do.'

'I suppose,' said Trevor, 'there is something curious about it.' This was a response that Jennifer had not expected. She had spoken to try to mask the contempt and irritation she was sure must be emanating from Trevor's side of the room. No one more than he detested zany female intuitive hunches.

Mrs Thomson felt no such surprise. 'And what do you think is curious about it?' She might have been trying to encourage a rather leaden student.

'It's shaped, like a novel. The usual diarist is concerned with the immediate emotion. This one starts in the past, of course, giving her background and childhood and so on. But one does come across that. What is unusual is the looking back to the past while recording the present. You remember her remorse about playing polkas on the organ on Good Friday? There is a very bare entry for that actual Good Friday, but that apparently traumatic experience isn't mentioned. She only remembers it when she is wondering whether she is worthy to be the new Lady Benbow. And it's odd to write a diary that leads up to a climax – her guardian's proposal of marriage – and then stop there. If you're given to writing diaries you go on. And as this one finishes in the middle of an exercise book even the Fleming Society seems to have sorrowfully accepted that there probably isn't anything more waiting to be discovered. This marriage was unhappy, we know that now. But it's as if the writer realized it was going to be unhappy and stopped at a point where the future still seemed to have promise.'

'But a girl, another girl, an outsider, who had read plenty of novels that end with wedding bells, she might think it was a natural climax and stop there, when her hero proposes?'

'I suppose so.'

'And being a Victorian girl would be unable to imagine what wedded bliss might be like. Or perhaps would not wish to contemplate it.'

'If you like.'

'But you don't propose to discuss it. You think I'm mad. I'm used to it, don't bother to apologise or pretend that you don't. I know that look; everybody has it on their face nowadays when I talk to them.' She waved the cigarette packet in their direction. 'I never asked . . .'

'No, we don't.'

'And I do, sixty a day. It was bad enough in Tommy's day but now without him to nag and throw up the windows to let out the smoke I'm rushing to destruction full pelt. I remember on a London bus once the conductor – a Cockney, of course – shouted at every stop "Full up downstairs, upstairs for the cancer ward". Oh well, I've certainly no wish to live for ever, and it might as well be cancer as anything else. But it's one of the things that haunts me about that diary, the writer's feelings about time the great annihilator. I know it's a cliché, everybody has said it, every writer you care to name. But she feels it exactly the same way as I do. So I agree with you about the underlying melancholy. If Tosswell and your society don't see it they must be blocks of stone. "And year by year our memory fades within the circle of the hills." Remember?'

'But that's Tennyson, not her.'

'Of course it is. But she makes me really *feel* it, the awful obliteration, the anonymity of death. Did you know that the worst curse in the Hebrew language is "may his name and remembrance be obliterated"? It shows what an elemental fear it is. Though you could say they're deceiving themselves, that you've only got to wait a generation at the most and the last flickering spark of a memory of you is gone, for the likes of you and me at any rate. Even if all your virtues are recorded on a tombstone *you* don't exist for anyone, it's just the quaint language, or the carving on it. That's what I mind about death, the being snuffed out, of ceasing to matter to anyone, being reduced to a ramshackle collection of furniture and a wardrobe of old clothes that have somehow got to be disposed of. And that's what whoever wrote that diary seemed to feel; if she had any thought of an afterlife and heavenly rewards she didn't say so. I'm the same, I haven't any comforting illusions.'

She spoke with passionate intensity. They looked back at her, ill at ease as one usually is when a total stranger bares her soul. 'I suppose,' said Jennifer, always the first to be unnerved by this sort of situation, 'that the writer, if she wasn't Louise Fleming, must have been very familiar with all the same people and places. It seems to ring true.' As she spoke she was ashamed of the triteness of the comment, the chattiness of her tone.

'Of course she was. Oh I can tell you I've thought about it a lot. Obviously it was someone who lived in Ludwardine. What really surprises me is that nobody has pointed out that Mairwood is three or four miles from Radnor Forest where they were always riding. It's certainly not the natural place to take exercise from Mairwood. Or perhaps people have said this – I'm not in touch with these things. I did have the curiosity to go and look at the log of Ludwardine School for the 1880s. Louise Fleming is never mentioned, not once. And yet by her accounts she was in and out of the school every week.'

'Do you think it was someone who knew the school well?'

'Not necessarily. I suppose it could have been done from hearsay – there's nothing now to show whether it's accurate or not.'

'It's only fair to say that the log of Clyro School doesn't mention the Rev. Francis Kilvert either, and yet he by his own account was in almost daily attendance. And why write about Ludwardine school at all? Surely it must have been someone who was fairly closely concerned with it?'

Mrs Thomson looked at Trevor contemptuously. 'Obviously you've never lived in a village. It's all one soap opera, which everyone watches and everyone comments on. And the Welsh love drama; they can extract excitement from somebody paying too much for a cow. A set-to about the school theatricals would have provided meat for the whole of Ludwardine for a week. There wasn't any television to watch in those days you know. I'm not saying the characters didn't exist. Tommy filled his copy of the diary with notes about their descendants in the village.'

'I hope there aren't many of those left. Wittering will be expecting me to interview them all. I certainly don't intend to, but I'd rather there weren't myriads of sources I'm leaving untapped.'

'You needn't worry, there are hardly any of them left now, they've all been driven out by the "retired" brigade, from the Midlands mostly. It makes me think of the red squirrels and the grey squirrels. (Do you know there *were* red squirrels in my childhood. Yes, I really can remember them.) God knows why they should want to retire here; they don't like walking, they don't go in for gardening even. And there's no public transport, you're six miles from the nearest chemist shop or hairdresser for your blue rinse. I suppose they've seen the place in happier days on their way to Aberystwyth (car loaded to the gills with kids and rubber dinghies). And back they come and build themselves grisly little bungalows called Chrislen or Shangri La; perhaps Septembers or Mimulus if they're a bit up-market. They hang coach lanterns outside and instal two-tone doorbells. There's always a patio, of course; most of them have been to the Costa Brava. They don't mix with the natives, they spend their time giving each other coffee mornings and cruising round to look for freezer bargains in Llandrindod or Crick – they wouldn't dream of patronising the village shop. And until you've heard people talking about what's in their freezer you don't understand boredom. They've turned the village into a sunset home. They all pretend they like it, but they must loathe it – all the hills, which they never set foot on, and the wind and the rain. And the dark, my God the dark in winter. You don't know what night is until you try to feel your way just a hundred yards down the Gletton road on a winter evening. Yes, the grey squirrels are killing off the red squirrels, I can tell you. All Tommy's old patients are extinct, pretty well. We look round at each other and wonder who will be the next to get struck. And as soon as the children leave school they go off somewhere else; they have to if they want to get a job. Soon there won't be anybody left to dish out the pensions and serve the *Daily Mails*.'

Both Hancocks made separate efforts to distract their hostess from her Cassandra mood. 'It's not just here that the OAPs are the màster race, you know,' remarked Trevor. 'Though it's worse than racism or sexism to say so. You can't get on the trains or the buses for them, they get concessions in everything – from cinemas to dry-cleaning, and they still natter away as if they're the forgotten generation. All I hope is that it lasts my time, and then you'll see what a bloody-minded old geezer I'll be, forever travelling between Penzance and Inverness on my Senior Citizen's railcard and griping away about modern youth.'

'Did any of your husband's patients, the people he talked to, ever mention Louise Fleming?'

'Nobody. But then as she left the district in 1890 I have to admit that it wasn't very surprising. They remembered her husband and the Mairwood church. He was regarded as a harmless eccentric with a bee in his bonnet about church services. One or two of them thought it mildly shocking that he should put his wife's face into a stained glass window and a holy subject, but most of them had never even been to the church. You're from a town, so you've no idea how country people stay in their own little run, feel patronising about people who move around. But I always think that the stained glass window was a touching idea.'

'Which couldn't keep her. You know that she went because the marriage failed?'

Mrs Thomson lit another cigarette. 'Did it now. Perhaps that's what happened to the Sleeping Beauty and her Prince Charming too. I always look at houses, especially the ones with trim matching curtains and flowers in the window, and wonder just what happens when the curtains are drawn. Perhaps all those Victorian marriages that are supposed to

54

have been domestic bliss were just one living hell. You know, I think a lot about those Victorian women living their tight, frustrated lives, their minds just eaten up with resentment – all those babies, you've no sooner laid one in the cradle than your husband's filled you with another. From the wedding night till the menopause – how they must have longed for that. Or not having babies and being relegated to spinsterdom and good works at thirty. Not ever being able to have an opinion of your own but always being at the mercy of some man – your father or your husband – Charlotte Yonge even carried it to brothers. My God, whatever's happened to the world now at least we've got away from that.'

The Hancocks' faces expressed their discomfort. Even the most forthright expect the talk of an older generation to conform to a fairly sedate and predictable pattern. 'At least the diarist got away with only two babies,' said Trevor with uneasy jocularity.

Mrs Thomson paid no attention. 'Frustrated women – do you know there were two of them, classic examples, living down at Knulle well into our time. The Ladies of Knulle they called them, Miss Mortimer and Miss Boys Talbot, crazed old witches who terrified the local kids. "I've seen one of the Ladies", they'd say, as if they'd met Beelzebub. I used not to give them a thought, they were just part of the village scene – every village has got its barmy inhabitants, people are very tolerant of them. But now that I'm turning into a crazed old witch myself I think of them. Especially as Miss Mortimer once lived in this house. Tiger, do you remember? The clever girl of the family, too clever by half according to our Louise, with a sharp tongue and a dominating manner – she was heading for spinsterdom even then. Think of the life she led here, brothers far less able than her scattered all over the world living independent, moderately successful lives, and she tied to aging parents and a suffocating little village like this.'

'But you imply that she did break away in the end.'

'Even Victorian parents seem to have died. But by then it was too late for a proper life, I suppose, so she settled down

55

the valley with this other woman.'

'You said Boys Talbot – any relation to him of the monument?'

'It was his daughter.'

'I'm not sure that I would have cared to be the daughter of a visionary and a philanthropist.'

Mrs Thomson sat up and leaned in Trevor's direction. 'You feel that? Now that is very strange because it is precisely that that affects me.' she spoke with the passionate intensity of one who had discovered a twin soul.

With uneasy flippancy Trevor tried to dissociate himself from affinity with Mrs Thomson. 'Well, of course I don't know anything about him, but it must be an uncomfortable business living with a visionary, and I wouldn't exactly have welcomed a philanthropist as a parent. Shades of Mrs Jellyby and all that.'

'Margaret Boys Talbot found it an uncomfortable business, as you say. In fact the local story is that her father chased her down the village street in her nightgown.'

'You mean he turned her out of the house for misbehaviour?'

'I mean,' said Mrs Thomson, staring at him fixedly, 'that he made improper advances to his own daughter. Incest.'

'Oh well, they always say that it's a commonplace in the country.' Trevor spoke in the light tones that one uses towards the deranged. 'Because of the boredom, I suppose – and the dark you were talking about.'

'He died soon afterwards so she got free. But it was part of the burden of being a woman then.'

'I honestly don't think that . . .'

'If it wasn't that then it was emotional incest, like Elizabeth Barrett and her father. Your parents possessed you, until your husband took you over. But all this is beside the point; what I was going to say is that I think that the diary was written by Margaret Boys Talbot.'

This statement was again delivered in the unemphatic tones of one uttering a truism too obvious to be discussed. The Hancocks stirred uneasily, gave each other a fleeting, surreptitious glance. 'Have you any reason –?', Trevor began carefully.

'Oh no reason at all. It's just an instinct, though I've thought about it a lot.' She looked at them with a measure of defiance.

'Her name doesn't occur in the Journal.'

'Exactly. Nor does her father's, which is odd when you think that he must have been important in Ludwardine. He lived up at the Court – that's the house that used to be across the Ludd opposite the battle mounds. It's burnt down now, nothing left of it. He brought the railway to Ludwardine and ruined himself in the process. The diarist talks a lot about the history of Ludwardine, about the battle mounds and the castle and all that, as well as sketching in the local characters. But she never mentions Boys Talbot's name. So she must have had some good reason not to, like hating him.'

'I see.' There did not seem to be much else to say.

'Perhaps, Trevor, we ought to go now. As we have the rest of Ludwardine to see.'

Both got to their feet with alacrity. Mrs Thomson made no effort to move, she stared at them broodingly. Then she stood up. 'Come and see the garden.'

As they followed her they gave each other covert glances. They were led through the conservatory, out into the long, dead grass, and then were plunged into the shrubbery, ducking to avoid the branches, trying to pull brambles from their legs.

'Look, here.'

Under the wall was a series of small headstones. Children's graves? Into both their minds came the sudden thought that they had been led here by a madwoman to share in some necrophilic rite.

'They're pets! Jennifer's voice had an almost hysterical note of relief in it as she stooped down and scraped at moss with a fingernail. 'I remember them like this at Ecclesfield vicarage.'

'You went there because of Mrs Ewing? Do you know her books then?'

'Oh no, not really. When I used to go to stay with my granny near Ecclesfield she took me to see the village. I was very taken with all the gravestones in the vicarage garden. In fact I was always asking to go back, just to cry over them. Children don't feel the death of people, it's the death of animals they mind, and there was something that really got me about those animals that had mattered so much to their owners that they had put up gravestones with their names on.'

'That's what I say. Particularly when I know that when I'm a handful of ashes these will still be here saying 'Caesar'' and "Pompey" and "Alas, poor Brock". You ought to read Mrs Ewing; *Mrs Overtheway's Remembrances* at any rate. I did it because of the diary, I wanted to see why the writer felt it so much. It was the story of Mrs Moss that she wept over, do you remember?'

'Under the cedar tree with old Lady Benbow fussing her all the time and wondering whether it was too hot or too cold.'

'When I read the story of Mrs Moss I knew it was no 17-year old that wrote that diary. It's the story of a child who longs to see the radiant beauty that she has heard her grandmother talk about, a beauty in rose brocade and green silk shoes with pink heels – and she is shown an ugly old woman in a horrible brown dress. And the child in the book who is told this story just falls asleep out of boredom, she doesn't see anything sad or interesting in it. Nor would any 17-year old. When you're that age you know perfectly well that you'll always be young and pretty, that old people were born like it and have only themselves to blame. Shapeless old bags, you say, *you'll* be different. I know, I was like that and I know perfectly well that nobody under the age of twenty believes that I ever was young or might have been pretty. I daresay you don't.' She stared at them with smouldering eyes.

'Do you know,' said Trevor a few minutes later, 'when she pointed to those gravestones I was quite sure for a minute that she was going to tell us that it was her what done it. Murder on the moors and all that.'

'What I'll never learn is what to say to mad people who tell you that they know you think they're mad.'

Chapter 4

JUNE

'If Mr Wittering tells me again that it was very good of us to come,' said Trevor, 'I'll begin to believe him.'

They stood in the Stores at Ludwardine and surveyed the village street. 'Is it my imagination, or has the June traffic the edge over the Easter traffic? That's when we were last here, April.'

Since there was no particular indication of whom he was addressing there was at first silence. Then – for surely his wife must be reckoned not to need this sort of reminding about the recent past – the shopkeeper recognized it as a statement to which she was expected to reply.

'It starts up like this in April and goes on till September. The end of September. Of course there'll always be the lorries, but that's when the caravans stop.' She gave the information without any particular feeling, in a brisk, matter-of-fact way; her enquiring look referred to what they might be expecting to buy rather than to any interest she might take in their presence in Ludwardine. She was young thirties, in a Marks & Spencer nylon overall and jeans, her voice West Midlands rather than local. Trevor who, with his ingrained, wary suspicion that he was besieged and threatened, was always trying to sign on allies, was clearly not going to get any support from this quarter. But he went on trying.

'Do you reckon they bring in any trade?'

'Oh yes, they come in for soft drinks and ices. And the caravans come to stock up.'

'So it's worth putting up with all this racket in the street outside?'

'You get used to it. And the old people like it, it gives them something to look at. When there was talk of a by-pass they got up a petition against it.'

'Do they like something like this?' Trevor pointed out at the cars parked on the opposite side of the road, the cluster of animated backs on the pavement, 'The Fleming Society on its annual walk-about? It's a pious pilgrimage over the route that a young woman took on a ride a hundred years ago. Through Mairwood and right round the hills to Black Mixen and back to Ludwardine again. Quite a pretty walk, though you wouldn't expect the natives to bother with it."

She looked out between the pyramids of detergent and pet food in the window at the cluster outside the Three Pigeons. 'Well, I don't expect they notice this very much, with all the cars there are about already. It's the pony trekking they like. We get that in August, they come and tie up the ponies outside the Talbot Arms. And there was that fire in Harley Valley six years ago, there were fire engines in the street for a week then.'

'I suppose there'll always be the chance that the Fleming Society will drop matches today. And the hills are dry enough and there's a strong breeze.'

'Yes, there's always a danger of fire except when it's really wet.' She remained coolly uninvolved.

'Oh well, we can't go on skulking from the society much longer. We've been using you as a fall-out shelter. So we'd better buy our fruit and go and chat them up. What have you got? Is it really only a choice between Golden Delicious and an Outspan orange? Then we'd better take a couple of cans of fizz as well to slake the thirst.'

On the opposite side of the road Mr Wittering was surrounded by a happy group of chatterers. Blazers had given way to open neck shirts for this less formal occasion, worn under nattily checked sports coats or pale golf jackets. The ladies were uniformly in trousers. Hands were plunged in pockets – June in Ludwardine was not warm, a stiff west wind blew down the village street, the sky was overcast and threatened rain.

'What would their mothers have said?' Trevor surveyed the ample buttocks across the road.

'No, trousers don't do anything for them, as my dress-shop auntie used to say.'

'Your auntie didn't *tell* her ladies that, did she? She wouldn't have been able to retire to Southport with her little pile if she had.'

'What she told them was that the thing they were cramming themselves into *did* something. If it plain didn't then she kept quiet or waited to tell us at home. She had a way with her and customers believed her.'

'I suppose if we crude northern types say anything remotely nice it sounds convincing because our voices aren't made for flattery; not like soft insinuating southern voices. Well Edgar, here we come.'

The cluster on the broad pavement outside the Three Pigeons made way for them smilingly, and others standing by their cars further down nodded. Nobody could say the society was not a friendly one. The Hancocks looked conspicuous. Both were equipped as for climbing Snowdon — orange cagoules, rucksacks, climbing boots.

'And here,' said Mr Wittering, 'we have our newest members. Mr and Mrs Hancock, all the way from Bradford. Which I think is the furthest afield today. Am I right?'

'None of us would presume to contradict,' said the stout military type by Trevor's side.

'Ah, but somebody might have road mileage at his fingertips. But I think I'm safe, Nottingham is our next furthest. Our usual group from Birmingham, a lot from Hereford and Worcester, of course, and Cardiff and Cheltenham. No, we can't beat Bradford today. Though for our September Saturday of Remembrance we shall have visitors from Canada and the States this year.'

'Are you expecting the Warden and Mr Tosswell?'

'Not at our June meeting, no. They're very busy men. This is just an extra little jaunt for those of us who like to get out in the fresh air.'

'Yes, they have weaknesses, but over fresh air they are notoriously strong-minded.'

One or two of Trevor's neighbours tittered, but the atmosphere generally was of uneasy embarrassment. Mr

Wittering sailed in to rescue the situation. 'Mr and Mrs Hancock are going to do the whole walk on foot, they tell me. Isn't this the first time? Does any one remember it being walked before?'

'I don't see how else it could be done. Do you mean the rest of you ride?'

Trevor's truculent facetiousness slid off Mr Wittering like a pat of soft butter. 'Now that would be an occasion. No, most of us are getting on a bit so we do it by car. Taking our time, of course, and getting out to walk here and there. We leave it to everybody to suit themselves. We just meet up for lunch at Beggar's Bush, and for tea at Ludwardine. It's quite surprising how far you can get by car. Even up to Black Mixen – to see the circle of the hills, you know; we all make a point of that. There's a road up through the Forestry Commission, a bit tricky to find, so we usually go in convoy. And then the road along the top to the radio mast. Now, do you two young people reckon you know the route? We don't want to send out search parties, do we!'

Other people's facetiousness is always distasteful. Trevor showed his irritation. 'I fancy we'll be able to manage fifteen miles of easy country without losing a limb.'

'Compass, survival kit, he's got the lot,' said the stout military party.

'What about Very lights?' said another. 'Bound to need them. I never travel without them myself, always have one or two handy in my pocket.'

'And a walkie-talkie radio.' said a bright lady who wore her spectacles like a necklace. 'Then we'll all come running to rescue them.'

'Depends where they were. If it's teatime and they're still up by the Great Creigau then yours truly stays where he is.'

'There is nothing more tedious,' said Trevor savagely as they marched down the Gletton road, nail-studded boots clattering, 'than middle-aged skittishness. The idea of facing them all again at lunch gives me the very great horrors. I think we'd better try to lose the way.'

'I used to be a dab hand at losing the biology mistress on school field expeditions. But I'd be ashamed this time, they'd put it down to bad map-reading.' Jennifer stepped back to let a car go past. A horn was tooted and a hand waved out of the window. 'How many more have got to pass us? It's getting tiring.'

'At least 20 more, I'd say. And the next one that coyly offers us a lift will get a V sign.'

'You'd better prepare to genuflect,' he said half an hour later. 'Mairwood is coming up.'

The blue slates of the spire could just be seen above distant trees, and now as they rounded the corner the little lodge with its comically tall chimneys came into sight.

'And here's the school. A fastidious conversion this time, better than the usual holiday cottage DIY. And not even a coach lantern.'

'Poor Edward Benbow. I wonder what he was really like.'

'A visionary, like him of the monument. I envy the Victorians, they could be. I'd like to believe in progress like they did. I'd like to have a vision.'

'You!' said Jennifer incredulously.

'Yes I would. Communism or the Church, I wouldn't care what it was as long as I thought it was going to save the world. That's the awful thing about being young now, there just are no viable visions. Everybody ought to have a chance of youthful illusions, it's against nature to be a cynic in your twenties.'

'Perhaps when you're middle-aged you'll get them – like Edgar and co.'

'If I get like that you can put paraquat in my tea. God, how old and worldly wise they make me feel. But that's just slushy sentimentality. Benbow wasn't like that.'

'How do you know?'

'I've read enough to recognize the type. I like him. He was a romantic, he did things on a grand scale. The more I think of it the more extraordinary that church is – an anachronism really at that date – much more the sort of thing you'd have expected a generation earlier. And to put your own wife into a church window – fifteenth-century Florentines might do that, but pious Victorians on the whole did not.'

'I hope his illusions and his beautiful church kept him

64

going when the congregations didn't come and his wife left him.'

'My guess is that they did. I reckon there was a tough, determined streak in him. It wasn't illusions with him, it was conviction.'

'You're only guessing.'

'I said I was only guessing, didn't I. But I can really feel him, in a way I can't feel the writer herself. It's what Mrs Thomson said, mad though she is; a lot's being kept back. Though it would be as much as my life was worth to say so to Wittering and his little friends. How Benbow would have winced at that brisk young parson, who sees church as an extension of the youth club. I mean, damn it, if you're going to have beliefs you ought to have an element of mystery, not behave as if you're sitting on a committee of time and motion experts.'

'You ought to set up a rival society of Benbowites.'

'The disadvantage of that being that we would all have to meet in the same shrine.'

'Then you'd better hurry and get off this road otherwise they'll all come pouring out of Mairwood and offer you lifts all over again.'

'Oh we're safe for a bit. They've got to make their salaams at the sacred fane, discuss Mr Wittering's plans for the memorial tablet, and imbibe from their flasks of Nescafe – elevenses is coming up.'

They left the Gletton road at the Evancob turning and took the path through the woods on the shoulder of Burfa Tump.

'We're safe here now,' said Jennifer. 'It's all field paths till Beggar's Bush. None of them are wearing shoes that could cope with this. A lot of the ladies had high-heeled sandals.'

'But they could cope with this,' said Trevor some thirty minutes later as they climbed over a gate on to a narrow metalled lane. 'It's the old road from Evancob to Gletton, and a pretty scenic one too. Just the sort of route that Edgar would recommend to his henchman – such hills and views.'

But no vehicle passed them, and there was no sound except the shrilling of larks, and the murmur of distant farm machinery from fields below where hay was being mown. The ridge ended and the road began to descend.

'There's Paradise Farm,' announced Jennifer with satisfaction, pointing to a sunlit group of buildings at the edge of the woods that covered the upper slopes of the valley to their left.

'Of course it's Paradise Farm. You always behave as though landmarks are in their right places by some miraculous intervention.'

'I still do think it's miraculous when I'm in the place where I meant to be. But do you know, I don't want to cause alarm and despondency, but it does look as though there are cars up by the farm.'

Trevor tried to reason the horrifying possibility out of existence. 'They couldn't get cars up there. Anyway, nobody passed us.'

'They might have come from the Gletton end.'

'My God, they'll be searching for Miss Fleming's cankered rose. Do you remember that bit? She finds it growing in the farm wall. A sort of sub-Hardy touch. They'll be wallowing in emotion – I can't bear it, we'll have to turn back.'

Though said violently, it was, as both of them knew, a rhetorical statement. Both continued marching down the hill; neither wavered more than fleetingly when they had to turn off into the track that led up to the farm. The cars were now obvious, sprawled in the grass by the side of the macadam.

'I suppose it's a point of honour to totter the final steps on one's own feet.' Trevor stared up at the cluster that stood by the farm buildings a couple of fields away. 'Now we're not going to stop and chatter, get that clear.'

'Have you found a rose?' called Jennifer as they approached the farm yard. After self-consciously hauling themselves up the slope with thirty pairs of eyes focused on them it was a relief to be within hailing distance. ('Shut up, Trevor, we've got to say something, haven't we.')

Mr Wittering stepped forward. 'How very sad. We would have waited if we had known you were so near.' He gestured towards the farmhouse.

There was no life to be seen there; windows and blistered door were impenetrably shut; a sea of uncut grass in the narrow garden surged up to the flaking white walls. There was a desolate sound of dogs barking in a nearby barn, a hollow noise that bounced off tinny walls. The Hancocks stared round them, at a loss.

'Our annual little ceremony.'

Jennifer had gone up to the low wall that bounded the garden. A spray of dog-rose had been laid there. She half-understood. 'This?'

'It has become a tradition,' said Mr Wittering.

'From our very earliest visit,' said Irene softly. 'The very first time that Edgar and I came we thought we ought to make this little gesture.'

'Only then as it was winter there were no flowers, so we promised ourselves that come the summer we would return, like the swallows, and bear our offering of wild rose. We feel that it symbolises the spirit of the diarist.'

Irene spelt it out for them. 'She found a rose with a canker. But she should have found a rose in bloom, we all feel that.'

'It seems so very fitting that we should remember her in every way we can,' said one of the ladies. 'She was so afraid of her memory fading. That's what I always think when we come here – that we are doing something for her that she never expected, but that she would surely have liked. There is the Service of Remembrance, of course. But it was when she was on this ride that she felt the fear of being forgotten.'

Orange cagoule, muddy boots, confronted the array of shining car-borne trimness. 'And what about the sheep that she saw being flayed – surely in that byre over there?' said Trevor chattily. 'Why not make a gesture of that? Have you ever thought that you may be commemorating the wrong lady?'

It was Jennifer who plunged into the chasm of silence. 'He doesn't really think that, he's teasing.'

But she was overtaken by Mr Wittering. 'I can see our young friend has been talking to Mrs Thomson. I should have warned him about that good lady.'

67

The recriminations that followed developed into the worst quarrel of the Hancocks' marriage. It absorbed the rest of the ten miles and the four hours that it took to cover the terrain, with momentary lulls when silence was demanded for map-reading, an exercise in any case fraught with irritation as the wind was now stiff, and buffeted the sheet so that they both had to hold it, both bitterly resenting the enforced proximity.

At first the acrimony was not remarkable. Jennifer did not speak until they were well inside the woods behind the farm. She tried to be circumspect, to keep her voice light.

'I didn't know that you took Mrs Thomson that seriously.'

'In some ways she has a great deal more insight than Wittering and his friends.'

'Do you think that somebody else did write the diary then?'

'You ought to know. You have just told them all what I meant and what I didn't mean. Why bother to ask *me*?'

'I'm interested. From what you said in April I gathered you thought Mrs Thomson was crazy, you said that lunatic hunches and *a priori* reasoning were typical of women like her – typical of all women really.'

'Since you remember it all so well it seems quite futile for me to say anything more.'

'I just thought you might have changed your mind.'

More map consultations were called for as they approached the crossroads that were the venue named for lunch. 'We'll have to avoid Beggar's Bush. They'll all be sitting there now at their little folding tables eating veal and ham pie and tinned potato salad with knives and forks.'

'And it's intellectually so much more respectable to eat salami with your fingers.'

'I should never have taken you away from Buxton. That's the only milieu you understand – where you live life with your chapel gloves on. We'll have to turn off here. I know it's a mile's detour, but even you would admit that it's better to keep our distance from all that horde.'

'Why,' said Jennifer conversationally, 'do you say things

that you don't believe and don't mean?'

He had no difficulty in knowing what she referred to. 'Nobody's on oath at a social occasion. Surely at your age you should have learned the difference between the light-hearted remark and the serious opinion. But I suppose it's impossible to expect a scientist to see anything except literally.'

'I don't see why you have to set out deliberately to rile people.'

'I've got as much chance of riling them as of riling an eiderdown. God, I wish I could think that there was some-one who could appreciate the beauty of it all; you couldn't have a more perfect illustration than that of what I mean about the Fleming Society.'

'Than what?' How stupid to provide feed lines like that, she thought angrily. But time and experience never seemed to teach her anything about how to handle him.

'Than the bland determination to make something pretty out of every aspect of the diary, to turn the writer into one of those crinolined ladies they used to daub on to blotting pads and tea cosies and lampshades fifty years ago (which you could say was the formative period for the Witteringites). They'd be the first to trot out the hoary clichés about Victorians veiling piano legs, but that's exactly what they are doing themselves. Perhaps the greatest interest in that diary is the underlying note of sadness, but as soon as there's a whiff of it – like the description of the cankered rose – they spray it with their ghastly little aerosol cans of sentimental optimism.'

An hour later they were beginning the climb up from the valley floor near Twiscob. Walls of Forestry Commission conifers pressed round them, mile upon mile to every side of them, obscuring the distance they had come, concealing the way they still had to go to reach the top of the forest. They were lapped in a silent world of pine needles and bare tree trunks that must continue, it was to be supposed, until they had climbed some 2000 feet. Jennifer's anger had by now evaporated, replaced by an insane desire to laugh at their predicament, cooped up here with their quarrel and no prospect of release from each other for hours yet.

'What I think is so funny,' she said conversationally, 'is the way Mr Wittering always manages to deflate you. So far he's always been a jump ahead.' She did not mean to be particularly provoking; at that moment it did strike her suddenly as a joke that could be shared. 'Every time you think you're being particularly daring, he turns out to know all about it.'

The quarrel at this point took on a new dimension. Up till now they had managed to confine it to the particular, the encounter at Paradise Farm. Now it became more fundamental – their reflections on each other's characters.

'What I never get from you is support. Today was absolutely typical. You had to contradict me, humiliate me in front of all those people. And now gloat over it.'

It was of course natural then to remind him that he had brought it upon himself, to muse upon the contradictions in his nature: his childish wish to shock and be contrary; his native aggression that would go so far and then take fright; his need for approval. 'You're always so surprised when people you don't like turn out not to like you either. What you would like is to kick them and then to be told how very daring and interesting you are, and how flattered the victim is by your attention. And for Teacher to tell you you've been a very clever boy. Can't you ever face up by yourself to the consequence of what you do?'

When at last they heaved themselves over the barbed wire that bounded the edge of the woods, into the open ground, a west wind was blowing a thin, stinging rain into their faces. The last few hundred feet of the ascent lay over heather and rough, tussocky ground where you had to concentrate if you were not going to break an ankle. They climbed in silence, each following a separate path.

'This must be the point where she looked out on the circle of hills.' Jennifer on the stony track that had been laid at the top braced herself against the wind and looked east. The only indication of the vast conifer plantations through which they had moved was a thin dark line drawn along the rim of the slopes below; the rest had vanished in the precipitous descent of the hillside. Beyond, grey hills veiled by rain melted into a grey sky.

'I suppose,' said Trevor some few paces behind, 'this is just another attempt to bait me.'

She began to giggle hysterically. '"So all day long the sound of battle rolled" – how's that for a line of Tennyson from a biochemist?'

Chapter 5

OCTOBER

For the young there is no more effective *memento mori* than a visit to their former place of education. Obviously, the greater the affection for it the keener the sense of desolation when it suddenly dawns that one is totally forgotten, has ceased to matter – at a place where one's most intense life to date has been lived; that even if the present denizens were told of one's identity they would find it wholly irrelevant. Teachers and the taught alike concern themselves only with the present. Once the results of the last examination are known the pupil dies, becomes just a name that persists for a little on a flapping class-list pinned in a college lodge during the high tourist season, a name for whom the tutor may later find himself wearily inditing references (though the more satisfactory the pupil the fewer, in general, of these that are required, the more swiftly he vanishes).

Even Jennifer who had only experienced Oxford vicariously (though intensely) through Trevor felt the melancholy of the occasion. It was a melancholy that neither of them had expected, since the mood at Bradford had been elation, though neither of them would have confessed to it, at the Warden's invitation so suddenly and unexpectedly extended.

'What do you know!' Trevor had crowed exultantly. 'I thought that with banishment to the provinces my name had been blotted out forever down there. A.A. regards provincial universities rather as the Victorian upper classes thought of board schools – necessary for the masses, but not things that one need ever oneself take cognisance of.'

'I suppose it was obvious to ask you – the first performance of the Louise songs and you a Fleming author. And weren't you secretary of the college music society once?'

72

'That's right, pour cold water,' he said bitterly.

'I'm sorry, I didn't mean it like that. You're so touchy. I was only trying to please. I meant that it was obvious to ask you to the concert. But to ask us both to dinner too. I suppose it couldn't be. . . ? I mean, you did say that Colin Cooper would be retiring soon.'

'No, impossible. Things aren't settled that way.'

'You always said they were settled quite informally – a nod or a lift of the eyebrow signified everything.'

'The trouble with you is that you always take me so literally. There's more to a college fellowship than the Warden's nod, I can tell you. And anyway he has no power.'

Of course she saw through his finality. But she abandoned the topic; in any case it had probably been unfair to show that she was aware of this his most cherished daydream. 'Will you be taking the Fleming piece with you?' She spoke warily. Since that June day in Ludwardine the topic had never been raised. She was aware that he had been working on it during the last three months, sensed that it mattered to him as much as anything he had ever undertaken, but knew that she must, if ever she referred to it, speak of it lightly as though of some ephemeral journalism.

'What do you think?'

She was surprised, but recognized that he wanted approval for something he had already planned to do. 'I think you should. It would be only polite to show it to A.A. and Tosswell. I mean, they needn't read it.'

'Trust you to remind me of that. But I think I will. There are a couple of things I'd like to explain to one or other of them before Wittering starts in on it. I'm assuming that Stern and Chantrey are bound to send it to them.'

So they had set off from Bradford in high spirits. These were still sustained when they reached north Oxford and the friends with whom they were to spend the night. Jokes were exchanged about the royal command that had brought them so far to eat their dinner, but it was conceded that if it had been Aberdeen rather than Bradford they would have had to have done the same.

'You'll be too early. Stay and have a drink.'

'Surely you don't grudge the poor exile his chance to stroll down memory lane again. We can walk there and pretend we are part of the place again.'

But as they progressed south down the Banbury road and the sober villas of Victorian tradesmen gave way to the preposterous fancies of Victorian academe the melancholy crept over them. By the time they were scuffing through the drift of chestnut leaves outside the Parks they had each withdrawn into silence. It was impossible to feel part of Oxford, they had no place there; they were tourists, outsiders. They had to step out of the way to avoid animated clusters, people called to each other over their heads, moved between them. It was not until a youth sidled up to them and asked confidentially to be directed to Lady Margaret Hall (it was only the second Sunday of term) that Trevor temporarily recovered his habitual jauntiness. But he explained in unnecessary detail; indeed at one moment Jennifer thought he was going to draw him a map.

'In a week he'll be calling it LMH and despising everybody who doesn't do the same. God, how old this makes me feel; everybody here seems two generations younger than I ever was. And how desperately important the trivialities of the moment seem,' he said as they stepped over the legs of a group sprawled with beer mugs on the pavement outside the King's Arms. 'I remember that all right, and how pleasantly condescending one felt to the people who couldn't appreciate it. That's Oxford epitomized, of course; intense concern for all the minutiae inside its walls, total disregard for what's outside. It never seems to occur to anybody outside the walls. They think that the whole world has its ear cocked for their little mouse squeaks, their budgerigar twitterings.'

'You liked it while you were here.'

'Of course I did – don't you ever listen to a word I say? It's precisely what I was saying, isn't it. While you're in it you're lulled into thinking that this is the only reality. Oh it's wonderful while you're here, all right, and it stays wonderful for those that manage to stay on – so long as they don't step outside. If they do they feel the draught, especially if they're people of consequence here. That really was brought home to me at that do we went to last September – the one we skipped this year.'

'The Fleming Remembrance Service?'

'The same. A.A. was out of his element. I know they were making a fuss of him and he put up a bloody good show of enjoying it, but it was because he'd written a piffling introduction that they were lionizing him – not because of his mystic position as Warden of Canterbury College, the doyen of academics too fastidious to put pen to paper, the leader of what Oxford bachelor society there is left. Of course they couldn't grasp that at all – so little that they had to try to invent an importance for him and call him "doctor". That was the first time that I really realized he was the same flesh and blood as the rest of us. It was like seeing the Pope in bathing trunks.'

'Do you know,' he said as they turned into Canterbury Lane, 'I made a mistake in marrying you.'

'So you've often told me.'

'I mean in A.A.'s eyes. While I was unmarried I had a certain interest. I was crude and unpolished – I always knew that I'd got the worst sort of lower middle class Christian name and an accent that grated and of course I'd read English which must mean that I had either been to a secondary modern or a girls' school. But I could be invited to his big crushes and displayed as an example of how broad-minded and broad-based and tolerant Canterbury was these days. I do honestly think that A.A. believes that anybody who talks Yorkshire must be the son of a miner. And then I went and got married and showed that I was just humdrum and bourgeois.'

'That's what I can't understand – him asking me. Are you sure he really is expecting me? It was put in such a queer way, "your wife if she would care to come", like a sort of afterthought, but he hoped I'd be tied to the kitchen stove and the kids.'

'He knows you're coming now because I wrote and told him so. For heaven's sake don't let's go over all this ground again.'

'Who else do you suppose will be there?'

'Rouncey presumably will be the hero of the hour since they're his songs that are being performed. Tosswell of course because they're his words and anyway he's A.A.'s alter ego. Of course you don't need telling that there isn't a Lady Rouncey or a Mrs Tosswell. Or a Mrs Adeane.'

'What about the Witterings?'

Trevor's cock-sparrow assurance momentarily left him. 'Surely not – this is an Oxford occasion. I mean, they'd be completely out of their depth.' With only a few yards to go before the college lodge he made a visible effort to come to terms with the possibility. 'Well, it can only be a very short affair, the concert's due to begin at 8.30. Anyway, I dare say it will be a vast crush and we can keep out of Edgar's way.'

But it was clear to Jennifer that the Witterings would be more than an embarrassment, the very fact of their presence would turn the occasion – of which he was expecting so much – into a meaningless *omnium gatherum*. It was odd it seemed never to have occurred to him that they might be there; it had been her first thought. With an effort she had restrained herself from voicing it before. But it had slipped out now.

They passed the lodge. A porter who was a stranger lifted his head from the evening paper and glanced at them incuriously. There was a fleeting hesitation, and then Trevor led the way round the grass of the quad rather than over it. His efforts to sustain a jaunty manner were almost painful.

'I suppose I ought to have told you that there is a butler.'

'Thank you for warning me.'

'And not a Filipino houseboy. One of the old school. He looks at you so that you know he's thinking "I bet in the circles *you* move in you've not seen one of *my* sort before.'

'Not many people would.'

'Aha, but like his master he thinks that anybody who presumes to cross his threshold ought to have.' Aggressively bracing his shoulders – his habitual preparation for a daunting encounter – Trevor put his finger square on the brilliantly polished brass bell-push.

When the butler showed them into the library it was instantly apparent that far from there being a vast crush where they might be unnoticed they were in fact intruders into some intimate occasion. There was a small cluster of men at the far end, standing in front of the fireplace and its leather-upholstered fender, all laughing immoderately. The butler departed, closing the door behind him ('with the air of having tossed a bit of stale meat into the lions' den,' Trevor was to say later when the whole occasion had at last been transmuted into one of his favourite dinner-party sagas. 'We started at love-thirty so to speak.') The Warden detached himself with almost visible reluctance from the group on the hearth rug and came forward.

'Trevor, how good to see you again.'

'My wife, Jennifer.'

'It is very good of you to come, Mrs Hancock.' (They had in fact met before; it was impossible to tell whether he remembered.) 'From so far too. I am afraid you will be the only lady. And as it is on the whole a bachelor occasion we are as you see in the library.'

'It's a lovely room to be in.'

'Yes, if you're not intimidated by books. Do you know Rousham? The Cottrell Dormers' house north of Woodstock? There one of the ladies who married into the family made her husband empty his entire library so that she could hang her family portraits where the books had been.'

'Jennifer,' said Trevor, 'I'm sure apologizes for her sex.' He didn't quite make the remark lightly enough; it sounded like a comment on the Warden's well-known prejudices.

Adeane smiled fleetingly. ('love-forty,' as Trevor put it.) 'Come and meet the rest of us.' Of the three men who leaned against the chimney-piece, two looked at them with ill-concealed incuriosity. ('We'd interrupted their games, they couldn't have been more bored by us.') 'Henry of course you know, Trevor. Just back from the Antipodes.' Tosswell stepped forward. His notoriously ravaged face, which had been variously alluded to as a battle site, a ploughed field, crumpled parchment, broke into a charming and boyish, almost deprecating smile; with it went an unexpected air of not being altogether at ease.

'And this is Hugo Rouncey.' Rouncey ('who looks more

like a bank manager than any real bank manager would consider decent') regarded them impassively. And Peregrine Thorpe.' ('Rouncey's attendant jackal, did all the talking for him.') A sharp-faced forty-year old smiled toothily. 'Trevor used to be our Lothian research fellow. But he has come from Bradford today.' ('All of which had naturally been outlined to them before, together with a summary of my career, personality and characteristics. But anyway I was wearing quite a decent suit that day so foiled them there – fifteen-forty, I reckoned.')

'We were comparing,' said Adeane blandly, 'honorary degrees.' ('The hell you were. Game and set to you.') 'Henry had countered your Columbia, Victor, with Melbourne. But what about nearer at home?'

'Durham,' said Tosswell, smiling almost apologetically at the Hancocks.

'Snap,' said Thorpe. 'Yes, Victor, you did you know. Don't you remember the macedoined vegetables in aspic and the lady at the lunch party who gave you a blow by blow account of her daughter's piano grade III?'

Rouncey, smiling faintly, shook his head.

'Well, I can vouch for it that he was there, and nearly late too because of me missing the way somewhere round about Bishop Auckland. Poor Victor, he gets the impression that every university is the same one. The same vice-chancellor making the same otiose speeches, and the same caterers' posh at the reception afterwards. And the same mothers nobbling him about their prodigies of children.'

'I once got nobbled,' said Tosswell dreamily, 'at a guest night by an Oxford lady – not at this college, Nat, I hasten to say – who lectured me from the tinned turtle soup till the strawberries in meringue baskets on the importance of breast feeding.'

Even Rouncey joined in the gales of laughter. ('We couldn't of course. It would have looked snide for us to do anything but smile politely.')

'I'm glad you haven't impugned Canterbury, at any rate,' said the Warden. 'Now let me take the last trick with Lampeter.'

'Victor's Stirling trumps that. He hasn't actually got it yet, but he's going to next summer.'

'No, I must insist on the exclusiveness of Lampeter. What would you say, Trevor?'

'Lampeter every time. When are we going to start on foreign decorations? Does the Purple Heart that my mother's GI boy-friend got for having chickenpox on D-Day count?' ('The frisson that went round the room could have been felt as far as Merton. Jen was having fits that I was letting the side down, but A.A. always expects that sort of clowning from me.')

'And if we couldn't compete over medals and decorations before dinner, dinner was even worse, because they talked about food. The whole time. The history of ice cream – you've no idea how much there was to be said about that – *sarbotières* and bombe moulds. About how eating out in France has become a travesty. They cook the scallops to cinders, the salad oil is no longer olive, and Rouncey and co. had an *oeuf* which stuck to the *plat. And* there are frozen vegetables. And all the time we were being served unspeakable food at breakneck speed. The melon was like frozen mangel-wurzel, and A.A. went through the motions of sending it back. "Is there any better melon, Charles?" "I'll go and enquire, sir." "No, sir, I'm afraid there isn't." Which of course we'd all known before he started. And when the uneaten melon was whipped off the table it was replaced with uneatable little birds, one per person on a piece of fried bread. Only nobody could drag a morsel of flesh off them so they went back as they came in. I said "Well, they'll make nice soup" but that didn't go down too well either. Then there were frozen strawberries which somebody had forgotten to get out of the freezer in time, and while we were chomping our way through the only course that actually could be masticated – a dried-up cheese soufflé – they were talking about the importance of roasting one's own coffee, the best place to buy green beans, and in what quantity, and where to go for your roasting machine. And the coffee when, choking on our last morsel of dried egg, we were hustled back into the library? It was no mere Nescafe, it was a thin, tepid, bitter concoction that might equally well have been tea or cocoa. But poured out of Georgian silver, of course. Talk about mind over matter! I began to see the truth of the clichés about intellectuals being remote from reality.'

To Jennifer, sitting between the Warden and Hugo Rouncey (whom everybody so tediously called Victor) the speed of the meal had been the one thing in its favour – though she found herself admiring the aplomb of the host who never, after the initial gesture over the melon, once referred to its shortcomings. She knew that she herself would have been breathless with apology. Indeed, one might even bemusedly suppose, observing his contented urbanity, that the inadequacies of the food were hallucination.

Placed where she was conversation was difficult. It was not only that the table was some fifteen feet long so that vast wastes of polished mahogany yawned between you and your neighbour. But Rouncey made not the slightest effort to speak to her, so that it would seem impertinence for her to speak to him. Besides, there is always the difficulty of knowing what to say to a celebrity. To treat him, at first at any rate, as an ordinary man is surely presumption or deliberate affectation. But to say 'What a masterpiece your Requiem for the Children is' is a conversation-stopper if ever there was one, and she did not fancy nearly falling off her chair to shout it to him over the Brussels carpet. So she had to sit silently and wait for such attention as the Warden, who was exchanging badinage with Peregrine Thorpe and through him with Tosswell, was prepared to give her. Trevor had always explained that the difference between Oxford and all other universities was the cultivated flippancy and lightness of tone, so profoundly irritating to the outsider, but so much missed by the exile. She found herself fervently on the side of the outsider.

Nor, surreptitiously watching Trevor, could she suppose that he was very much more in his element. Of course he had had far more practice than she had at such occasions, but he seemed to have difficulty in keeping afloat. Every time that he struggled to heave himself into the conversational boat, the Warden, Thorpe, or Tosswell sent it skimming away in a different direction. He would flounder after them, but to Jennifer's way of thinking he never got anywhere, and the loudness of his voice and of his laugh showed his desperation.

'Trevor would have us think that in the north you live on tinned ravioli and chips.' The Warden had at last turned in her direction. 'And that his life is one long high tea. But we know our Trevor. What is it the young favour nowadays? Is it pulses and so on? What might be termed the "ethnic" diet?'

What could one say to this? Explain that Trevor never allowed dinner to be served before eight o'clock in case it might be supposed that the meal was tea? That he saw to it that she cooked from Elizabeth David, Jane Grigson or Michael Smith? This would be playing into the Warden's hands.

'It was Oxford where I remember them being so keen on health foods,' she said warily.

'Yes, I believe you are right there. I remember a long conversation with one of our fellows' wives about the merits of brown rice which I rather gathered was a philosophy of life in itself. At any rate she told me she bought it by the sackful, which seemed to argue great devotion. And the cult might even have started here. Do you remember, Henry – or was it in your California days? – that shop in the High that sold yoghourt when it was still so very avant-garde even to know what the word meant? There were all sorts of herbal remedies and unguents too, and it was presided over by two deaths-heads, one male and one female, who looked such a very poor advertisement for their products, I always thought – yellowed skin stretched over bone.'

Tosswell, smiling, disclaimed knowledge of the establishment, and returned to discussion of the Sydney Opera House with Thorpe. Jennifer felt that the ball now lay in her court.

'Is' (Hugo Rouncey? Sir Hugo? Victor?) . . . 'Will the composer be playing his own songs this evening?'

'No, on this occasion he will be a spectator. He has

entrusted the performance to the college music society. It is a very great privilege for them, but we have a dynamic secretary at the moment who used his not inconsiderable powers of persuasion on Victor.'

(Trevor had been considered dynamic in his day, she thought; has he been totally forgotten?) Aloud, she asked if they had some particularly good performers among the undergraduates.

'Tim Hallows is singing, one of our choral clerks who has an outstandingly fine voice. And the pianist is James Kelly who left us two years ago. He's *répétiteur* at Glyndebourne at the moment. He'll go far, Victor was very impressed at the rehearsal.'

There being nothing that Jennifer could contribute to this line of conversation she searched for another topic. 'Did you go to the Fleming Remembrance service this year?' It was curious, she felt, that this had not been touched upon before now, since it was the only occasion that linked them all.

'Not this year, I'm afraid. Henry was in Australia – indeed he only got back a few days ago – and I was committed elsewhere. And you?'

'No, we couldn't either.' (A lie, of course. Trevor, though she had certainly never expected him to go, had made a great issue of refusing when the invitation had come.) 'How disappointed Mr Wittering must have been not to have the President.' She had intended this as a polite tribute to Tosswell, but realized too late that it sounded like malicious comment on Wittering.

'Yes, it was sad. Edgar read out the message that Henry had written for the occasion; it was the first one we had had to miss. But we'll be seeing them next month. Henry and I thought we would organize a little dinner party for Edgar and Irene, they have been so extremely hospitable and kind. And he's so enormously interesting – there never seems to be time at the more public functions for proper conversation.'

The implication of all this was shattering. Trevor, who always felt that life was permanent warfare where you lined up allies, dug yourselves into defensive positions, had, she knew, been confidently proceeding on the assumption that Oxford must inevitably be on one side, the provincials on the other — the Romans peering down from Hadrian's Wall at the woad-bedizened natives, the British raj in India. But it was perfectly clear from what Adeane had said, had intended to be understood, that the Witterings and what might be termed the Canterbury set were on terms of easy familiarity from which Trevor was totally excluded. She remembered that terrible game Diplomacy she had once been made to play, where you would suddenly and painfully find that your apparently friendly ally had been lured from your side by a player you had been regarding as your bitterest enemy. It came as a relief when the butler arrived at this moment to announce that coffee had been taken into the library.

'Then perhaps there'll just be time, Nat,' said Thorpe, 'for you to show us your modern dress photos.' He pushed back his chair with a great show of eagerness. 'You've tantalized us unfairly.'

In the library they stood holding Worcester porcelain cups of stewed but almost cold coffee in one hand, and passed photographs with the other. Jennifer had often heard about the Warden's notorious aversion for the way the present young clothed themselves. But he was apparently not content with merely observing their dress in his own college precincts or in the street, he had commissioned photographs of extreme examples so that he could, in the privacy of his own library, fuel the fire of his distaste. How this could be reconciled with the appearance of Tosswell, who always dressed as though he had just risen from the floor of a squat, Jennifer could not think, but looking at him furtively she could not see that he was in the least embarrassed or apologetic. Indeed he was passing round the prints with seeming enjoyment. Perhaps like the food it was a further instance of hallucination.

Scrutiny of the photographs ended when the French clock above the fireplace elegantly and melodiously tinkled out the half hour. The Warden glanced in its direction. 'Correct time; we must now adjourn to the hall.'

'You keep Greenwich time in the Lodgings then?' said

83

Thorpe. 'Did you realize, Victor, that Canterbury time, from time immemorial, is five minutes behind the rest of the nation? It seems an admirable arrangement, Nat; you can just stroll out on the hour from your own place and be a few minutes early for whatever you're doing in college.'

The chattering in the hall stopped as the little procession moved down it towards the high carved chairs that had been placed for the Warden's party just below the dais. The atmosphere was still steamy with gravy fumes, but the vast refectory tables from which dinner had been eatern had been pushed back against the walls, and benches piled on them for the audience who were lolling back against the dark panelling and the portraits of Canterbury dignitaries.

'Fancy sitting in the front row with the nobs,' Trevor said in Jennifer's ear. 'After all those years of being perched up in the gods. I remember the time when I almost put my head through Warden Henniker-Hadden and the JCR had to underwrite the picture-restorer's bill.'

As they took their seats the Canterbury clock on the gatehouse outside rang out the first seven notes of its ancient hymn tune. A moment later and the performers walked on to the platform.

It was an exceedingly long programme, as all undergraduate concerts tend to be, and with absolutely no concessions to popular taste. Jennifer did not attempt to listen, but after an hour the jangling of the harpsichord penetrated even the defensive wall behind which she usually managed to isolate herself on occasions that bored her. Its noise fretted her almost physically. The polished oak of the chair beneath her was in any case acutely uncomfortable; ruefully she began to remember that future queen who, not yet schooled to royal standards of propriety, had complained that her 'bottom had pins and needles'. In every way this seat was unsuitable for prolonged occupation; it was too large, too slippery, too high. Discomfort became anguish; there seemed no reason why the concert should ever end. By the time the singer and the pianist reached the platform for the evening's climax, the Rouncey songs, the Canterbury

84

clock was already intoning eleven o'clock, and she could only console herself in her despairing exhaustion by reflecting that it was the last item on the programme, and there were only six songs. And surely a song, unlike a sonata, implied brevity?

Walking down Parks road half an hour later she had nothing to say. The whole evening had been so painful that it seemed better not to comment on it. Anyway, it was Trevor's college and even she knew that it was not for her to utter the first words of criticism.

But Trevor seemed in a curiously elated state. 'You know, that music's really good.'

'Which?'

'The Rouncey of course. Good is not the way you go about describing the Goldberg Variations, or Wolf. But he's knocked the bottom out of Tosswell.'

'What do you mean?'

'The Louise poems.'

'Wasn't that what they were singing?'

'Oh come off it. I know you're pretty well tone deaf, but surely you can read programmes.'

'The programme seemed to say that the poems were by Tosswell.'

'Of course they were, but it's the ones Rouncey chose that are significant. He's left out all the ones so dear to the heart of the Fleming Society -- the Latin lesson, Harley stream, above the Vron, and so on, and kept the ones that hint at tragedy: the four blossoms, the solitary foxglove, the dying of the year, the cankered rose. Only Rouncey has brought about a transformation; you forget that the originals are only vapid little jingles. And he seems to have got Tosswell to write him a new one, the sheep flayer. You must have noticed that.'

'I was feeling like a flayed sheep myself by that time. Anyway, I don't know the original poems so I wouldn't know if anything had been added.'

'Didn't you notice the Tennyson even, right at the very end?'

'"I climb the hill" and something about 'some gracious

memory of my friend"? That was Tennyson was it. I did think it seemed a bit different.'

'Of course it was, the difference between Mozart and Salieri! But what Rouncey's done is to change a sort of pastoral idyll (if you could dignify Tosswell's crap by that name) into an elegy. Rouncey really understands, behind that poker-face there's real sensibility. He's the only person who seems to feel what I feel about the Fleming Journal. I want to tell Tosswell that – well, tactfully, of course, but he won't mind, he and Rouncey are twin souls, more or less – when I go to see him tomorrow.'

She was startled out of her weary apathy. 'You're going to see him?'

'While you were saying your farewells to A.A. he waylaid me and asked me to come. So I'll take this.' He tapped the pocket of his coat. Jennifer had seen him as they set out slip in the bulky envelope that there had never, throughout the evening, been the slightest opportunity to refer to.

'So when are you going?'

'Tomorrow morning, I suppose you could come too.'

'No fear. It was perfectly clear that I was never intended to go to the dinner party. I'm not going to make the same mistake again.'

'What do you suppose that he wants to see you about?' she asked next morning as they wandered down through the Parks.

'I don't know.' But Trevor's mood seemed buoyant. 'I'm glad though. There wasn't a chance last night to say anything about my Fleming piece.'

'Are you pleased with it, now that it's finished?'

'So so.'

So he was. She ventured a little further. 'What did you say in the end – about the identity of the girl who wrote the diary? I mean, did you ever think there was anything in what Mrs Thomson said?' No mention of what Trevor himself had said to Mr Wittering, that was too painful, best forgotten.

'It's really that that I wanted to prepare the Tosser for. To get him on my side before Wittering can start on him.'

'Why, have you said very controversial things?'

'Not what any sane person could call controversial. I have just hazarded a guess that the diary may have been in a sense a work of fiction, in that it was written when Louise Fleming was Louise Benbow living in France in middle age and perhaps looking back with nostalgia to a time when she was happy and young and in love with her husband – probably using some sort of journal she had kept when she was living at Mairwood. But why don't you read it if you're interested instead of catechising me like this?'

'You've never offered to show it to me.'

'Because you've never asked. Can't you see it's humiliating pressing things on people who are obviously bored?'

'I wasn't bored. I just didn't like to ask you, there was a time when the very word "Fleming" seemed to give you apoplexy.'

'Surely you can't blame me for that, with Wittering wittering on. But he has quietened down now, though I suppose it will all start up again when Stern and Chantrey ask for his comments.'

'Will they?'

'Pretty well bound to. Which is why I want to get Tosswell on my side before I send off the typescript.'

'What is his cottage like?' she asked as they crossed Broad street by the Clarendon Building. 'Is it very chi-chi and full of *objets*?'

'You couldn't be more wrong. It's utterly aseptic. Like the room in the gospel that was swept and garnished. It's as if he's purged himself of all worldly goods since he's become a reformed character. It's furnished I should think with bits and pieces left over from undergraduates' rooms, and there's not a thing that looks as though he took any pleasure in it. If you're curious come and see – you could always arrive and call for me in about twenty minutes.'

'No. I'm going to the paperback shop. You'll find me there somewhere.'

*   *   *

He came up behind her with such violent suddenness as she squatted on her heels surveying the cookery books that she nearly overbalanced. 'I've been fired.'

'What on earth do you mean?'

'What I say. That I've been fired. Look, are we going to stand here forever?'

'I just wanted this book.' She took a look at the knot of people at the sales counter and then at Trevor's face. 'No, I won't bother.'

'I could never have believed it, even of Adeane.'

'Hadn't you better talk more quietly,' she said in an undertone. They were barely out of the shop and there seemed a lot of curious bystanders.

'I will not be quiet, I don't care who hears it. Adeane has behaved like the rat that he is, and has even allowed Tosswell to do his dirty work for him. And that dinner last night – it seems to have been designed as a sort of tactful approach to it all.'

'Tactful! I thought it was just about the most insulting occasion I had ever come across.'

'Then you've got more perception than I gave you credit for. But in fact it was designed as a softening-up operation.'

'But what for?'

'To tell me that Stern and Chantrey have retracted.'

'Do you mean from the Fleming book? But haven't you got a contract?'

'Oh yes, they'll buy me out. Wittering, it seems, has written imploring them to get Adeane to write it, Adeane has agreed, and Tosswell as President has been deputed to break the news to me. I imagine it's all been decided for months, they've just been waiting for Tosswell to get back from Australia. Tosswell did it all very gently as he thought – he's a soft-hearted old slob, he's like that Aldous Huxley character with a heart of pure hogwash. He said he wanted me to know before the Stern and Chantrey letter came.'

'You mean Wittering's won?' But on every occasion he had held the ace of trumps.

'Wittering's won, all right. Do you know what he called me? Tosswell told me because he thought it would make it

easier (easier! the man must be an imbecile – he is of course).
He called me an outsider.'

Yes, thought Jennifer, that guileless pink face masked
cunning all right. Or was it plain luck to discover the barb
that would wound most?

PART TWO

Prologue
JUNE, 1883

Mr Jenkins, who was embarrassed himself, did not suspect that his visitor was far more so. As she had specially sought him out – at the SPG meeting at Gletton the week before – and had earnestly asked if she might come over to Cascoed to speak to him about something that was troubling her, he supposed that she wanted this meeting. He was a simple man, learned in Welsh antiquities but with very little knowledge of human nature.

But Margaret had hardly slept for the past few nights for thought of the ordeal ahead. Once the request had been made and a day fixed there had been no going back. She had stepped up to Mr Jenkins as they all left the church hall and had asked her favour. And why Mr Jenkins? Partly, she supposed, it was because the Cascoed valley was so remote that a secret confided there might be expected to stay secret. There was also the great advantage that she barely knew Mr Jenkins. Nor had her father ever known him. Fellow clergy they might be, and historians – historians of Wales at that – but their interests barely touched, and neither man had ever moved much from his study, let alone his parish. Margaret could therefore feel tolerably certain that her affairs would not be discussed.

So a week after the meeting in Gletton she had driven the pony cart the five miles from Ludwardine. It was an unexpectedly fine afternoon; really heavy rain perhaps might have excused her, or sudden illness, or the pony going lame. But these were not to be; there was absolutely nothing to prevent her from keeping her appointment at Cascoed Rectory.

The road to Cascoed skirted the shield-shaped mass of hills that made up Radnor Forest (its upper reaches bare of trees despite its name), on this side gaunt and bony and carved out into hollows black with shadow under an overcast sky, but today almost soft, and radiantly green with young bracken shoots. It was a little-used road and she had met nobody, though no one who might have seen her would have been surprised; Miss Talbot was known to drive or ride all round these parts. After Beggar's Bush, the highest point, the road plunged steeply downhill and she had known that she was nearing the time of trial; once at the bottom you were nearly in the Cascoed valley.

The hamlet of Cascoed, if you could call it that, consisted of the rectory, a white three-storied building that looked like a farmhouse, and a couple of farms visible from the road. There were besides half a dozen other dwellings hidden somewhere on the slopes of the heavily wooded hills on either side of it, Ack Wood on the one hand, Litton Wood on the other. If you went on down the road you came to the church and the little schoolhouse, standing above a stream that was culverted below the road, but which after heavy rains inevitably rose and poured down it; and usually at least once or twice during spring and autumn Cascoed was cut off from the rest of the world. There was no other way out of the valley. Beyond the church the road dwindled into a track that carried on until it reached Fossidoes Farm at the very furthest end of the valley, where it was only a field or two wide, and hemmed in by hills that climbed steeply to over 2000 feet.

If you were sure of your pony, or of your own legs, and sure too of your direction, you could climb up through the woods, and then on to the bracken and heather above, and make your way over the bleak moorlands of Radnor Forest back to Ludwardine. Nobody who lived in Cascoed would have dreamed of doing anything so foolish. They did not care for the hills, regarding them as obstacles which had to be climbed to fetch in the cattle or the sheep. Perhaps in August the children would be sent up to pick whinberries. But even this was regarded as a waste of time, for what was there after half a day on Black Mixen but a couple of baskets of berries; you had to spend sugar on making them into pies that were gone before you could turn round. The hills were an unfortunate fact of nature which had to be endured. Cascoed in general got no pleasure out of them, they left that to the leisured classes – not that many came that way; just occasionally the doctor's young gentlemen from Ludwardine, making the circle of the hills on foot or on pony back.

They would have counted the Rev. Mr Jenkins among the leisured classes, of course, marvelling at the amount of time he chose to spend 'just reading a book'. Nobody saw him at it, but it was generally known that he did, and known that the postman grumbled about the weight of the parcels of books he had to carry. The thirty or so souls in his congregation had no strong feelings about him. They were vaguely gratified that he was a scholar who had put his name to a book, and thankful that he had never attempted to interfere in local matters. It did not matter that they could not hear his sermons which he crouched over and mumbled; it let them off trying to follow.

And for his part Mr Jenkins was satisfied with his lot, and always had been during the twenty-three years that he had held the living. Only now had be begun to feel that time was getting short and so little achieved, and the Ecclesiastical Antiquities of Cymry still half complete. He was a conscientious man and allowed himself to shirk none of his duties; he knew it was his duty, for instance, to leave his study from time to time – he abhorred recluses, such as Price the Solitary of Painscastle had reputedly become. And he knew it was his duty to receive Miss Talbot and hear what she had to say.

He had been in no doubt of the purpose of the visit when she had spoken of something 'that was troubling her'. But the same spirit that made him deplore immoderation, that saved him from being the recluse that he had it in him to be, made him also very wary of this occasion. It sounded almost as if she had confession in mind. The fact that her father had always shown himself infinitely removed from Puseyite extravagance was no guarantee that his daughter might not be ensnared; young women are notoriously impressionable.

But when he had Miss Talbot actually seated in his study he discovered that there was to be none of the outpourings he had feared. Indeed as she made fluttering little comments on the view of Ack Wood from his window, asked about the school, about the repair to the steeple struck by lightning the previous autumn, he began to wonder bemusedly if he had been totally mistaken about the purpose of her visit. It seemed that the whole afternoon might be consumed in chit-chat about Cascoed affairs that did not interest him, nor surely her. At last he made a move to deflect the conversation towards her own affairs.

'And are you writing anything just now?'

Her face flooded with colour. 'Well, yes, that is . . .'

He was somewhat surprised at this modesty. After all she had three or four little tales to her credit. Not that he had read them himself but he understood they were well thought of in educational circles. He would have supposed she was used to authorship by this time. He tried to put her more at ease.

'And what is the theme this time? I understand you take great pains to be accurate in your history.'

'It was that that I wanted to ask you about,' said Margaret. There was a pause and then she rushed on. 'I wanted to know what you thought – about imagination.'

'About imagination?' He was puzzled.

'I mean . . . about whether it is wrong.'

He was still at a loss. 'If you mean, is it wrong to use one's imagination to supplement history, to imagine events and set them in a historical context, then I am sure everybody would agree that it is perfectly justified, especially' – and here he bowed rather clumsily in Margaret's direction – 'when the result gives so much pleasure.'

But the compliment seemed to arouse even greater unease. 'But I really meant,' hesitated Margaret, 'was, is imagination wrong in itself to the person who uses it? Could it be . . . a sin?'

He began to have some inkling of what she must mean, and was amazed. Mental impurity was not a vice that he could ever have connected with a young woman, especially one of Miss Talbot's background; nor would he expect to be consulted about such a matter.

Margaret, though mercifully unable to understand why Mr Jenkins seemed so put out, sensed that the word she had used was perhaps too strong. She had come out with the firm intention of showing that she recognized she could be gravely at fault. But 'sin' might not be the word to use here. 'I mean,' she faltered, 'The Bible tells us that the imagination of man's heart is evil from his youth . . . so should we perhaps try to drive it away?'

Mr Jenkins was enormously relieved.. He was also deeply ashamed of having imputed such thoughts to her, even fleetingly. 'I understand you. Our ancestors, even my own father, were brought up to regard that as God's prohibition against imagination; they held that anything set down in print that was not a fact was of necessity a lie and therefore evil. I gather that there are certain bodies of thinkers who believe it still and allow themselves to read no fiction whatever, not even moral tales. But this need not trouble you. It is not the line taken by the Church of England nowadays, though I believe there was a time when the Religious Tract Society was doubtful about publishing fiction, even of the most uplifting sort. Not now, however, and certainly not the SPCK who I believe publish your own work.'

'No,' said Margaret absently, 'Griffith and Farran.' She was puzzling how she could make herself clearer.

'An excellent firm. I believe our own school gives prizes from their list.'

'But is it wrong to *enjoy* imagining?' she persisted. She could not forgive herself if she were to leave feeling she had failed to make herself clear.

'I certainly do not think that because something is enjoyable it follows that it is wrong. Much of what is innocent is enjoyable.' He reflected that much that was sinful was also probably enjoyable, but that need not concern either himself or her. 'Besides, I think that a work of fiction would be dull to the reader if he felt that the writer had not taken pleasure in it.'

Margaret disregarded the last rider and concentrated on the other remarks, which gave her the reassurance she had craved but had not dared expect. 'But if it absorbs one's thoughts – all the time?'

'I suppose that any work of creation absorbs the mind most of one's working hours.' Mr Jenkins thought ruefully of the afternoon already gone and the article on the ruins of Ednol church promised to Archaeologia Cambrensis these three weeks. 'Of course one should not neglect spiritual matters, but provided one is satisfied that one has done one's duty there it seems quite proper that most of one's thoughts go to the matter . . . shall we say, in hand.'

There was a pause, in which Margaret realized that the topic was reckoned to be exhausted. She rose, and Mr Jenkins rose with an alacrity that well might have discomposed her if her mind had not been still on her own matters. Would her conscience be satisfied with this interview, satisfied that she had put her case honestly and fairly? But she was being given no further openings; inexorably Mr Jenkins was leading her towards the front door. As he stood on the step he recollected himself.

'Your father. . . ?' He paused awkwardly. 'Your father is in reasonably good health I hope.'

'He is quite well, thank you.'

Her brisk cheerfulness surprised him. He was on the point of further enquiry, but then thought better of it. 'Well then, I will wish you a very good day. Thank you for calling.' For he was indeed grateful that the visit had not been as taxing as he had feared.

'Oh no,' said Margaret earnestly. 'It was very good of you to allow me to come.' She turned and went down the path to the footbridge over the stream, and the relief that the ordeal was over seemed to carry her on wings. But it was not until she reached the top of Beggar's Bush hill that the last doubts were resolved. It suddenly came to her that she had gone further, agonizingly further in baring herself than she had ever done before. Heaven was merciful and would set the pain she had endured against any failure of hers to explain the full nature of her dilemma to Mr Jenkins. Margaret's theological thinking had always been hazy.

'I saw Margaret Talbot today,' remarked Dr Mortimer over the dinner table that night. 'Driving herself along the road from the Bush.'

'She is out and about all over the place now,' said his daughter. 'Independent. Quite a change from the old days.'

'She looked . . . well, one might almost say radiant. Could it be that she is in love?'

His wife looked at him, surprised. The comment was out of character. He rarely took notice of human emotions.

'She'll never be in love with anybody,' said Tiger contemptuously. 'Only shadows, like that frightful cousin of hers.'

'Boys Talbot. I concede that he was frightful. But he was more substantial than a shadow unfortunately.'

'What I mean is that it was impossible from the start.'

'Not surprisingly, since he was more than twice her age and married.'

'But she would never want anything that was not impossible. Reality frightens her, she lives in a dreamworld.'

'Have you ever read her books?'

Tiger shrugged. 'The first. She gave it to me. It's about Cavaliers – Talbot Cavaliers, as you might expect.'

'And dastardly Roundheads, I presume.'

'No, that's the trouble. If she's got any feelings or opinions she hugs them to herself. It's what makes her, and her books, so futile, just milk and water.'

'That seems rather hard,' said her mother. 'You used to be fond of her.'

'Not hard,' observed Tiger. 'Just realistic, that's all.'

The doctor was losing interest in the topic. 'She has certainly always seemed a low-spirited girl to me. However, there is evidently some joy in her life, judging from her appearance this afternoon. One can only be thankful that this much has been vouchsafed to her. Her existence must be dreary enough – living in the shadow of the good rector's disintegration.'

'She may not notice it.'

'Then there'll come a day when she won't be able to help noticing. Mary, I do wish you could persuade Mrs Tilley to make *adequate* quantities of caper sauce. This amount wouldn't garnish a woodlouse.'

Chapter 1

1882

It was true that Margaret Talbot and Lily Mortimer – whose family nickname of Tiger conveyed more of her true nature than her baptismal name – had once been intimates. When you are young it is assumed by your elders as well as by yourself that if you are contemporaries that is enough. The friendship had been declining ever since Margaret, having left school, had become a permanent resident at the rectory instead of being just a holiday visitor whose arrival was to be greeted with excitement. This was some nine years ago, so Mrs Mortimer had had plenty of time to grow accustomed to the coolness between the two girls. Their temperaments were now obviously imcompatible, like vinegar and oil, you might say. The exuberant frankness that had been an attractive feature in Tiger the schoolgirl had turned into disconcerting abrasiveness. As for Margaret, there is a limit, even in the meekest, to the amount of putting down that can be endured. She took to keeping out of Tiger's way, and it became a habit.

But because she had once appeared to accept Tiger's ruthless denunciation of her faults of character, it did not follow that Margaret had not resented it. She was shrewder than Tiger gave her credit for, and she knew she was, and was irked that she seemed to give such a poor impression. By the time she reached her late twenties she was resigned to the fact that if anybody noticed her at all it was as somebody insignificant and unsure of herself. Very well then, she would not expose herself to their contempt. As the only child of the rector, in a small community where there was no squire now, and few gentry, she could not avoid society; in fact she nowadays had to represent him at every local gathering. But she could always keep to the background, observe, and record. Her diary comments were very different from the demure historical tales that the public saw, and which, being written for children were filtered from all impurity such as trenchant comment on adult folly.

'Mistress Meg in Van Dyck costume and all that,' Tiger had said contemptuously to her brothers after a reading of the first story. 'Curtseying to her king or bravely hiding him in a closet. It's a pity Bonnie Prince Charlie never got to Wales – but not even a Talbot could claim that. Mistress Meg would have had a giddy time dressing him up as a dairymaid and kissing his hand. Well, one thing you can be certain of, she'll never kiss anything more than a hand, and a dream hand at that.' At this point Ernest, flushed and angry, had told her to hold her tongue, 'not even the worst fellows at school dared speak of a lady like that.'

But Tiger, sharp-tongued though she was, did not invent, she had not the imagination for that. It was true that Margaret had spent much of her adolescence telling herself stories in which she always played the principal part. Tiger was mistaken, however, in assuming that she believed what she dreamed. She was perfectly aware of herself as a dreamer of foolish dreams. When she had fallen in love at school she sensed how ludicrous it would seem to the beholder and that it therefore behoved her to be certain that no one should ever have an inkling of her devotion. Only once had she lost her head and her judgement – over her own cousin, a married man of some thirty years her senior. She would not allow that she had 'fallen in love' as Tiger had described it, but the strength of her emotion had surprised and indeed shocked her. He was dead now, and had died ignorant of her feelings, but she still remembered them with shame. It must never happen again. So that she certainly had not allowed herself to fall in love with Edward Benbow when in 1882 he came back to Mairwood as both squire and parson.

Edward Benbow was indeed, as all Ludwardine conceded, a fine figure of a man. He was also an unexpected son for Sir Samuel Benbow to have sired. Sir Samuel's Hereford breweries had provided him with the wealth to acquire in 1857 the square, solid Georgian house in the hamlet of Mairwood some three miles to the east of Ludwardine, on the Gletton road. They had also provided him (via prudent support of the Tory party) with his baronetcy. Once in Radnorshire he had zealously set about turning himself into a model landowner. He had been accepted by the Radnor gentry, but not much liked. He had been irascible, that was a fact. They said he was pompous, which was more a matter of opinion. And the rumour had been that in spite of the lavish way in which the Mairwood estate was run he was a close-fisted old devil who disputed every tuppence-ha'penny at home, and was far more interested in the stabling of his bloodstock than in the welfare of his tenants.

That had been cottage opinion. The gentry disliked his competitive attitude, the way he seemed to take up every activity with the idea of outstripping the rest of them, whether it was over the extent of his glasshouses or the amount he subscribed to charity. Though Sir Samuel had done all that he should in the way of supporting the local hunt and sitting on the bench, he could not be said to have made many friends in the neighbourhood, and his sudden death six years before had not afflicted anyone in particular. Indeed there had been a certain amount of ribald laughter amongst the more profane about the fitting way Sir Samuel had departed this life. Having implacably opposed the building of the Ludd Valley Railway, he had died of a heart attack upon seeing the first train run down it. ('Blown up with rage like one of those there engine boilers', was how somebody in the Three Pigeons had put it.)

Margaret remembered Edward Benbow as a fair-haired, unsmiling schoolboy, standing beside his mother at a Christmas party at Mairwood, receiving the guests – all obviously asked for his sake, since they were his contemporaries – with politeness, but with marked lack of interest. His mother however, a large and impulsively cordial lady, amply atoned for it by the warmth of her greetings.

That was the only time Margaret had been in Mairwood during Sir Samuel's reign. When he died in 1876 the house was, to all intents and purposes, shut up. Edward by this time was at Oxford, a studious boy, they heard, winning prizes, and his mother had moved to be near him. Mairwood, which had never really been on the Ludd Valley map so far as the local gentry were concerned, now was totally forgotten, somewhere behind the magnificent oakwoods that one passed on the way to Gletton. If Edward did visit Mairwood during the vacations it was not mentioned. He would not in any case have occasion to go to Ludwardine; Mairwood was in the parish of Knulle and, socially, looked down the valley towards Gletton and England rather than up it towards Ludwardine and Wales.

And then at the Fancy Fair at Gletton in the early summer of 1882 she had found herself sharing the artistic and literary stall with Lady Benbow. The fair was being held in aid of the Working Men's Library at Gletton, and it was assumed that Miss Talbot, as a lady author, would be interested in promoting such a cause. The committee could have wished that she was a more dominant personality; they could have lionized such a one, made her the focal point of the occasion. But without discussing the matter it was tacitly agreed that she would never fill such a role, that she must be asked to take a stall and provided with a companion of sufficient stature to assume responsibility for it. The obvious stall was the one which purveyed paper in some form or another. There would be watercolours, Margaret was told, and writing paper decorated with little sketches of Gletton church; blotting pads and letter racks and objects in papier-maché, and framed copies of Beatrice Orde-Wilson's verses about the Ludd. It was not suggested that she should provide any of her books, only her presence, and she was aware that the favour was being conferred by the organizers rather than by her.

Margaret was intensely proud – something that nobody realized but herself – far too proud to allow it to be guessed that she felt slighted by anything whatever. She took care always to let it be thought that she had little opinion of herself. By now she had realized ruefully that people easily accepted her apparent evaluation of herself, but she shrugged it off with not much bitterness. Somewhere there lurked at the back of her mind a feeling (she was still young enough for such visions) never actually formulated but which obscurely comforted her, that one day she would do something to confound them all, and would blaze among them as the comet she really was. In the meantime she consciously followed the precept of the Gospel (uneasily feeling nevertheless that she should not be absorbing worldly wisdom from Holy Scripture) and took the lowest seat. She wanted to escape the truly terrible mortification of being sent down lower.

So she had written back to the committee, deprecating her ability to do sums quickly, and in return had been told that she would have an assistant, Lady Benbow, who had recently come back with her son to take up permanent residence at Mairwood. It would be very pleasant, the letter went on, to launch Lady Benbow back into local society in this way, and what better person could be found to begin this process than a member of one of the leading families of the area? Margaret was not taken in, but was content to hover in Lady Benbow's shadow, if this was what was required.

Lady Benbow obviously had no idea that she was being favoured by the companionship of one of the Talbots of Ludwardine, or indeed by an authoress. (The vicar's wife had in fact told her that it would be a kindness to partner Margaret, who was rather diffident, and was to be pitied nowadays with the poor rector on her hands.) Not that she was patronizing, she was merely very friendly. 'Such a warm nature,' Mrs Hunt had said in an explanatory aside to Margaret, and this was evident at once. Margaret felt she was being taken under an umbrella of kindness, an umbrella she was inclined to suspect. For under her unassuming manner was a conviction that she was an interesting individual, worthy of being liked for her own sake, and she habitually felt hostility to the sort of careless cordiality that was extended to everybody indiscriminately.

Since Lady Belbow barely knew her, her warmth must mean surely that it was lavished on all she encountered. She remembered how at the Mairwood party Lady Benbow had moved among her son's guests urging them at supper to partake of more of this or that, implying what a gratification it would be to her personally if they did so, what a disappointment if they did not. She had toured the perimeter of the ballroom, dragging out shy girls huddled among the gilt chairs and presenting them to cowering and unwilling youths. She had seemed to make herself responsible for wrapping up each departing guest and urging them all not to take cold.

'Winter parties,' she had said then to Margaret, 'such a very dangerous season. Now, my dear, just let me lend you an extra shawl for the drive back. I always think of Ludwardine as so very high and cold.'

And now, fourteen years later, she was deeply concerned about the wisdom of Margaret's removing her mantle. Would she not feel the draughts of the Drill Hall? She had come all the way from Ludwardine by train? That was exceedingly enterprising of her. She had to confess that she had come from Mairwood in a closed carriage but would be delighted if Miss Talbot would accompany her back in it, Thomas could so very easily take her the extra three miles to Ludwardine. Would not her father prefer that she should be brought back thus?

Margaret was aware that her father, even by now, had forgotten where she was, if he had ever taken it in. She had told him, of course, and he had nodded vaguely. At five o'clock he would be asking the servants fretfully why she did not come and pour his tea for him, but an hour after that the episode would have gone from his mind and he would be forlornly wandering round the study searching for some book he thought he had lost, which was probably lying on his desk. Work on the history of the Talbots de Ludwardine proceeded very slowly these days, indeed was stagnant. Margaret herself put it down to the fact that he was nearing the end of it and dreading the moment when the last word would be set. For her own part she could not conceive how his days would be filled; the work had occupied him all her conscious years. It was, she thought, no bad thing that he should be hesitating over its completion, and she did not worry about him unduly. He had never been a very vigorous or active man and he did not seem markedly less so now.

'I really think Papa quite trusts the railway,' she told Lady Benbow, 'and it is so very convenient, and the station not at all far from the rectory.'

But nevertheless she found herself travelling back to Ludwardine in the Benbow carriage and accepting the pressing invitation to come to visit Mairwood.

'Edward is so taken up with his schemes – it would be a kindness, my dear.'

But Margaret knew that the kindness was Lady Benbow's.

A week or so later she had gone over to Mairwood, driving herself in the pony cart. She had never seen the place by daylight, and it was with a certain sense of excitement that she turned down the fine avenue of wych elms by the little lodge with its pointed Gothic windows. Mairwood House became visible when she emerged from the trees; square, three-storied, matter-of-fact and unappealing – rather reminiscent of Sir Samuel himself.

'Not at all a pretty house, I'm afraid,' said Lady Benbow, who received her in the square drawing room where the light glared in through four deep windows. 'But perhaps Edward will improve it in time. The place is like a barracks and the garden looks like a parade ground.'

Margaret, looking out at the expanse of grass that extended beyond the windows, featureless except for the occasional random flowerbed, could only agree.

'Though it will all have to take second place to his schemes for the church and the school and what have you, of course. That is what really matters to him, he has such very high ideals, you know. Young men do have extravagant ideas, and it is a blessing that Edward's are like this. I mean it could have been horse-racing – or worse, I suppose. An acquaintance of ours in Hereford has had terrible trouble with his sons, they got into such reckless company at Cambridge. Edward was at Oxford, of course; I don't know whether that makes for difference. Cambridge is near Newmarket where there are racing people, and Oxford is so

High Church – at least some of it is, though by no means all.'

Lady Benbow's conversation flowed on, rather as she herself flowed over the chair in which she sat. Margaret studied her surroundings. The furniture, in the style of about forty years ago, had clearly all been bought from the same shop at the same moment; that declared itself at once. The rosewood-framed sofas and chairs that were sprinkled round the room had all been upholstered in the same sharp acid green which the years had not been able to subdue. There were draped classical statues, chosen it seemed to fill space, of a deadening white uniformity, alternating with glass-fronted cabinets in the French taste, containing fussy bits of porcelain. All this must have been removed for the ball – for it was the same room, she remembered the organ in its white-painted case which stood, rather incongruously, with white and gilt pipes, something like a very large wedding cake, as the odd man out, the only object Sir Samuel had not purchased from his emporium.

'Yes, our organ,' Lady Benbow was saying. 'Sir Samuel would have liked to see it go, I know, and there was many a time when I thought he would have had it torn out. But in the end he let it be. And now Edward is glad of it. He plays quite nicely, you know, and we always have prayers in here and he plays for the hymns. I suppose I ought to be able to do it, but though my papa sent me all the best masters somehow I never did have much music in me. Do you play, my dear? How do you like to pass your time?'

Margaret had to admit she did not play, neither did she paint or draw. She had always felt great uneasiness under direct personal questioning; it threatened the anonymity which she wore like a protective garment. She found it difficult to respond easily even to the ordinary gambits of polite society where few are interested in the answers to the questions they feel bound to ask. Lady Benbow's questions were quite outside this convention, she asked because she was implacably interested. Nor was it mere curiosity, Margaret recognized that, even while recoiling, though unable to remove her eyes from those brown ones opposite, the only colour in the large pale face turned towards her with such inexorable benevolence. The feeble attempts she made to extricate herself from the suffocating warmth of Lady Benbow's apparent concern for her were of no avail. She was aware of their feebleness, aware that a stronger personality would have been able to shake itself clear.

And then despairingly she had indicated the picture over the chimney-piece, a group of little girls in white dresses, blue ribbons in their fair hair, grouped round a basket of flowers. It indeed diverted Lady Benbow, though in a direction Margaret would never intentionally have chosen.

'Our dear ones,' she said simply. 'Sir Samuel had it painted for me – afterwards, you know. Of course it had to be taken from likenesses of them, Mr Grant had never seen them. But he did it so very well, don't you think? And it really is very like. Chatty, that is the one on the left, our eldest, was always so very protecting to Jessie, our baby. You can see how she is holding up the flower for her to play with. And Addie, she was the second one, always had that look of mischief on her face. Sir Samuel gave it to me on Jessie's anniversary – she was the last, you know.'

'I am so very sorry,' Margaret managed to get out, horrified at her clumsy blunder.

'No, it is a long time now. I thought it never would be a long time, I wanted it to be a long time because they said time healed. It was before we left Hereford, there was bad scarlet fever that year. Of course we did all we could to keep them from it, but it got into the house somehow. That was really why Sir Samuel decided we must come here. It was partly to shake off the memories, but also to bring up Edward in the country. He was just a tiny baby then – the only one to escape. But you mustn't let it make you sad, my dear, it's all over now and they're in a better world. Besides, I tell myself that I can remember them as always young – such loves they were too. Addie, the little rogue, how she did make us laugh! She could wheedle the very shoes off you. But it was Betsy – that one who's watching her – who was her papa's favourite, no doubt about that. She was the delicate one, the one who was so frightened of things and had the bad dreams. He could be stern with the others –

when their spirits got too high as children's do – but he never was with her. Our four blossoms, we called them. I never minded that they were all girls though I felt it for Sir Samuel – not having an heir, you know. And then there was Edward, and we were so happy. But there were only those three weeks when we were all together, and then Chatty sickened and a month later they all were gone. I used to think it was a judgement on me for being too happy.' Tears flowed down from the brown eyes over the pale, fat cheeks. She wept without heaves or sobs, her face uncrumpled. Margaret watched with acute dismay.

'But there'll be grandchildren,' said Lady Benbow. 'I always tell myself that.' She wiped her eyes, and her moon-like face was as tranquil and cheerful as ever. 'Of course Edward isn't married yet and he does sometimes tell me not to hurry him. But one day there'll be children here, I'm sure of it.'

Margaret felt she could steer the conversation now to the surely safe topic of the surviving child. She was right; Lady Benbow could, it seemed, expatiate happily on the history and achievements of Edward forever. But Margaret liked listening, had always far preferred it to talking herself. It was not opinions she wanted to hear, it was histories; she got the same pleasure from them as she had from the stories her father had told her as a child.

Edward, Lady Benbow told her, had been a source of anxiety to them as a child because he had seemed delicate. Indeed, that was why she had moved to Oxford after Sir Samuel's death, so that she could keep an eye on whether his bed and his linen were aired properly. Well, not just that, of course, but she did like to be near him now he was the only one she had left in the world. Edward's career had been all that anybody could have dreamed. He had achieved such distinction as an undergraduate, and had won so many prizes, and now was a fellow of his college. And yet he was not a mere pale, stooping scholar either, he was fond of sport, he played cricket – he had played it for his university. She was so glad that he did not hunt. She had never got used to it with Sir Samuel. Hunting days had always found her waiting by a window, expecting to see a body carried past her on a gate. She could laugh at herself now, but it had been very real at the time. But Edward had not played much since he was in holy orders, and probably he would give it up altogether now that he had left his college. She looked doubtfully at Margaret.

'Perhaps your papa has views about the clergy taking part in such sport?'

Margaret reflected that her father, in the days when he had had the energy to discuss such matters, would have been more likely to have commented peevishly on the pretensions of a brewing family. He was old-fashioned about these things; coming from an ancient family himself he set great store upon long lineage. She accepted this quirk uncritically as a characteristic shared by all men of his generation and background.

'I don't think Papa would be against a clergyman playing a game like that.'

'Of course he does not play now. There is not the time for it, for one thing, and I suppose not the people either, though when he has his school perhaps the little boys will play.'

'This is a school for Mairwood?'

'The church school. He wants to have choir boys in it who would sing service every day. He is so very fond of music and ceremonies. At Magdalen College he had the music but not the ceremonies, and at St Barnabas (I don't know if you know it in Oxford but really it is almost popish with all its incense and vestments) he had the ceremonies but not the music – not good enough for Edward, at any rate; he is so very particular. But I don't know; what is all very well for Oxford will not quite do out here. That is why I hope that Edward will some day think about cricket again. I mean, one would not want him to be wholly serious – though it is a very good thing to be serious and I would not have it otherwise for the world.'

When Margaret rose to go she notice for the first time beside the portrait of Sir Samuel in hunting costume (broad-shouldered, masterful, and with an irascible expression that the artist had not been wholly able to dismiss) a smaller portrait of a ringletted girl with mild brown eyes, in the low-cut dress of 40 years ago, and realized, with a sense of profound shock, that it must have been Lady Benbow at about the time of her marriage. The cruelty of time, to swathe her in all this middle-aged flesh, to muffle and distort the slight figure. Which was the real self – the slender, fresh-faced girl or the massive putty-featured woman with a widow's cap on the iron-grey hair? Did one mind changing thus; hate the present and look back longingly at the past? Would *she* mind? Would her spirit change to match her body? Or would there always be the feeling of being imprisoned inside a carapace that one despised and resented?

'You must come again, my dear,' Lady Benbow was saying. 'We shall be having Edward's young ward to stay. Yes, he is a guardian – the little sister of a college friend. Both her parents are now dead, and she is to spend her school holidays with us. You may well meet Edward on your way out. But don't be surprised if he doesn't remember you. I am afraid that he takes more interest in ideas than in people. I suppose it is the way of all men.'

'Why, there *is* Edward.' They were standing on the steps at the front of the house, where the pony cart had been brought round for Margaret. 'Edward, my dear, you remember Miss Talbot from Ludwardine?'

He was in riding dress, making his way over the gravel from the direction of the stableyard. Margaret was thrown into miserable confusion. There was positively no reason at all why he should remember from fourteen years before a shy girl he had once been introduced to at a party. She found herself blushing and making deprecating murmurs, and resenting Lady Benbow's unconsidered warmth of manner. Edward Benbow, now approaching the steps, was without doubt a most attractive young man. As a boy of sixteen he had seemed overgrown, bony. Now his face had filled out and the strong features which had been too decided in a boy gave him a look of distinction. The appearance of willowy frailty had gone; he was broad-shouldered and robust. He had his mother's pale complexion and brown eyes, but whereas hers rested on one with amiable goodwill his were abstracted. He looked politely at Margaret but she felt that he had certainly not registered her identity.

'I have been telling Miss Talbot about our dear Louise and asking her to come and see her. After city life Louise may well feel cut off out here. I would like to show her that there is young life in Radnorshire.'

It was, Margaret thought, a singularly inept remark, since she must surely be at least ten years older than the unknown Louise. Nor did she regard herself as young any longer. At 26 she knew herself to be looked upon as the rector's spinster daughter. She felt nettled. Edward Benbow said nothing. As he passed her on the steps he bowed gravely and went on into the house.

'Just Edward's way,' said his mother happily. 'He has less to say than any man I know. Of course I know that men say less than we do – I did all the talking when Sir Samuel was alive. But Edward never says anything unless he feels he has a serious contribution to make. So please don't mind him, my dear.'

Chapter 2

JULY, 1882

But Margaret's journal did not begin that day – her first encounter with Edward Benbow. It needed Louise, and Margaret did not meet her for some weeks.

By then it was July, July in a summer of uneven warmth, interspersed as so many Julys are in mid-Wales, with a good deal of rain. A note had arrived from Lady Benbow saying that dear Louise was expected at Mairwood when her school term finished on July 20th, and she would be so pleased if Margaret could spare the time to come over and take tea two days later.

'I am going to Mairwood again, Papa,' Margaret had said to her father as she poured his tea for him at breakfast that day.

Sir Jonathan roused himself from the stupor of silence in which he now habitually sat. 'To Mairwood?' he said vaguely. 'That would be to see the Walshams?'

'Not the Walshams, Papa.' (They had been living there in her father's boyhood when he used to come to Ludwardine for his holidays.) 'The Benbows live there now. Sir Samuel Benbow, do you remember? But he is dead now, it is his son, Sir Edward. Though it was his mother who asked me.'

'Sir Samuel Benbow!' The rector spoke with unusual vigour, but anything touching on the baronetage could stir the embers. 'He owned a brewery, did he not? I hardly think we have any obligation to call there.' He had made the same remark a few weeks before.

'I do not think the family have any connection with brewing now. His son is a clergyman and a fellow of his college, Magdalen College, I think.'

'There was a time,' said the rector with some heat, 'when one could be assured that the Church took none but *gentle-*

men. I will take my second cup of tea in the study. Pray ring the bell for Sarah to carry it there.'

Reflecting on the display of petulance unusual in her father who nowadays seemed to feel, to experience so little, Margaret realized that with his deep veneration for the sanctity of ancient families, particularly his own, he would take it very much amiss that only three miles away there was another baronet who was also a clergyman. She should never have contributed to her father's mortification by mentioning Magdalen, his own college, and she sighed at her clumsiness. Naturally none of this would make any difference to her visit to Mairwood, about which she was neutral; she did not particularly look forward to it, but neither was she apprehensive; if Lady Benbow had a young visitor then presumably she would have less time to concern herself with Margaret. At least, she told herself she was neutral, suppressing with severity the thought that had intruded into the back of her mind that she might on this occasion also see Edward Benbow.

She drove over in the brilliant light that so often clothes the Radnor countryside in periods of unsettled weather. In the summer when the glass stands at Set Fair (which it has to be admitted rarely happens in mid-Wales) then the hills are softly blurred, almost melting into the sky. Now they stood out, sharp-coloured under a sky that was for the moment piercingly blue but would soon be dense with cloud. The road to Mairwood lay away from the hills, towards Gletton, following and sometimes crossing the alder-fringed Ludd. It also followed the railway, now at last settling down in the landscape which had for the first few years been sadly scarred by it. Sir Samuel had sworn that it would never cross his land. Inevitably it had done so, had, one might say, brought about his death. Yet now even he would have been hard put to see it from the road. The fields had grown up to it, the raw embankments were clad in grass; it looked as if it might have been there as long as the burial mounds on Radnor Forest standing out against the western sky.

It was a drive that Margaret particularly loved, but one that she did increasingly little now that the railway would take her to such points as Knulle and Cwm Hir on the valley road. And today she did it with a surprising sense of exhilaration, a lifting of the spirit that surely could not be attributed to the prospect of seeing Lady Benbow or her young visitor.

As she approached the Mairwood lodge she saw Dr Mortimer driving out past it. Her immediate reaction was one of relief that there was no need for them to exchange verbal civilities; even in the days when she was daily in and out of the Grove she had been thrown into panic confusion in his presence. But then, safely past him, she wondered. Who could be ill? It surely could only be Lady Benbow – but then would not a message have been sent to the rectory to tell her not to come? She could not, however, turn back now merely because of a guess.

Lady Benbow was there to receive her, but distrait and in a state of simmering indignation.

'It is just what I supposed of schools. My papa would never have allowed me to go to one. We always had governesses, and there were masters to teach us the subjects they could not provide. It is really monstrous what they have done to that poor child. Dr Mortimer has called yesterday and the day before. Of course we sent for him as soon as she arrived.'

'She is ill?'

'It is that dreadful school, overworking her, not allowing her sufficient exercise, underfeeding her. I know it is a place quite well thought of, but Dr Mortimer says he would not put one of his dogs in their charge. It seems that she has had these headaches and fainting fits for a long time, but the school said that it was hysterical nonsense. Such a very sad life that she has had – and now to be used like this!'

'Her parents are dead?' ventured Margaret.

'Her parents both died in India a few years ago. Of one of those dreadful diseases, I don't remember its name. So she did not really know them as she had been brought up in England ever since she was a little girl. There was just her and her brother – I daresay there were other children who died in that climate – I don't know how any of them survive

116

it, I'm sure. Her brother was a great deal older, Edward's age. They were at college together, indeed they were very close friends. But he always had a weak chest, and he took no care of himself, and there it was, he died of consumption. Edward persuaded him to go to Madeira, but it was of no use. So there is that dear girl, quite alone in the world. You would think any school would try to make it up to her – all that she had lost, you know. But they have bullied and brow-beaten her until they have brought her to this pass. It is monstrous, quite monstrous.' Lady Benbow then recalled that earlier tragedy. 'I dare say there was no one to see that his bed was aired either,' she said sorrowfully. There was a silence as she considered the terrible implications of this. 'I have brought up Edward to pay great attention to that – his bed *and* his linen – but that poor young man had no mother near him for most of his life.'

Margaret felt ill-equipped to comment upon all this sadness, anything she could say would be so inadequate. So she allowed a second or two of sympathetic silence before she ventured a remark. 'I hope Miss . . . is not so very ill.'

'Dr Mortimer says that it is nervous exhaustion. Poor Edward feels very responsible. He agreed to become her guardian when her poor brother felt himself to be so ill.' Tears started to fall as Lady Benbow remembered. 'It was at Oxford station, on his way to Madeira. He knew he would never come back. To think if it had been Edward himself! He used to visit the school, you know, though they did not like him to see Louise by herself. I think they thought he was very young to be a clergyman, at least I can only suppose it was that. I said as soon as we got settled at Mairwood she must come here for her holidays. But I did not think she would come like this, indeed I did not.'

'I am sure she will get well very quickly here. She will be so well cared for.'

'Oh yes she will get plenty of care. I have not often seen Edward so concerned for a person.'

'Perhaps you would allow me to come and read to Miss . . .'

'Miss Fleming. That is a most kind thought.'

'I am very used to reading aloud. I often do it for Papa in the evenings. He spends so much of his day with books that he is glad then for someone to read for him.'

'It is a delightful idea. I was wondering how we should keep her amused and that would be the very thing. Perhaps in a week's time. Surely she will have taken a turn for the better by then.'

It was the remark about Edward's concern that kindled the spark, so to speak, though the fire did not spring into flame until a week or two later. But when Margaret drove back towards Ludwardine, she was so engrossed by pleasant imaginings that she let the reins fall slack on Daisy's back, in a way that would have horrified old William the stableman, who made no secret of his view that Miss Talbot was no hand with horses, not even driving them, let alone up on Sunbeam, who always came in with a sore back if Miss Talbot had ridden her any distance at all.

It had never occurred to Margaret that love or marriage would enter her life. It was a curious fact that her boarding school which aimed, so far as it aimed at anything, at turning out girls to be sober ornaments of society, never in any of the homilies forever addressed to its pupils, mentioned marriage – which was the most likely destiny of all of them. Nor, even more curiously, did the girls speak of it among themselves. But they did marry, of course, some of them almost as soon as they had left the schoolroom, and it gave Margaret considerable unease to think about it – those people who had seemed to exist for school alone had turned into something completely new. Or had they always been different, just managed to conceal the fact while she had known them? She did not envy them, any more than a Frenchman might aspire to be a Hottentot; they were just a totally dissimilar species. But as a Frenchman might be interested in reading of the habits of Hottentots, find them on paper fascinating and delightful, so Margaret did enjoy romance in novels, a select few novels, particularly those of Miss Austen. For in all things she disliked the extreme, and she felt that most contemporary novelists exaggerated if they touched on affairs of the heart. She could not imagine, for instance, why girls should go into a decline through thwarted love – like Lily Dale – or die of it like Emily in *Sir Harry Hotspur*. So she did not want to fall in love with Edward Benbow herself; she could not allow that, it had been so painful, so humiliating over Cousin Richard. What she desired was to imagine somebody else so doing – and obviously this should be the as yet unseen Louise.

When she presented herself at Mairwood precisely a week later she was more than a little apprehensive. Would Lady Benbow have totally forgotten, feel that her visit was an intrusion? Would the unknown Louise resent it? She had gone to great pains to choose a book. It was not only the invalid that she was considering; she also had the guardian's opinion in mind. Religion she rejected; it was not incumbent on her, surely, to play the role of district visitor. But Edward Benbow might well have prejudices about fiction, she knew that some people did. There was poetry, there were school prizes such as *Famous Girls*, and Tupper's *Proverbial Philosophy*, and *Sesame and Lilies* (which last the school gave to every girl as a leaving present). None of these was at all suitable.

In the end she picked out *Mrs Overtheway's Remembrances*. It had been given to her the Christmas she was 14, when she should have been too old for children's books, by an aunt who never seemed to have much awareness of her age. But in fact for many years it had been her best-loved book. In the accounts of family life she could experience vicariously what it might be like to be one of many (reality as she had seen it lived by the Mortimer children across the road could be rather daunting). And if she wanted comfort it was there in the final story, where the father returned to the small daughter who thought he was dead. But she could have found similar satisfaction in a score of other books; what was unique was the way it had conveyed to her the poignancy of passing time. Until then she had not given old age any thought; she might *know* otherwise, but what she *felt* was that the old had chosen to be old. In the story of Mrs Moss the narrator had been brought up against the cruelty of old age; the belle that her grandmother had recalled to her as a radiant breaker of hearts had turned into a hook-nosed old witch.

This was not the episode that Margaret read most often, it was too painful, but it had been her first experience of the *lacrimae rerum*, and since this sense of the sadness of time's passing was the emotion that affected her most deeply, she remembered Mrs Ewing's book with particular feeling. It was an indication of how much store she set upon this occasion that she should have chosen this book so close to herself which she had never hitherto shared with anybody.

She held it self-consciously as she made her way behind the servant, through the house to the garden where Miss Louise, they told her, was to be found. There was a cedar tree at the far east end of the house, the only vertical feature in the considerable acreage of lawn and garish flowerbeds that surrounded the house. Under it she could see a sofa and the figure of Lady Benbow poised beside it. Lady Benbow was welcoming enough.

'Why my dear, how very kind. I had quite forgot. Louise, this is Miss Talbot from Ludwardine – an authoress, Louise, just think of it! How many books is it you have written? Louise may well have read them, she is a famous reader. We are just trying to decide whether she is too hot or too cold, and whether an extra shawl is needed. And is that one of your own books you have brought? She is going to read to you, Louise – now is that not kind! As soon as she heard you were ill she thought of it.'

The head of the sofa concealed the invalid, and Margaret had to step around it before she could see the object of Lady Benbow's agitated concern. Louise was not at all what she had expected. She had visualized a pale and hollow-eyed wraith. The girl propped up on cushions on the chaise-longue had a pale brown skin under a sprinkling of freckles which were no blemish, Margaret thought, but enchantingly pretty. Her hair was coppery red, she had long dark eyelashes and large dark eyes. Exotic was the adjective that first occurred to Margaret, and she instantly understood that such a personality might well have found life very difficult at school. Girls' schools, if her own was anything to go by, were deeply distrustful of pupils who seemed to possess talent or appearance out of the ordinary; who looked as though they might resist being herded down the path of docile conformity. Miss Fleming at the moment looked docile enough as she lay there, But Margaret could sense even now that she was an individualist, and felt apprehensive. Was this the person to whom she had thought to read a children's book?

'Now,' said Lady Benbow. 'All we need is a chair. You must stay and talk to Louise while I find someone to fetch it. And I shall bring you a nice shady hat, Louise. So hard to know whether the sun is a friend or an enemy.'

The invalid gave no appearance at all of wishing to be talked to, but Margaret knew she must attempt it. 'I have brought a book by Juliana Horatia Ewing. Did you ever read her? It was a book I used to like particularly, and I thought it might be easy to listen to. I mean, one does not want anything very taxing when one is convalescing. At least I never did.' There did not seem to be a flicker of response from the chaise-longue. After a pause Margaret ventured on a question. 'Do you like books very much? If you could tell me what you care to read then I would try to find something of the sort at home.'

Large brown eyes looked at her blankly. 'Books?' It was as though Margaret had said cuneiform tablets.

'Well, do you like history?'

'I didn't like history at school.'

'Perhaps poetry then?'

'Yes.' But the tone was less than enthusiastic.

'Or travels or natural history. I think we have some books of those.'

The eyelashes had dropped again. 'I expect the book you said you had will be very nice.'

'The Mrs Ewing?'

'I thought you said Juliana someone.'

'Yes, that is Mrs Ewing.'

'Oh.' Disappointment was manifest in that single syllable. 'If it's Mrs then I expect she preaches. Juliana sounded pretty and young.'

'She was only two years married when she wrote this book.'

'Still . . .' Nothing apparently could atone for Mrs Ewing's unfortunate state of matronhood.

Margaret persisted. Surely Lady Benbow must have had some reason for averring that her guest was a great reader. 'Do they read to you here?'

'Edward reads poems. They're churchy sort of poems, I think he said they're called *The Christian Year*. And the evening service each night. He is very kind.'

'Of course Edward is kind to you!' Lady Benbow had now reached them, accompanied by a servant with a chair. '(Yes, Joseph, just there, where the sun will not catch Miss Talbot's eyes.) He feels that he has become an elder brother to you. And he is to take over her lessons, you know, because it has been quite decided that she must not go back to school. Now Louise, here is a garden hat of mine, pray put it on. I know it is not the latest *à la mode* thing, but there is no one here to see you but the birds and Miss Talbot, and she I know will overlook such things in the interest of your comfort – will you not, Miss Talbot. And now I will leave you to your reading.' And Lady Benbow billowed away towards the house.

'Would you like me to begin at the beginning? It is the stories that an old lady tells to a little girl who has been ill.' As she said it, Margaret was deeply conscious of her ineptitude; no doubt Louise thought it had been chosen because of the supposed similarity to herself. But she did not know her well enough to laugh about this, and instead hurried on into a literary defence of the book. 'It is not at all a children's book, though I suppose it was intended as one. Indeed I think children would find it difficult, it is very reflective.'

Louise had taken off the hat and was playing with the ribbons as it lay in her lap. 'I don't really like prosy books. Is it very prosy?'

Thus was Margaret's confidence completely undermined before she ever started. But she had nothing else to offer, so launched into the account of little Ida's acquaintanceship with Mrs Overtheway. Her voice might sound steady, but as she turned over page after page she became increasingly horrified by the unsuitability of her choice. Whatever she might have said, this part of the book was aimed at children and young children at that, and all the talk of Ida's illness and the sadness of her bereavement made the parallel with Miss Fleming absurdly close. 'That is only the introduction,' she said at last, lifting her head. 'It is the next story that becomes so interesting.'

Louise was lying back on her cushions, staring up into the branches of the cedar. The hat had fallen on to the grass. She did not appear to notice that Margaret had stopped reading, or even to have heard her comment. So Margaret hurried on to Mrs Overtheway's reflections about the unrecognized vexations of childhood – and was dismayed; all her listener's fears about promises seemed justified. When one read the book oneself one's eyes glided over it, no doubt, for she had never noticed this before. She had only retained the story's essence – the bitter disappointment of the child who had expected to see a radiant beauty in hooped petticoat and powdered hair, and only found an old and ugly woman in a hideous brown dress. She tried to speed up such action as there was by skipping here and there, and then, angry with herself at the way she was betraying *Mrs Overtheway* to a stranger, she stopped quite suddenly in mid-paragraph.

She had been going to excuse herself by saying that she thought she must be tiring the invalid, but when she closed the book it seemed that the invalid was totally unaware that the reading had come to an end. She was turning her head very slowly on the cushion, backwards and forwards, still watching the branches overhead. Then she looked at Margaret, and seemed to become aware of the silence.

'That was a very pretty story. Thank you very much.'

'I expect I shall find Lady Benbow inside,' said Margaret, standing up. 'Oh, there I see her coming down the steps.' She was hesitating about how to take her leave without referring to the depressingly unprofitable half-hour both of them had just endured when the invalid startled her by raising herself on her elbow to look at her pleadingly.

'You will come back another time, won't you? Everybody is so old here and I never see anybody else.'

These were much the most animated words Margaret had heard her utter yet. Instantly they erased her gloomy sense of failure, and with warmth she assured the girl that of course she would return. And she could tell Lady Benbow quite positively that she had enjoyed herself and would come back another day since that was what Miss Fleming seemed to wish. No, she would not stay for the refreshment that Lady Benbow pressed upon her (realizing as she won the battle that she could not have fought off the urgent offers of hospitality if there had not been another, and much more delightfully needy object of interest out there under the cedar tree.)

'Well then, since you really will not (oh that naughty child, she is still bare-headed) . . . I have told them to have the pony-cart ready for you out at the front. And I am so very grateful. It is good for dear Louise to have some young company, and some young reading too. Edward is sometimes, I think, perhaps a little serious. One should not say it of course, but I do wonder if a girl like Louise does not want something other than the Psalms. And now if you will forgive me I must run and tell the silly child to shade her eyes. Goodbye, goodbye, and so very many thanks.'

The pony-cart was there indeed, and she was climbing into it when she heard her name called; Edward Benbow was approaching.

'Miss Talbot, I just wanted a word with you before you left. (Yes, Thomas, you can leave now.) Miss Talbot,' (he spoke in a lowered voice) 'I wanted to ask you about my ward, Louise Fleming.' He was frowning, fingering the whip.

Margaret was startled, yet flattered by the confidential voice. 'I hardly know her,' she said deprecatingly. 'Indeed I only met her for the first time today.'

'Yes, of course. And I hardly know her myself, for she says very little. But I thought that you, having been to a boarding school yourself, might understand . . .' He paused, seemingly at a loss. 'I mean, she was so unhappy that she cannot bear to talk about it. And Miss Elliott, the lady in charge, has given – well, unfavourable reports . . .'

Instantly Margaret understood his predicament, his desire to think well of his charge, his distress at what the school might have said about her, his embarrassment at broaching the subject to a stranger. She spoke with warmth. 'I think girls' schools are often very strange, they are so inward-looking. I mean, they sometimes seem to forget there is any life outside the walls, and outside their rules. And the rules matter so dreadfully, much more than any real wrongdoing. The teachers nag and fret so, over such silly little things, and if they think that a girl thinks these things are silly they can be so harsh. Cruel, even.' She stopped, feeling that she had said too much, but he was looking at her with respect and interest.

'You obviously understand. Do I take it you were unhappy yourself?'

'I could keep the rules without very much difficulty. But I was always afraid of breaking them, even by mistake, because the consequences were so terrible. And there were girls with spirit, the interesting ones, who were in trouble the whole time, without meaning or wishing to be.'

'Miss Talbot, you have done a lot to set my mind at rest. I was very angry at what Miss Elliott said – about Louise's frivolity and lightness of mind – it seemed inconceivable in Robert's sister. And of course I could not speak to Louise herself. But now I realize from what you say that such persons as Mrs Elliott are – shall we say charitably – over zealous.'

'I really feel they think of nothing else but details of girls' conduct. I used to think this was quite normal. It is only since I left that I realized how very strange it is, to spend your life thinking only of girls.'

Edward Benbow smiled. It was then that Margaret (but as Louise, not as herself) fell in love.

Chapter 3

AUGUST, 1882

At first she had no particular plan in view, no idea of making it into a proper journal, and it was not until several days after meeting Louise, and then Edward Benbow, that she could bring herself to put down on paper what she told herself were absurd daydreams.

But the fact was that at that time she was starved of writing. All through her adolescence and for long beyond she had kept a diary, which had recorded her emotions so faithfully that she blushed to remember it. If ever she had re-read it she had been acutely dismayed, it had seemed so foolishly egoistical. The schoolgirl period had been the worst of course, swinging from sententious reflections to emotional outbursts of love or hate. (She wondered that she had been so bold as to write it at school, but the diaries had a lock and people displayed very little curiosity – perhaps because her companions were so little willing to read or write anything themselves.) She had kept these she hardly knew why – perhaps because it would have seemed a betrayal of an earlier self to have destroyed them.

Her later diaries she knew to be an improvement. She had attempted character sketches which were sometimes quite apt; she had recorded conversation – she had a good ear for that. She still did not care much to look back over them; any diary must have an element of self in it, and Margaret was profoundly bored by herself. Even so she would have let them be if it had not been for the episode of her cousin Richard Talbot. It had hardly been an episode, either. It had lasted for all of four years – four years of records dominated by her emotion if she met him, dismay if she felt she had acquitted herself badly in his eyes, admiration for his achievements, resentment of his critics. She had supported him through all the setbacks which she had regarded as temporary, but which had finished in the disaster that all his enemies had predicted. But she had never had the courage to tell him so, or indeed to tell anybody else; only the diary mutely received her outpourings. She had never felt emotion such as this before, and she would never allow it afterwards. She was deeply ashamed, partly that she had failed him, but mostly – and she could freely admit to herself that it was all part of her supreme egotism – that she had allowed herself to give way to such feeling.

On an impulse of acute self-hatred she had destroyed the diaries, all of them. It would not normally have been so easy to dispose of half a shelf of books, but there was a fire at the bottom of the garden that day; they had cut down the old sycamore and had been burning the branches – she could see the leaping flames from the windows of her room all afternoon. In the evening when the men had gone she went down. It was mostly ash now, but the heat was there and a breeze sent lines of flame running through the embers as she had carried the volumes through the darkening garden. Two journeys, and ten years had been destroyed in as many minutes.

She had gone out to the fire the next day. It was still warm, she could feel it through the sole of her shoe, and as she stared down she could see a few corners of charred paper in the feathery grey ash. Nothing could be read on the piece that she picked up, you could not detect that writing had been there at all. All her youth had been consumed, there was nothing left of it all; nothing to tell anybody of the person she had been. Despising herself as she did she ought not to have been sorry – and yet she felt melancholy. Normally she lived in the present and enjoyed it, for she had an easily contented, incurious temperament. But just occasionally, as now, the clouds that cocooned her were rent apart and she would have a sudden vision of an infinite and desolate cosmos, of time whirling past her, gone irretrievably as she tried to grasp at it.

There had been a story of her childhood called *The Warning Clock*, of a little girl who, when her nurse tried to rouse her, delayed getting up. All day long as the hands of the clock inexorably moved forward she slept on, and then, instead of the figure of the nurse at the bottom of her bed there was a shadowy figure with a scythe. It had been one of her father's books as a child and was, of course, a call for repentance in the style of the moralists of those days. But Margaret, reared in a gentler tradition, had not been impressed so much by the thought of the doom that awaited the procrastinator as by the sense of the terrible, relentless passing of time that the story had first wakened in her. She was only 21 when the diaries were burnt, but she felt that a quarter of her life lay destroyed, and there was very little ahead.

She had kept no diary since, and had felt the lack of it. So often she wanted to set down something that had amused or impressed her, some village character, some comment on the passing of the seasons; she found these so beautiful that she hated the thought of them slipping away without record. So it was curious that she should begin to do this twice over at about the same time, August 1882.

She had set aside an afternoon to visit Louise Fleming about a week after that reading under the cedar tree. When old William told her that the pony was lame, and Sunbeam, the mare that she rode up on the hills, had cast a shoe she determined to go forward with her plans just the same. There was no particular need to, she had not specified any particular day, but she told herself that she disliked setting aside any arrangement, even if it was only with herself. And so she set off down the Gletton road. She was a strong walker and enjoyed it, and the day was soft and cloudy so it was no hardship. She was put out rather than pleased when Mrs Mortimer in the Grove governess cart stopped by her, and hearing that she too was on her way to Mairwood, insisted that she should be given a lift.

The Mortimer establishment, once so much a part of her life that she could not have imagined how she would have filled her day without contact with one or more of its members, had now so far receded to the outer fringe of it that she was positively ill at ease if she met any of them. She had to be aware of them of course; Ludwardine was a small,

128

relatively isolated community at the last point in the Welsh Marches where the English could be said to be dominant. The English themselves might have said that Ludwardine was the last stronghold of civilisation, meaning that north and west of that the Welsh looked after their own affairs without the help of English gentry. But even in Ludwardine the English tended to close up and cling together, an atavistic instinct perhaps inherited from the centuries before when most church towers also served as points from which lookout was kept for the mutinous Welsh hordes who might sweep down from the hills. The Mortimers and the Talbots were certainly both of them ancient Marcher families with strong folk memories of having to defend their holdings against the natives. They were also the old gentry in the parish, and though the heads of each family had, to put it mildly, no great liking for each other, there were many occasions on which they found themselves thrown together.

There had been a time when Margaret had run freely from the rectory to the Grove, had almost considered the doctor's seven sons as brothers (from whom she could always comfortably retreat into the quiet of the rectory when things got too boisterous). And with Tiger she had been on as close terms as she had ever been with anybody. Which was not very close, she would freely admit, for she had always shrunk from intimacy.

But the boys now were nearly all grown up and scattered: Alfred in India, Claud a railway engineer in Swindon, Ernest the only white man for a hundred miles in Basutoland, Arthur in the army, Only Johnnie at Osborne and the twins, Charles and Julius, now at Cheltenham, returned to the Grove in the holidays. The others seemed to have put the greatest distance they could between themselves and their father. Some of them had been afraid of him, the others were merely rebellious. But certainly none of them seemed now to have any affection for their home. When they had all been young there together they had been united in a sense of solidarity against their father, but once the eldest had departed the family seemed to fall apart. Dr Mortimer, habitually saturnine and silent, seemed hardly to care, and his wife, who had always given more of her mind to her garden and her plants than to her children, seemed not to notice. Indeed it was a rare event to see her away from home, and Margaret could only explain her presence on the Gletton road that August afternoon by supposing that it must be a dead season of the year so far as gardens were concerned. And this indeed turned out to be the case.

'Of course I should have called months ago, but what with one thing and another I put it off. But there really isn't much you can do just now – in the garden that is. Heigh ho, what a bore it all is. But I always tell myself that once it's done it's done forever. At least it is with me, perhaps you are more conscientious about the formalities of life.'

She was, Margaret thought, refreshingly unlike most women of her age, whose day seemed to be structured by afternoon calls, and who employed much of their daughters' time in writing social notes for them. Nor did most ladies drive themselves out in their children's governess cart.

'Is yours just a social call?' Mary Mortimer continued, 'or are you involved with the church?'

'The church?'

'Edward Benbow's church. You must have heard about that, surely. He is planning to have quite a little monastic community there – well, perhaps not quite monastic, but there'll be a church and a school and a choir school if he has his way. What I do wonder is what all the Mairwood people – all two of them, there aren't many more, are there? – will make of it. I mean, he's very ritualist, isn't he? And I do wonder how he's going to find the boys to put into the choir.'

'I had heard a little.' Margaret was uneasy. Though Mrs Mortimer and Tiger were to be seen in church on Sundays, she had always felt that they were to some degree affected by Dr Mortimer's openly professed scepticism. She always fancied she detected a faintly mocking attitude – and then would reproach herself. 'I was going to see Louise Fleming, Sir Edward's ward. It was nothing to do with the church.' She tried to shift the conversation on to Mortimer ground.

'How is everybody, all the boys? It's so long since I have heard.'

'And we don't hear so very often, they're none of them great correspondents. Nor am I, I suppose. There was a letter from Alfred this morning telling me that he didn't want just a list of new plants in the garden, why couldn't I write as if I was talking to him. It sounds so easy when you say it, but I find it quite impossible; when I get a pen in my hand all thought quite vanishes. Poor Alfred, he is feeling pretty low just now.'

'I'm sorry.' Margaret remembered him as the gentlest, the least turbulent of the Mortimer sons. It might have been because he was the eldest, and so had early assumed a mantle of responsibility for the others. The younger ones had seemed naturally adventurous, she would have expected them to scatter to the far ends of the earth as soon as they could. They had enjoyed coming home for the holidays, but only because it was a blessed release from school, and they would have been equally happy if home had been the Surrey hills, or even a suburb of London. But she sensed that Alfred really cared for the place. He said very little, but she had noticed that whereas the others used the countryside for destructive forays, birdsnesting, or pigeon-shooting, butterfly-catching or fishing, he went off for long solitary walks, culminating, whatever the weather might be, in an expedition from one end of the forest to the other the day before he returned to school. He used to talk about his destiny in the Indian army; in the end he could not face army life, but had gone out to India as a civilian. Margaret was vague about what he did, but thought it had something to do with forests, if there were forests in India.

'He's had one of those things that people get in India.'

'Malaria?'

'Or even more disagreeable, I never like to ask Henry too much about them. It seems to have pulled him down a very great deal, and he really sounds dejected. And so homesick. I suppose it will be better when he is on his feet again, but at the moment he's just lying there behind straw matting or whatever it is they use to keep the bungalow cool, and fretting for Ludwardine. A nice grey sky, he says, and the smell of summer early morning. And gentle colours that don't hurt your eyes.'

Margaret then could see it, the harsh glaring light, the stupefying heat, gaudy colours. She spoke with feeling. 'It must be dreadful. I don't know how I could bear it – not to be here.'

'Do you feel that? I'm not sure that I do. In fact I think I would be very happy to be in a place where the winters weren't so long, where the wind didn't blow so hard, and where there wasn't so much rain. And I daresay Alfred would wish himself elsewhere if he had to spend any length of time here.'

'I'll write to him, shall I?' When Margaret said this on the spur of the moment she had no notion of anything else but how she would enjoy evoking to an exile the sights and sounds that he longed for. 'Unless you think it would make him even more homesick.' At the moment this possibility seemed to be the only drawback. It was not until much later it occurred to her that the suggestion was hardly conventional, indeed was open to grave misinterpretation.

But Mrs Mortimer was not the person to make such misinterpretations. She accepted the offer at its face value, and if the thought did creep into the back of her mind that Alfred might take a warmer view of Margaret's impulse than was really warranted, she could see no harm in this; indeed it might all work out very well.

'Yes, that would be very well received, I'm sure. You could tell him just the things he wants to know – the little things about the village that I never seem to be able to put down. And Tiger isn't any better, she just lectures him with her latest theories. (I must say I always wonder how on earth letters get from Ludwardine to Upper Burma, it must be a very winding route.) Now I do hope you aren't proposing to stay very long at Mairwood; I feel that what I have to say to Lady Benbow could hardly cover a farthing.'

Margaret suspected, though she hardly liked to say so, that Lady Benbow would not be daunted by so little a thing as that. Nor, as they later sat in the drawing room did there seem at any moment to be any cessation in the flow of conversation that came from the back of the room, where the two elder ladies were sitting facing the fern-filled grate. She and Louise sat by an open window. And in Louise there was an amazing change. She was animated, she sparkled, indeed she bid fair to out-talk Lady Benbow herself.

'It was so amazingly kind of you to come when you did. And you read me such a pretty story. I'm afraid I can't remember its author or much what it was about, but it was very pretty. There was somebody called Ida, that I do know because it made me think of Ida Lowestoft at school. It's funny to think I shall never see her again, when we sat next to each other every day for eight years. Oh well, I can't say that I mind particularly.'

'You won't want me to read to you anymore. But if there is anything I can lend?' Louise had not evinced any great enthusiasm for reading on that previous occasion, but she might have more energy now that she had recovered. 'What sort of books do you like?'

There was a dreamy expression on Louise's face. 'There is a book called *Comin' Through the Rye*. A friend of mine has four copies – one for school, one for home, and one in each of her grandparent's homes. I've only got the one though. I love it, I read it every day of my life.'

'I don't think I know it. But then I don't see very many novels.'

'Of course we wouldn't have been allowed to read it at school. I covered mine in brown paper and wrote Marmion on it.'

'Marmion?'

'I thought there was a poem called that – that's what my friend told me. She wrote Blair's Sermons on hers. But I didn't like to do that – not to say it was sermons, I mean.' She looked at Margaret doubtfully. 'I mean I do not think there is harm in saying something is a poem. But sermons – I know she would have got into quite terrible trouble for that. Still, nobody did see. Not that I wasn't always in trouble.'

This seemed to be a topic to avoid, surely. 'What is *Comin' Through the Rye* about?'

'It is so delightful.' Louise lay back in her chair with a rapt smile. 'It is about how terrible fathers and clergymen are.' Margaret's stunned silence roused her, and she sat up anxiously. 'I mean of course not all clergymen, at least she did not say that. But the one in the book has a smile which would butter the whole neighbourhood – I know *just* what she meant. And his sermons are so dull – and some sermons are, you know, at least the ones we had to go to. And the father in the book is quite terrible, just like a tyrant, and the children hate him so and are so frightened. I suppose fathers can be like that.'

'Oh not always.' But Margaret did remember the Mortimers' fear of theirs.

'No, I suppose not. I never really knew my papa. I came home from India when I was eight so I can't remember. Except that mamma used to say that she would have to tell papa if I behaved badly, so I used to get frightened. And there is quite a lot about love in the book – which is why we knew Miss Elliott would be so fearfully angry if she found us reading it. The girl who tells the story loves a man who lives near them. But perhaps you don't care for that kind of story.'

Margaret could well imagine that Miss Elliott would find it very subversive. But she herself was touched, both by the artless way that Louise seemed to assume that they were both on the same side, and by her endearing childishness.

But Louise was beginning to realize that she might have gone too far. 'Of course you have a father and I am sure he is quite different. And he is a clergyman too. And Edward is a clergyman, but I never really think of that, he is so immensely kind. You know he has begun to teach me Latin. Lady Benbow does not like him to because she says she does not want my brain to be teased after I have been ill, but I really feel quite well now most of the time.'

'Do you like Latin?'

'Well, I have only had one lesson, and I do like Edward teaching me, you cannot think how kind he is. I think I might like Latin – if only I knew what nom., voc., acc. meant when he writes them down before "columba". Don't you think that is a pretty word? It means "dove". He told me what the Latin for "girl" is too. I think it's "puella". He says he will teach me Greek if I make progress with the Latin, so I do hope I will understand – about nom. and voc. Miss Talbot, do you know about Latin? If you could give me a little help I might get on and please Edward.'

It would have been impossible to resist such a request. Margaret knew no more Latin than the odd phrase she had picked up when she had been helping her father, but surely with the aid of a grammar she could sort out some of Louise's perplexities.

'I daresay if I could find some of my father's old school books (I think he may have kept them) I might be able to puzzle out something.'

'Could you do it pretty soon, do you think? Edward is to teach me every day and I should so like to understand what he says. I mean, he does explain of course, but I am listening to his voice not what he says and I don't like to ask him to repeat. But I shouldn't in the least mind asking you.'

By the time Mary Mortimer had caught her eye and both ladies had risen to go, Margaret found that she had promised to return the following day to elucidate the mysteries of the Latin cases. Louise seemed to have no notion that she was asking a favour of any consequence; the tyranny of the weak is often impossible to resist. And Margaret had no wish to resist, she found this eager dependence upon herself both touching and flattering.

'Curious how that child is no relation,' remarked Mary Mortimer on their way home. 'That sort of breathless silliness . . . ah well, I daresay I won't have to endure any more of Lady Benbow for a while. There's no one better than me at being not at home when visitors call and I am in the garden; I've taken great care to plant my shrubs in strategic positions and there are a lot of them.'

As she put Margaret down by the rectory gates she reverted to the subject of Alfred. 'I'll be writing tomorrow. If you've got time for a letter bring it over and I'll put it in with mine.'

Chapter 4

AUGUST, 1882

Mary Mortimer spoke at dinner that night of her visit to Mairwood. Meals at the Grove had never been notable for conversation, even in the days when there were seven boys round the table. The forbidding presence of Dr Mortimer whose very silence seemed to convey distaste and disapproval always discouraged easy talk. He took no part in any exchange himself, appeared completely abstracted from it, but was, as all his sons knew, ready to wither the maker of any remark that seemed to him foolish or impertinent or merely ill-considered. With the result that talking was generally confined to those places and occasions where their father was not present. Now that the boys had departed and only three places were laid, at one end of the table, even less was said. Tiger sat engrossed in her own thoughts which she no longer cared to communicate to any of her family. At the age of 25 it was becoming increasingly certain that she had inherited her father's temperament, and the burden of the black dog that habitually crouched on his shoulder. It was not clear whether Mary Mortimer was aware of or even cared about the bilious moods of her husband and daughter. She had never been known to refer to them or to alter her manner in any way. She continued placid, unruffled, saying little. One would have said that she was not so much deterred by the moodiness around her as indifferent to it.

'I took Margaret with me to Mairwood. She was walking.'

'I thought she usually drove herself,' remarked Tiger.

'The pony was lame, and she had promised the girl they have there now.'

'Oh yes, Meg was always dutiful that way. What is the girl like?'

'I hardly spoke to her, but ineffably silly,' said Mary Mortimer serenely. 'And very beautiful.'

Dr Mortimer lifted his head. 'I can corroborate that. The emptiest head I have encountered, bar none. But beautiful certainly.'

'What on earth is Meg doing with her then?'

'I asked that myself. I really cannot think. But she seems fond of her. I noticed an offended silence when I commented on the silliness. So I said no more.'

'Meg is unpredictable in some ways,' said Tiger. 'She seems such a straightforward plodder, and then she suddenly surprises you.'

'She surprised me today. She offered to write to Alfred.'

'Offered? How do you mean?'

'I said what a homesick letter we'd had from him, and that he was ill and so on and had complained about the dearth of proper letters from home, and she suggested that she should write.'

'Affie was always rather spooney on Meg, he'll think she's coming round at last.'

'But I don't think she is. I really don't think it crossed her mind that he would look at it in that way.'

'Meg's simplicity is almost eerie,' said Tiger dismissively.

'It would be no bad thing.' Dr Mortimer spoke reflectively. 'In fact I am surprised nothing has come of it before. Margaret Talbot would seem Alfred's obvious choice. He could do a lot worse, and so for that matter could she.'

'But he'll never get her,' said Tiger flatly. 'Nobody will. She doesn't want anything like that.'

'That is balderdash. Of course every woman wants to marry. After all, what else has the sex been created for?'

The dinner table took on its usual aura of sullen gloom.

Margaret brought over her letter to Alfred early the next morning. It had not, she found, been very easy to write. It was inhibiting to know that it was going under the cover of his mother's letter; she imagined it being discussed, perhaps even mocked by mother and daughter before it was ever dispatched. Since she felt she was writing as much for their eye as for Alfred's she dismissed topic after topic as unsuitable. Mairwood for instance and its inhabitants – Alfred would no doubt already have received caustic reports upon that. She did not want to write about anything that mattered to her – such as her feeling for the Radnor scene – if they were to see it. She hardly thought that chatter about her various parish duties, the Bible classes, the Thrift Club, the village school, would amuse a man and a Mortimer at that. In the end she had written a self-deprecating account of her experiences with Sunbeam, the mare the rectory had acquired from Ludwardine Court after their cousins had left, and for which she had no aptitude for riding though she took her out for expeditions over the hills. In that way she was able to provide glimpses of the countryside – the Mawn Pool on Bache Hill now reduced to cracked black mud by the summer droughts; the stream in Upper Harley in its customary August state – a dried-up bed with isolated pools here and there; the children coming down from the hills with stained fingers and baskets full of whinberries.

And – a sight that had moved her inexplicably though she had no hope that Alfred would understand, and was afraid that the Mortimers would scoff – the solitary foxglove growing out of the precipitous bank above a hidden waterfall in what they as children called Heron Dingle. The stream in Heron Dingle always ran; however dry the season it was constant, tinkling over the stones on its way down to Harley Valley. For old times' sake she had scrambled up to see whether she could find the heron fishing. But she had gone no further than the first waterfall where white water fell three feet or so over rock dark green with liverwort and kept the tawny pool below in perpetual motion. It was not just the lulling sound of the splashing that had kept her there, but the perpetual trembling of the foxglove just above the commotion of the water which had had a hypnotic effect on her senses.

The letter in her hand, she pushed open the gate that said 'Beware'. Once it had read 'Beware of Badger', but the badger had long ago been dispatched, too savage even for the Mortimers. Indeed the livestock that the Grove had once held had disappeared even as the children had scattered.

You no longer had to run the gauntlet of Polly, sitting in the conservatory and ready with sharp comment and even sharper beak. There were no rats, no white mice. The pack of dogs had been reduced to Caesar and Pompey, now aged and somnolent, and no longer even with the energy or curiosity to bark at visitors.

There was a time when she had run through the 'Beware' gate and into the house with no more thought than if it had been the rectory. Now she hesitated before she pushed open the door into the conservatory. Perhaps she would be expected to ring like a visitor at the front door? Caesar and Pompey, in their baskets below the staging that held Mrs Mortimer's choicer geraniums, looked at her but did not raise their heads from their paws. She stepped into the hall, paused, and then knocked at the door into the morning room.

To her relief Mrs Mortimer was there, at her desk. The room, tidier now that there were no longer boys to sprawl around in it, had not become any more comfortable or feminine. The springs of the sofas and chairs still sagged; they had not been re-covered. The stamp albums, the model soldiers, the pots of glue, the butterfly nets and killing bottles, the apple cores and pocket knives that had at one time strewn every surface had all vanished, making the worn patches in the carpet and the stains on the table seem more intrusive. It had once been the most lively room in the house; now it was as still and dead as any in the rectory. Mrs Mortimer turned.

'Oh Margaret, I might have known I could rely on you. You are just at the right moment, as I was about to close the envelope. I may say that I have cut down on my usual four sides (I somehow feel that one must tiresomely go on to a second sheet if one is writing abroad) since I could count on your supplementing my effort.'

The letter was handed over, pushed into the envelope, sealed. So nobody else did see it after all. Margaret lingered.

'I was wondering,' she hesitated, 'whether you would still have the books that the boys learned Latin from. I seem to remember that Tiger taught Charley and Julius from something.'

Mary Mortimer never showed surprise nor asked unnecessary questions. Margaret had known this and had been glad to find her alone. Tiger now, she would have cross-questioned, probed, commented.

'Why of course we must have had something.' She rose and came over to the bookshelves. They were sparsely filled; the Mortimer boys had all put action before reading. There was Marryat, Fenimore Cooper, Kingston, Manville Fenn, all in remarkably good state compared to the rest of the room. Mrs Mortimer looked at them vaguely. 'The trouble is I don't really know what I'm looking for; I'll have to find Tiger.' And she went out in the hall and called.

'A *Latin* primer?' Tiger's black eyebrows, so like her father's, met in the frown that Margaret knew well. No doubt it merely indicated surprise, but to the apprehensive it seemed to express contemptuous disapproval.

'I thought my father might have kept his, but I can't find it anywhere in the study and his memory is not very good these days.'

'But why on earth should you be needing it?'

'I daresay she has to help her father with old manuscripts, Tiger. There really is no need to be so ferocious.'

'It was not for my father. It was to help Miss Fleming.'

'Louise Fleming!' Even Mrs Mortimer was startled. 'That child we met yesterday? Whatever is she doing with Latin?'

'Sir Edward is teaching her and she wanted help. I thought I could master the grammar perhaps better than her, and help her a little in the early stages. I think very clever people don't understand the difficulties that beginners have. They can't get back – well, to the roots.'

'But of all things why should he want to teach her *Latin*? You might as well try to teach an ape metaphysics!'

'Oh come, Tiger,' remonstrated her mother. 'You have never even met her.'

'I know what you and Papa said. And I can perfectly imagine the type.'

'I think he likes teaching. And I suppose the classics are the things he knows best.'

'Well!' Tiger pronounced this monosyllable with such vehemence and contempt that no more could be said.

But, thought Margaret, wrestling with statements about the dative case being the case of indirect object or personal interest, it must be years before a learner could inch his way as far as reading a classical text, and she was doubtful whether Louise would have anything like the staying power. However, she would be able to solve the immediate difficulties, and since she had promised to bring help as soon as possible, she set off that afternoon.

Lady Benbow, it seemed, was not at home. 'But Miss Fleming?', hesitated Margaret. She it seemed was in the library with Sir Edward. Margaret had not expected this and was at a loss. 'But perhaps I should be disturbing them?' she hazarded.

She sensed contempt for one who did not know her own mind as the manservant answered that Sir Edward had left no instructions about not being disturbed. Apprehensively she followed him, certain by now that neither party would welcome her at this particular moment.

The library was a large room, lit by windows in two of its walls, and at the far end of it the tutorial was taking place. She could not see the faces, for the light was behind them, but the silhouettes seemed to Margaret's hungry eye to symbolize perfectly master and pupil; he indicating some point on the page on the table before them, she listening with drooping, acquiescent head. And then they were aware of observers and the picture was spoilt. Edward Benbow leapt to his feet, Louise pushed her chair away from the table. Put out by his presence, Margaret a little incoherently explained the purpose of her visit. It was difficult on two counts; she had to avoid suggesting that the teacher's explanations were too abstruse, or that the pupil was wanting in aptitude.

'We were just about to go to see the progress on Edward's church.' Louise enthusiastically shut the book that was on the table and jumped up. 'You will come with us? Yes,

Edward, you cannot think how well I feel these days. I am sure it will do me a very great deal of good to walk a little way.'

That evening the journal of Louise Fleming at Mairwood was begun. Margaret had determined to write it when she got home. As she had walked back towards Ludwardine there were phrases already running round her head, and she stepped out swiftly and eagerly, resenting the distance that lay between her and pen and paper.

But at the rectory her duties intervened. She had to give the rector his tea, and listen while he, in an unwontedly garrulous mood, tried to recall some detail of the pedigree on the female side of the Walshams who had owned Mairwood when he was a boy. And then Miss Garvett called, from the village school, to discuss the vexed question of what veils the girls should wear for the confirmation. This was not for many months yet, but Miss Garbett felt an early decision was advisable as an order would have to be placed in good time. Margaret succeeded in dismissing Miss Garbett, made happy now by the certainty that Miss Talbot (as she all along thought) supported her in her insistence that the new veils must be of the very plainest, and of durable material since they would have to serve many generations. Of course there would be opposition from the girls' mothers, to say nothing of the girls themselves (so bold was the present generation, quite unlike their predecessors, to say nothing of Miss Garbett's own contemporaries), all of whom wanted something more frivolous not to say vulgar. But Miss Garbett felt she could confidently quell such murmurings, now that she knew Miss Talbot's views. And if there might be one or two candidates who refused to present themselves on account of the veils, then this would probably be all to the good, since they could only be entering into it very lightly and with very wrong reasons. Still she did not really anticipate that even Lily Price and Grace Morgan, giddy as they were, would dare to withdraw themselves from the confirmation classes, and if they did, a word from Miss Talbot would soon set all to rights.

But hardly had the door closed upon Miss Garbett before

William Dugdale appeared. He was the latest curate, and sorely lacked confidence. In the past her father had been served by some stalwart characters who saw what was to be done and did it, a thing very necessary in this parish, since the rector gave no direction himself and expected his curates to assume control over all parish activities except morning service in Ludwardine church which his sense of duty insisted that he should preside over, though it was some years since he had preached there. All he asked was that they should have no 'tendencies', that they should not be markedly either 'high' or 'low'. Naturally, like all right-minded people, he deplored ritualistic practice or anything that smacked of Puseyism. But he also strongly disliked enthusiasm and emotion in the pulpit; it went with the evangelical cast of mind and suggested lack of breeding. The bishop knew his views well enough, and with one or two exceptions, had always sent him young men who had not, on the whole, wandered above or below the sober path of gentlemanly observance which Sir Jonathan steadfastly believed to be that of the true church ordained by God.

At least, this is how Sir Jonathan would have looked at it when he had been his old self. But latterly he had been failing and fading; very gradually, no doubt, for Margaret was hardly aware of change. He had never been a strikingly energetic man, but now (he was not yet 60, though Margaret thought of him as an elderly man) he was stooped, with a tottering step, and even his life's work on the place of the Talbot family in the history of the Welsh Marches could hardly keep his attention. He rarely strayed outside his study, so that it was more than ever desirable that his curate should be capable and confident. Capable Mr Dugdale might have been, but his self-distrust masked it. He perpetually moved with the air of a man who suspects that behind his back people are laughing at him. Admittedly Dr Mortimer referred to him as a dithering incompetent, and Tiger, who was involved with him over her Cottage Dispensary Club, railed about him as a half-wit, but in general people paid him far less attention than he imagined; it is frequently the most diffident who are the most egocentric.

Since it was axiomatic that the rector should never be consulted, it was usually Margaret who had to try to sort out Mr Dugdale's problems. On this occasion the trouble had been over the behaviour of some of the older boys at the last Literary Institute lecture. The Literary Institute had been established in the Town Hall some five years ago. It held a few books, a piano and a billiard table, all sent down from the Court when the Boys Talbots had left it. Normally it was little used, but Mr Dugdale had felt strongly that something should be done to rescue the younger members of the community from their deplorable tendency to loaf in the evenings. The loafing was most apparent in the summer, when the lads sat about in the street (the steps of the Boys Talbot monument at the bottom of Broad Street was a favourite place, from whence they hurled jibes at the passers-by; Mr Dugdale often found himself making elaborate detours round the village in the evenings to avoid running the gauntlet of that grandstand of idlers). He therefore decided to arrange a series of lectures in high summer, rather than in the usual winter season when, in a place like Ludwardine, most of the parishioners were sitting in front of their own fireplaces somewhere at the end of a muddy track in the hills. It was not easy to find lecturers, so sometimes there was a concert of local talent, and this week Mr Dugdale, unable to assemble any other diversion, had himself undertaken to give readings. He had chosen *Max Kromer*, that story of the siege of Strasbourg, but there had been interruptions, among other things there had been lewd remarks.

Mr Dugdale had come to ask whether Miss Talbot thought, in view of the levity displayed at this lecture, it might be best to bring the series to a close, and he probably would have discussed the pros and cons at far greater length if he had not been immediately overcome with dismay at the realization that he had uttered the word 'lewd' with its infinite powers of improper suggestion, in the presence of a lady. He was fair-skinned, and his cheeks flamed with embarrassment. (This propensity to blush when confused was one of the crosses he knew he had to bear.) So, muttering that he would leave Miss Talbot to consider the matter at her leisure, he had hurried away, and Margaret was free at last until dinner time.

But even safely alone in her room she could not begin. She brought the accounts of the Thrift Club up to date and prepared the lesson for next day's Bible Class, and these put aside she still sat at her desk with her pen laid on the empty page. She had determined that she could not start the journal proper until she had settled in her mind the smallest detail of its writer's beginnings, her parentage, her birth in India, her coming to England, even down to the names of the schoolmistresses who had taught her. But this was not what inhibited her, for already she had decided upon much of it; she could feel the shimmering heat of India, see the ayah in her white draperies, the kind brown faces that smiled down at her, the farewell to Mama, clinging to her before she hurried off the boat, the arrival in a damp, grey England. She knew the school, the cold, the chilblains, the voices that nagged though one no longer heard what they said, the food that one could not eat yet must, the incomprehensible lessons, the even more incomprehensible recreations, the continuous aura of disapproval.

But before she could set this down she had to write the words 'My name is Louise Fleming'. It had been so easy, so delightful, to supply the mental details. She had not realized how difficult it would be to transfer them to paper. All her life she had been schooled to regard any extravagance of behaviour, any deviation from the norm, with abhorrence. And what could be more preposterous than this assumption of another's personality? All very well to let fantasies whirl round one's head; that was merely akin to the dreaming at night that one could not control. But to pull them out, give them concrete shape by recording them on paper, that was to affect to believe them, as well as expose them to the world. It was the latter consideration that made her so reluctant; the thought of these pathetic imaginings (for she was still at this stage able to detach herself from them) being laid out for incredulous inspection by the cold eye of reason.

Nevertheless, Margaret's behaviour was at all times ruled

by a dogged determination to persist. She knew she would be tormented until she had at least made a beginning. She had decided that she was going to record Louise's life at Mairwood, and that to her seemed as binding as any promise to another – she did not stop to reason why this should be. And this must be prefaced by Louise's history of herself so that she could ease herself gradually into the other's personality.

And so on 15th August 1882, with half an hour to go before she had to tidy herself for dinner, Margaret smoothed the page of the large exercise book she had originally bought to write her personal reports on the children she taught in the scripture lessons at the school, and began. 'My name is Louise Fleming. I was born in Cawnpore on 3rd September, 1865 . . .'

Chapter 5

AUTUMN, 1882

When Mary Mortimer had remarked upon Margaret's 'offended silence' on the subject of Louise's intellect, she had not understood. Margaret had not been offended; it was just that she did not wish to comment. She had always felt that the Mortimers – that is, the doctor and Tiger and to a lesser degree Mrs Mortimer – set far too much store by cleverness. For her the futility of cleverness could be proved by the Mortimers themselves. There was the doctor (and there was no doubt about his intellect) embittered because he seemed to feel he had not made proper use of it; constantly infuriated by the stupidity of those around him. The same could be said of Tiger, unable to settle down to the usual feminine pastimes because of restless yearnings to undertake work that the female sex was never intended for. Margaret could see for herself that cleverness had endowed neither of them with commonsense nor good judgement, and it certainly made them far more difficult to live with. Dr Mortimer had always berated the boys for their stupidity (she could never understand why he, a scientist, seemed unable to grasp that the brain you were born with was a fact of nature, like the greenness of grass). But they seemed to have made far greater sense of their lives, and there was no doubt that they were both happier and better liked. The Mortimers (by which she meant the parents and Tiger) judged other people's cleverness by their own standards, and Margaret knew that their criteria were so different from hers that there was no point in discussion. What Mary Mortimer might have said would not have influenced her, but she chose not to listen to remarks that she guessed would be slighting.

She could see, of course, that Louise had little interest in things of the mind, but thought it to her credit that she did not pretend it. Besides, it seemed that this was because such things had never before come her way – they certainly would not at any ordinary girls' school – and for this reason she might be all the readier to absorb them in her new environment. Her eagerness to learn from her guardian was endearing, and Margaret dwelt repeatedly on the memory of the two of them in the library, the rapt pupil, the absorbed tutor. She liked Louise, even loved her. She had never before met anybody quite so artless and childlike, certainly no one so beautiful, and was deeply touched that so exotic a being should turn to her (she felt a faded spinster beside her) and seem to desire her friendship.

When Margaret began the journal she did not attempt to write it as the real Louise might have been supposed to do. She wrote it as Margaret Talbot, but not as Louise's contemporary, the Margaret Talbot of ten years ago, wordy and prosy and given to prim moral reflection and suffocating emotion. The person who wrote it had none of the silliness of sixteen, she was poised and confident – at least since she had put the ordeal of school behind her. It was not Margaret but an ideal of what she would have liked to be.

To begin with she was nervous of discovering details about Louise and her past that would conflict with what she had already set down. It would be impossible now to go back and alter; a life was taking shape under her hand and was becoming reality. Day by day she added a little to it and felt the character take on more substance. At no time did she ask Louise about her life before she came to Mairwood, and Louise, being essentially a creature of the present, did not much refer to it. But there had been a strange moment of confirmation. She had been speaking of the dead brother, Robert. He was all that Margaret already knew him to be, affectionate, concerned and protective, writing letters of wise counsel to her at school, sending her little books of good words which she treasured not because of the teaching they imparted but because he had inscribed them 'To Lulu, from her affectionate brother'. But Margaret had already set it all down.

148

'But the thing I'll never forgive Miss Elliot for, never as long as I live, was what she did when I was little and had just gone to The Laurels.'

'She took away the sugar pig he had sent you.'

Louise stared. 'However did you know? Had I told you that? Yes, that's what she did, and I cried myself to sleep for a week. He had asked somebody at his own school to buy it for me and send it to comfort me. And that old cat saw me open the packet and said it was unwholesome and made me give it up.'

In Margaret's version she had deprived the child of it as a punishment, but it made little odds.

The Mortimers were aware of Margaret's now habitual visits to Mairwood; little can be kept secret in a village community. 'It's the new church, of course,' said Mary Mortimer. 'Though it's hard to see quite why she is so involved with it when she has so much to do in this parish.'

'There is a very personable young squarson there,' remarked the doctor from the depths of his newspaper. 'Of course I think myself that his endeavours, though worthy, are wrongheaded, and that it is futile to provide a church where none is needed. But I would not expect a clergyman's daughter to see this. I would expect her to cheer him on, which she seems to be doing.'

'There's much more to it than a church,' put in Tiger. 'He's got such plans you can't think. He wants to set up a choir school, and a sort of hospital for aged pensioners who will troop into church two by two in blue cloaks and chant God Save Sir Edward, or some such. All living in a holy community near the house. Old Thomas told me while I was dressing his leg. He's a freethinker and a radical of course, and he thinks that something like this is going back to the Dark Ages.'

'I'm not as violent a man as Thomas.' (Dr Mortimer habitually thought of himself as mild and moderate.) 'But I would say it was old-fashioned. He might have got away with it forty years ago (always providing he had the money). But not nowadays, and not in Radnorshire.'

'But could she be in love with him, do you think?' mused Mary Mortimer. 'He's a veritable Sir Galahad, I believe.'

'Mary, please!' said Henry Mortimer with pain in his voice. 'I should have thought you would have known after 30 years of marriage how disagreeable I find this sort of speculation.'

The boys had always resented the way their father contrived both to have his cake and eat it. He would say what he chose, uncontradicted, and then deprecate the taste of anybody else who pursued the same line. Nobody ever complained, however; the boys because they did not dare, his wife because she did not care enough.

Margaret was not in love with Edward Benbow, not in any way that Mrs Mortimer would have understood. She was watching him fall in love with Louise, experiencing it vicariously but intensely, without any tinge of envy. At present she knew the girl was hardly aware of it, she was absorbing the affection and cossetting she had been starved of so long. She was a creature who blossomed and expanded when she felt people were fond of her, and Margaret, remembering how dull and unresponsive she was on the first occasion she met her, was reminded of those Japanese flowers that emerge from a tightly closed shell as soon as you put it in water.

Now that she was happy she was confident. Margaret had watched her with the men that day in August when the three of them had walked to the site near the Home Farm where the ground was being levelled for the church. They had paced out the line its walls would take, and then while her guardian was speaking to Margaret about such matters as the books that might be provided for a parish library, Louise had wandered off to talk to the labourers.

'What I do feel is that there is room for books with a specifically High Church line. Of course I know that there is Mowbray, and to a certain extent the National Society, but the books they put out don't catch the public imagination like the ones the Religious Tract Society publish, which have the sort of dash and spirit that the simple like. You might say that the evangelicals hold all the trump cards. Do you not feel able to do a little High Church corruption of youth, Miss Talbot? A little poisoning of the wells?'

So he had a sense of humour. Aloud she said that she did not think she could do it well enough, that it needed to be very well done otherwise it would deter rather than encourage.

'How true that is. I can recall a story in a series for choirboys, showing a starving clergyman in a decline, the bailiffs in the house, and the children crying for bread. The moral was celibacy for the clergy, but I thought that choirboys might be forgiven if they thought they were being warned against the priesthood.'

Almost as she laughed he had turned to graver things. 'I wonder if you were ever at Newland?'

'At Newland?'

'Near Malvern. I used to go over there from Oxford when I was an undergraduate. I don't know a place that I love more. It is something of Newland that I am trying to re-create here.'

'It is a religious community?' Margaret ventured.

'In a sense. It was the work of James Skinner, the vicar of Newland. He came from St Barnabas, Pimlico – notorious for its ritualism.' Edward Benbow smiled gleefully. 'Indeed there were riots. And then he came to Worcestershire, to a parish where there had not been a resident clergyman for 40 years, and where there was only a small wooden church and the sacrament was not even celebrated monthly. And of course the services were very bald and grim. The altar was not decorated, there were no vestments, no music except one old man playing a fiddle. But when I used to stay there – it was just before Father Skinner had to resign because of his health – there was a splendid new church and daily celebration, and the music must have been the finest in any country church. Father Skinner had seen to it that the choirboys had free places at a local school, and so he had attracted some fine voices. And he had built almshouses and the pensioners attended daily service. I would like to feel that I could achieve something comparable.'

'But the congregation? I mean, would there be enough

people to support such a splendid enterprise?' There was not, Margaret knew, more than the Home Farm and a few cottages within walking distance of Mairwood.

'I would hope to have the pensioners to make a core of worshippers. But at Newland people came from a distance because of the fame of the place. Indeed there had to be a rule that the true parishioners were allowed to take their places first. I think enthusiasm can work miracles, and that at least I feel confident of providing.'

Though not entirely convinced she could admire his vision. 'I would love to give you some support but . . .'

'Of course your loyalty must be with your father's church. I did not propose to come poaching, I assure you. But would you agree to be one of the school managers? I think you could give us enormous help there, especially as you are experienced, and I really have had so little to do with schools.'

She assured him with warmth that this would give her great pleasure, but sensed that his attention was withdrawn. She turned to see what he was looking at. In the distance Louise could be seen talking with great animation, while two or three labourers leaned on their spades and watched her.

'It is extraordinary what a way she has with everybody. Whoever they are, they all love her.'

Margaret knew that she herself had no such way. She could deal quite competently with Garbetts and Dugdales – the schoolmistresses and curates that a rector's daughter inevitably encountered – and rather less competently with the cottagers. She sensed that while none of these disliked her they were all indifferent. People smiled politely when she knocked on their door; nobody's face brightened. When she rose to go nobody pressed her to stay. She did her conscientious best to avoid the traditional faults of the rectory lady, the tendency to interfere and to criticise, but she knew that she lacked the cordiality of manner and above all the assurance that would make people warm to her. And this Louise, without thinking about it, clearly possessed. When she had come to write up that day in the journal at last she could refer quite dispassionately to the difference between them. 'While I spoke to the workmen Miss Talbot talked to Edward about serious things. She seems ill at ease with ordinary people, probably because she thinks too much about the effect she is creating.'

She could write about the village occasions much more readily than she could take part in them and she found herself describing them to Alfred with an easy fluency that she never had had in his presence. A reply had come from Upper Burma in October, eight weeks after she had written. It was addressed to her personally at the rectory, not sent under the cover of one to his mother. It was not very eloquent, but she had known it would not be – none of the Mortimer boys reckoned to express much through the pen. Touched though she was by his evident astonished pleasure at hearing from her, and his yearning for more news from home, she did find herself marvelling at the way he could fill both sides of two sheets of paper and yet tell nothing, absolutely nothing; not a single fact beyond a remark about the climate, and even that stopped at the vileness and left the rest to her imagination. There was some comment on what she herself had written, and otherwise only clichés and vague sentiments.

She wrote the day she received the letter. It was much easier now. Made confident by his appreciation (and also knowing that there was no possibility this time of anybody else setting eyes upon it, she could be expansive about the comedy of the school Christmas entertainment.

Price the School was a progressive man who had absorbed new methods, not from anything he had been taught himself, but from the educational journals he took in. And he had been struck with the idea of allowing the schoolchildren to act. But Mr Dugdale, when he heard about it, had expressed horror – the theatre to him was an instrument of the devil; he also thought that the Ludwardine children, who were already out of hand, would finish up by being completely uncontrollable.

'And how would any of the girls get situations in a well-conducted family if *that* was known to their discredit?'

Margaret, called in to arbitrate, had not felt that her opinion would be of enough weight. She could not see that much ill would come of Mr Price's proposed innovation, but with Mr Dugdale's amour-propre in mind, thought that this was a matter that should be referred to her father. She was reluctant to trouble him, and knew too that it would be difficult to get him to bring his mind to bear upon it. But without a decision from him neither side would be satisfied.

As she had surmised, it took some time to penetrate the clouds that hung round him these days. And then when he realized that it was a matter concerning the school he became testy.

'The school has never been my province, Margaret. I should have thought that you and John White could have settled the matter between you.'

John White had been the headmaster some twenty years ago, but she knew who he meant. 'I know it sounds very trivial, Papa, but it has become a matter of principle, and it would help everybody so much if we knew what your views were.'

All she really needed was the faintest glimmer of an opinion, something that she could build up fairly truthfully and present as the rector's fiat. But this she could not get; he muttered and grumbled, until in the end she realized that he had probably forgotten what they were supposed to be discussing.

'Mr Dugdale thinks that it is morally detrimental to children to act. Is this what you think?'

The rector flickered into life. He knew Dugdale to be the name of a curate, but the curate who came into his mind was one John Clements who had been with them a few years before. Clements had been far too evangelical for his taste, and he associated him with extreme attitudes and a fervour he found thoroughly distasteful.

'I think nothing of the sort,' he said sharply, and then went off into a rambling account of how the headmaster of his private school had every year put on a comedy of Terence in which the better classical scholars were allowed to take part. With that Margaret had had to be content.

She had conveyed to Mr Dugdale as tactfully as she could that while the rector felt that great care should be taken when children appeared on the stage he thought it permissible if it was something educational. To Mr Price she said that the rector had given qualified approval, and could they not present some tableaux vivants (this had been her own idea; it seemed a fair compromise and obviated the necessity of children having to learn lines, which she foresaw would be tedious to all concerned). The compromise had not particularly pleased either side, and then there had been a great falling out over the subjects of the tableaux. Mr Dugdale had wanted historical scenes; Mr Price had suggested fairy tales. Whereupon the former had dismissed these as frivolity with no moral content, and the latter had rushed hotly to their defence and had attacked the morality of much of history.

'I was reminded,' wrote Margaret to Alfred, 'of a small terrier yapping and snapping round the heels of a bewildered mastiff. Do you remember how Caesar and Pompey would run between the legs of dogs three times their size and bite them before they knew what was happening?'

When the dust of this had settled and Margaret had manoeuvred the two parties into a position where she hoped each would feel he was victorious (in that it was agreed some infants should present tableaux of nursery rhymes, and the others a blend of fact and fantasy, Columbus landing in America, but also Robinson Crusoe), she found unexpected difficulties with the children. 'Of course they have never seen any acting, and have never really been allowed to use their imaginations. We were always playing imaginative games (do you remember how we used to storm the castle mound pretending to be Owen Glendower, and how deliciously exciting, yet terrifying, it was to be the English garrison standing on top and waiting for the heads of the Welsh to show up through the bracken?) and so it is hard to put oneself in their place and realize how much it would have been discouraged at home and thought of as lying, even if it had ever occurred to them to pretend they were something that they were not. Their books too are so totally different, just sage little domestic tales about village life and how Edwin was a good boy and did not idle and swear or mix with bad company but gathered up firewood for his granny. So it is really hardly surprising that they find what we are asking them to do totally incomprehensible, and the Queen of Hearts and Robinson Crusoe just fidget and giggle. Perhaps when we can find them some costumes it will be better.'

When she had written out this saga it had filled four sheets. She read it over and was amused. The journal lacked scenes of village life, and so far she had found no opportunity for humour, except in Lady Benbow's clucking and fussing and marshalling of her lame ducks. Mairwood had little connection with Ludwardine. Their circle of acquaintances would be drawn from further down the Ludd Valley, eastwards towards Gletton. Of these people Margaret knew little. She met them on gala occasions, and she knew their names and their faces, and had sometimes a feeling for their characters. But she knew she could not invent a whole way of life for them. If it had been a novel, yes. But this purported to be life.

And so she turned the Benbows towards Ludwardine, to take part in the life of the parish until such time as Mairwood had its own church. It was not difficult to invent a reason why Louise, after three months at her new home, should only now come into contact with Ludwardine society. She had been ill, and Lady Benbow had taken a long time to allow her latest chick to stretch its wings a little. But since a position in the centre of the Ludwardine vortex was needed, Margaret brought her into the school, to take a scripture class under the supervision of Miss Talbot.

'Miss Talbot has manoeuvred this. She aspires to be progressive, and thinks that scripture might seem more attractive if not invariably taught by the elderly.'

And so the comedy of the school entertainment was played out in the journal some few weeks after in fact the best of it was over.

Chapter 6

DECEMBER, 1882

In that first half of the journal, Margaret was absorbed but not yet taken over by it. She was recording Ludwardine life, as somebody with Louise's gift for friendship might be expected to find it. What Margaret herself had heard as second-hand village talk was therefore put down as the result of direct confidence, imparted over the fireside cup of tea that in reality she was never offered. The legends of the district, the stories of bygone personalities that Margaret had absorbed over some 20 years were told to Louise, the eager enquirer, by such narrators as old Thomas the cobbler and Evans at the forge (crusty characters of strong views whom Margaret in real life would never have ventured to try to draw). There was so much that she wanted to set down that the time she had set aside for writing, the hour before dinner, was rarely enough, and she sat up at the desk in her room long after the rest of the household had gone to bed, driving her cramped hand over the cold paper. It was Ludwardine and its affairs that kept her there; of the life at Mairwood she said little, and she was still chary of much mention of Edward Benbow's name.

But this was to change after that Saturday in mid-December when the foundation stone of St Mary the Virgin's church was at last laid at Mairwood. The beginning of December had been mild and wet, and this had been succeeded by bitter cold and deep frost, with fog blanketing the hills. It had not been the weather to be out of doors; the cottage doors were shut tight, nobody lingered in the street; farm labourers in the fields with slit sacks over heads and shoulders to try to keep the damp from penetrating their bones blew on their fingers and slapped their arms across their chests as they cleared ditches, spread manure – the traditional dirty jobs of the back-end of the year. At the school Mr Price made the children do jumping and stamping exercises before they came in for he did not believe in an over-heated schoolroom, and there were plenty of infants who thought it must be their breath, puffing and panting out there in the playground, that made the air so foggy.

Then suddenly that Saturday the fog lifted and the hills could be seen again, the tawny brown of the bracken silvered by the frost and shining under the sun in a brilliant pale sky. The ceremony at Mairwood, which it had seemed would have no spectators at all, would go forward under conditions more favourable than in many a June. From the start there had of course been no question of the rector attending; the day was long past when anybody expected him to be present at such a function. He now seemed so feeble that it had become impossible to remember he might once have been vigorous. But knowing that Mr Dugdale was taking part in the procession, Margaret had suggested that they should go together in the rectory dog-cart.

It was a sacrifice. A lifetime spent in Ludwardine had still not blunted her sense of the beauty of that road down the Ludd valley. Every time she turned down it from the turnpike road between Ludwardine and Crick she had the same feeling of entering her own kingdom. If she went down the road alone she greeted each landmark with loving recognition, turning to each, almost bowing, lifting her eyes to the bald top of Burfa Tump (the site of an Iron Age camp and still standing clear above the woods that swarmed up the lower slopes); to the twin protuberances that marked even more ancient forts on Radnor Forest stark against the sky in the distance; to the twisted thorn standing in isolation on the skyline of Herrock Hill nearer at hand, and the smoothly turfed arena below it, that looked almost as if it had been man-shaped for a dancing floor, but never had anything on it but the moon-faced red and white cattle from Barlands Farm.

This time she must ignore them, in the interests of polite conversation with Mr Dugdale, and she felt as though she was slighting kind neighbours who deserved better of her. In spite of the radiance of the day, Mr Dugdale was obviously oppressed; she could feel him to be apprehensive. At first he nursed the carpet bag that contained his surplice and said little. But as they turned into the Gletton road by Tilt Cottage he could contain himself no longer.

'I fear that the proceedings may be of a somewhat ritualistic nature.' He frowned and looked straight ahead. He was not too sure of Miss Talbot's own views. Women were prone to temptation in this direction, even Sir Jonathan's daughter. 'I believe that Sir Edward used to frequent St Barnabas church in his Oxford days.' He glanced at Margaret warily, wondering if she understood. 'St Barnabas had a considerable reputation for . . . for extremeness of rite in my time, though perhaps not in your father's.'

'I believe he did mention St Barnabas. And also Newland, near Malvern Link. There was someone there called Mr Skinner, I think, for whom he has a great admiration.'

'James Skinner, of the Pimlico riots?' Mr Dugdale was indeed dismayed. 'Then it will certainly be ritualistic, positive Mariolatry. I wonder whether I should have . . . I was not told that the procession was going to be of that nature.' He lapsed into a silence that Margaret felt to be fraught with foreboding.

There were not many people gathered in the bare and levelled field on the site beside the tall white farmhouse and its outbuildings, and those that there were had chosen to scatter themselves in self-conscious, isolated huddles. There were the Howes of the Home Farm, who would presumably be the mainstay of any congregation there was to be; Mr and Mrs Duggan of Quarry Bank, always noticeable in a gathering of this sort by reason of the redness of their faces, the corpulence of their persons, and their expensive clothing – Quarry Duggan's silk hat shone almost aggressively, and his wife had more jet beads on her mantle than anybody else would have thought appropriate. The Proctors had come from Knulle, and the Thomases from Gryllis. Otherwise there only so far seemed to be a few unidentified cottage women with children clinging to their skirts.

The shape of the church that was to rise was traced by a deep trench, enclosing a space that looked surprisingly small. At one end of it a tripod of poles had been erected from which was suspended the block of stone that was to be laid in the ceremony about to take place.

'An apse apparently.' Mr Dugdale looked with evident disapproval at the curve of the trench at the eastern end. 'The architect seems to have a continental style in view. Well then, I had better make my way to the house. I understand the clergy are assembling there.'

With a brave show of being unselfconscious, Margaret stepped over the rutted ground iron-hard with frost, and walked up to the suspended stone to examine it for any inscription. There was none; the surface had been dressed but as yet was blank. Then hoping no group would beckon her to join them she stationed herself at the eastern end, behind the despised apse. Turning her head from the brilliance of the sun she saw Lady Benbow advancing, majestic in purple, but mercifully occupied with the Orde Wilsons.

The founder had chosen a noble site. The field rose slightly, and the church would stand on a mound overlooking the farm in its grove of sycamore trees, with Mairwood House just visible beyond, and behind it, over the tops of nearer hills, the darker range of Radnor Forest, a barrier against the rest of the world. No Cistercian monks had ever found more beautiful seclusion.

The procession when it came was not 'extreme' enough to unnerve Mr Dugdale but it wanted nothing in majesty. There was no incense – she guessed that this was what Mr Dugdale most feared – but there was a gilt cross carried high by a white-robed acolyte, and behind him a surpliced choir. 'Yea, the sparrow hath found her an house, and the swallow a nest where she may lay her young: even thy altars, O Lord of hosts, my King and my God. Blessed are they that dwell in thy house: they will always be praising thee.'

When the archdeacon had given his address Louise came forward. She was dressed in tawny velvet, the colour of the bracken on the hills; her hat was wreathed with a curling white feather and she carried a white fur muff. She moved over to the tripod, took the trowel from the mason standing by it and laid her muff on the ground. With easy unselfconsciousness she scooped up a mass of mortar from the hod that was held up to her, spread it and then stood back. The stone was wound down; the creaking of the pulley broke the stillness. As it fell into place she gave it three ringing taps with her trowel, turning a laughing face to her guardian as she did so. Margaret, always too readily moved, could only mouth the hymn that was sung after the archdeacon had pronounced the blessing. The procession re-formed and walked away. The sound of 'Jerusalem, my happy home' receded and died in the distance. The spectators left behind looked at each other uncertainly; they were unsure whether voices might now be raised, secular topics broached. Margaret was not left to doubt; she found Lady Benbow by her side clasping her arm with both hands.

'So beautiful, so really beautiful was it not. Sometimes I have wondered whether Edward was not rather hasty – I mean it is to cost twenty thousand pounds to build the church and endow it, and then there are all his other plans. But when I saw him, so really in his element I could not be anything else but proud. And Louise, you saw her, the dear child. You know, I have such hopes. Edward is fond of her, I am sure of it, and he really could not do better, I mean the sister of such a very old friend, she could not but be the best person, do you not agree? To be sure she is young, barely seventeen, but girls do marry young, I did myself. I sometimes think it is better that way, they can be moulded. Sir Samuel moulded me, I can tell you that, such a giddy little thing I was. Well, perhaps not giddy so much as just unheeding. I certainly learned to heed. The trouble I used to get into with my household accounts! You would scarcely believe it but I did not know the difference between a gross and a dozen. That is, I knew there was a difference, but not how much, I thought it was rather less than a score, and I ordered a gross of blacking brushes for the kitchen (of course a dozen would have been too much) and you should have seen how many there were! Poor Sir Samuel, he used to be quite out of patience with me, and I can't tell you how I dreaded Saturday evenings when we went over the house-keeping books. I used to creep away and weep. But that would never happen to Louise, Edward is so patient and she is thoroughly used to having lessons with him. It would really be like a romance in real life, do you not think, to marry your guardian! Oh there, I should never have let the word slip out, Edward would not like it at all.' She pressed Margaret's arm, looked around her and lowered her voice. 'So you must forget all that I have been saying. But I daresay you are well used to keeping other people's secrets. It is just that I feel so happy for Edward, and for Louise of course. It is like the time when Sir Samuel came to ask Papa for me all over again.'

Lady Benbow's breathless confidences lasted for most of the walk to the house, where the gentry were making their way, the lesser orders having been left behind to be supplied with beer and bread and cheese at the Home Farm. She was silent for a moment or two as they approached the house, and then as they were mounting the steps she brought her mouth confidentially close to Margaret's ear. 'Of course it is my dearest wish that there should be a new little Chatty, Addie, Betsy and Jessie in the nursery. They cannot come a bit too soon for me.' She gave a conspiratorial and emphatic nod, pressed Margaret's arm with much fervour, and hurried away to her other guests.

The dining room table had been spread with a lavish cold collation; raised pies, rounds of beef, hams, cold fowl, tongues, covered it; the guests – there were hardly more than a score of them – would surely not be able to make much inroad into all this. As everybody stood uneasily round the edge of the room, exchanging platitudes on the fineness of the day, the good fortune that it *was* today not yesterday, how it was really not too cold at all except for standing still, Louise ran up to Margaret.

'Oh I did enjoy that. I wish church was always like that, all processions and singing. I mean,' she lowered her voice, 'there is usually such a deal of *words*, don't you sometimes think. Though of course I would never say so to Edward, or indeed to anybody else. And do you like my velvet? I thought hard what it should be. I mean it would never do to be *particular*, so it could not be too bright colours. Lady

Benbow was very kind and took me over to a dressmaker in Hereford since we did not think that Gletton would do it properly. I thought of the white feather, and Lady Benbow added the muff. Didn't you think it was beautiful? Sometimes she is so kind. I mean she always is – and she does understand about lessons.'

'About lessons?'

'Well, how long they feel. Even with Edward.'

'How is the Latin?'

'I have given up learning things. I mean *columba, columbam* or whatever it is, which is a help. But we read together. Or rather, Edward reads it and tells me what the words mean and tries to get me to do the same only I can't, of course. What is rather dreadful is when we read the Psalms in Latin because I should know the Psalms, shouldn't I. And sometimes he sets me to looking up words. It is so difficult, for the words are quite different in the dictionary. English is so much easier because the words don't go on changing all the time. And he makes me write essays, and that is the worst of all, because I can never think of anything to say, and I would like to please him. It was Education the other day, and I really could not think of anything except that school was a very great bore. That is the trouble, the things I could say, I may not.'

'What would you like to write about?'

'About nothing really,' said Louise confidentially. 'At least, nothing that Edward was going to read, because I just don't have enough serious thoughts, and you know, it doesn't do to be light with Edward. But Lady Benbow understands, and sometimes she comes in and begs me off, says she needs me for something. Oh look, there's Clara Proctor. And isn't that shade of blue unbecoming, it makes her face look more mauve than ever, but I'll have to go and say I like it.'

As Louise flitted off to the group of Proctors who Margaret could see were impatient for her company, the clergymen, by now divested of their surplices, came into the room and the luncheon could begin. Margaret found herself sitting next to the archdeacon who asked, as all did, the ritual questions about her father's health, and then applied himself to carving the round of beef in front of him and sending it down the table. Occasionally he threw out a few remarks as though addressing a public meeting, and in the intervals between these Margaret looked round the table, at Mr Dugdale who for all his lofty principles and the spareness of his frame was capable of eating more and faster than anyone she had ever met, at Louise chattering away at Mr Proctor who was listening with tender attention, and lastly at Edward Benbow, his head gravely inclined towards Mrs Duggan who, from the animation of her manner, must be on the subject of her son's achievements at Eton.

But she did have a few moments' conversation with him. As the guests crowded into the hall, anxious to be on their way as soon as they decently could, before the afternoon became dark, he caught sight of her as she stood by the vast marble font-shaped object in the Greek style with which Sir Samuel, for some reason best known to himself, had chosen to place on a plinth in the middle of the floor. She was waiting her turn to take leave of Lady Benbow who, by the door, was detaining each stiffly smiling but impatient guest with particular confidences. Margaret was wondering how many she had told of her ambition to make a match between Louise and Edward. All the senior ladies, no doubt. Then her son, standing as always seemed his way, detached from the throng of chatterers, saw her and made his way over.

'I am sorry this is the first opportunity to speak – just as you are going. I am so pleased that you managed to come over – to a rival camp, so to speak.'

She murmured something about her enthusiasm for the project, knowing as she voiced it that he must have been listening to polite nothings such as these from all present. But hers were said with deep conviction. 'And the choir,' she added. 'I have never heard singing like that, not since my aunt once took me to Salisbury Cathedral.' She thought of the singing in Ludwardine church, led by boys chosen for the relative docility of their temperaments rather than by reason of any musical ability.

'The choir was from Newland. I must confess that has

always been a great ambition of mine – to have them singing here at this particular occasion. We have now fed them and dispatched them to the train, because it would never do if they were not back in time for their duties at Newland.'

'Do you think you will be able to train a choir like that at Mairwood?' Margaret ventured, wondering wherever he would find suitable material. Radnorshire might be a Welsh county, but in her experience the locality was totally devoid of musical interest – if he could hear the children bawling out the hymns at Sunday School! There was also the difficulty that there were so few boys of the right age living anywhere near Mairwood.

'I think given a good choirmaster and sufficient inducements to the boys we can do something of the sort, and reasonably quickly too. It is astonishing what musical ability is latent in most children – or so I have been always told. I hope you were not disappointed by the choice of music today.'

'Disappointed?'

'We did not include the hymn prescribed in the Hymn Book for the laying of a foundation stone of a church – you know, the one that asks "that we, who these foundations lay, may raise the topstone in its day"? You don't know it? Ah well, it extols the pitch-pine pew, or so I always infer. "Endue the creatures with thy Grace that shall adorn thy dwelling-place, the beauty of the oak and pine . . ." Now pine is all very well in the Psalms, and I concede that it may have beauty on Mount Lebanon, but I have an abhorrence of the material as used in the churches of today.' He smiled almost mischievously.

Mr Dugdale, who Margaret knew would think that a jest on a sacred subject was tantamount to blasphemy, mercifully did not hear this remark. He did not say very much on the way home. The air was very cold now, the sun a red ball just poised above the rim of the forest, the hills black. Their breath smoked, and the hooves rang on the frosty road.

'All things considered, the ceremony was more moderate than I would have believed. Really quite moderate,' said Mr Dugdale as they turned out of the Gletton road towards

Ludwardine and could see the lighted windows of the nearest cottages. 'Even the choir – and I gather it had been brought from Newland – was in perfectly good taste. That sort of rite often produces music that is little short of operatic,' he informed her with pious outrage.

Chapter 7

1883

Margaret walked in a trance of happiness during those six months at the beginning of 1883. It was noticed, though none of those who discussed it knew what the reason could be. Mr Dugdale suspected darkly that she had been perverted by Sir Edward and was – for all the fact that she was as scrupulous and regular in her duties as ever at Ludwardine church – becoming swept up into Puseyism. Mary Mortimer wondered, though she said nothing of this to other members of the family, whether Alfred could be responsible. He had written with feeling to his mother about the great solace of Margaret's letters. The domestic staff at the rectory remarked upon it and talked.

'I've never seen her like this, never,' Sarah told Dora in the kitchen. 'And it isn't as if the rector's getting any better.'

'Getting better! He won't do that in this life. I've seen it happen a lot. Not that he's the age it usually happens. He's no older than the doctor. I heard Miss Margaret say once that they were born on the same day in the same year.

Sarah marvelled. 'He could be Doctor's grandad! I always wondered how he came to be Miss Margaret's father.'

Henry Mortimer said something of the same sort to his wife when she spoke of the rector's age. 'Of *course* he's not an old man. He's my age to the day. I have tried to prepare Margaret a little for what is likely to happen. Usually the relations know without being told, but I honestly don't think she has noticed there is anything amiss. When she saw me yesterday she asked me if there was anything I could give him to help him sleep better. And then I discovered that he has lost all sense of time and has taken to wandering at night.'

'Didn't you tell her outright that his brain is softening?' demanded Tiger.

'When you have lived as long as I have you will realize that nothing is as straightforward as you young think it. Or at least I hope you will. No, I said as much as I decently could, but I knew I was making no impression whatever on her shining confidence that all was well and that her father was just suffering from temporary sleeplessness. I felt it was like trying to climb up a glass wall. She also said something about him being elderly and then remembered that he and I were contemporaries. But instead of this jolting her into realizing that there must be something wrong with a man still in his fifties who behaves as though he were 90, she was overcome with confusion at having implied that I was elderly.'

'Typical of Margaret,' said Tiger scornfully. 'She has a greater capacity for embarrassment than anybody else I know. You might say that her life was governed by fear of it.'

But at that moment Margaret's life was governed by her love, or rather the love of Louise, for Edward Benbow. It went far beyond her writing in the journal. Edward was with her whatever she did. He would come up behind her while she was writing, rest a hand on her shoulder, and she would lay down her pen and look up at him. She did not sit in her room at the rectory, the room furnished with the old-fashioned eighteenth century pieces and the faded rose and gold curtains that had come from her mother's home (together with the little pastel of her mother herself in low-cut blue silk and elaborately piled coiffure, timidly smiling, a picture which held neither reality nor emotion for Margaret, who had never seen her). She was at Mairwood in the room billowing with the white muslin that Lady Benbow thought suitable for a young girl of Louise's age, standing at the window watching as Edward walked over the gravel below. He would look up as he went into the house, smile and wave. Or she was in the library with the Latin dictionary open on the table before her, but at a loss – until Edward came in, pulled up a chair beside her and with swift explanation removed all difficulty. 'You understand now?' Yes, she understood. When she – as Louise – went into the school to give the girls their scripture lesson, he would come into the classroom, watch approvingly for an instant; their eyes would meet and he would be gone.

The more observant children saw those swift smiles that she gave in the direction of the door. Most of them accepted this as another of the inscrutable phenomena associated with the world of the gentry, whom few of them regarded as human beings in the ordinary sense of the word. Emmy Thomas, sharper and more daring than most, outraged the other girls in Standard Six. 'She's going the same way as her dad, soft upstairs.' This was held to be quite exceptionally shocking, even for Emmy. 'Going soft,' as Emmy called it, was not a thing that happened in Miss Talbot's sphere at all. In the village you might be born like it, like Loopy Lil who lurched round dribbling and making animal noises, but the gentry had money to see that such things did not happen to them. And the rector was just old, anybody could see that from the way he walked – on the rare occasions that he was seen at all.

Of this sort of speculation Margaret was mercifully unaware. She herself shared something of the children's incomprehension. The cottagers were an alien world to her, and try as she would she could not visualize the girls she taught, with their neatly braided hair and demure responses, as being children like, say, the Mortimers had been, or even the watered-down versions that she had encountered at her own school.

But she had not really been aware that her smiles had taken physical shape. These days, indeed, she hardly knew what was real, what was dream, and the truly extraordinary aspect of this was that she, who had always had such a horror of the abnormal, simply did not care.

The winter that followed that brilliant December day at Mairwood was not a particularly severe one. There had been snow on the hills in January, and then a wet and raw February. It was the time of the year that she found most trying, with the busyness generated by Christmas behind her, but the light still short, the hills sodden, and the lanes deep in mire. Her life at this season seemed bounded by the narrow limits of Ludwardine, and she understood a little of the passionate resentment her cousin Elizabeth had felt when she lived at the Court, of the hills which pressed in round the village, an implacable barrier against the rest of the world.

Nor was she over at Mairwood. There would be no meetings of the school managers until the school buildings were further advanced, and in any case she had become very reluctant to set eyes on the reality there. After some weeks when she seemed to have walked no further than the school or the parish rooms it was a great delight on a fine mild day at the end of February to ask for Sunbeam to be saddled and to take her up Harley valley. There was a clear light, the low cloud had at last lifted revealing a mild blue sky, and a fresh west wind blew in her face as she rode up beside the stream which had surged over its banks and now covered the grassy fringe where the black cattle from Lower Harley Farm usually grazed. At last she could shake off the claustrophobia that had afflicted her in the past weeks . . . for at Mairwood Lady Benbow's benevolence could smother, and only when she was riding could she be sure of being alone with Edward.

Margaret had taken to solitary rides some years before. It had begun in the days when her cousins had been living at the Court. Cousin Richard, ever concerned about the needs of his fellow-beings, had suggested that she might visit with him some of the remoter hill farms whose inhabitants had little contact with the rest of the world. He had put his daughter's mare at her disposal and together they had negotiated those steep tracks that were like a watercourse in the winter, a rocky stream bed in the summer. They had knocked on the doors of farms of whose existence she had been completely unaware, and had ridden along the drovers' paths over the top of the forest to isolated shepherds' hovels. In those days of infatuation she had been reluctant to see any flaw in her cousin, but she had felt guilty disappointment that he took so little interest in the scene around him and seemed only concerned with ways in which the rural economy could be improved. She knew she should admire his brisk energy, and she blamed herself for her foolish sentimentality about the picturesque, but she was dismayed by his repeatedly expressed wish that all the heather and bracken should be ploughed up and grass planted for the sheep.

The mare had later become her own and she had continued the rides by herself. These were, she half-realized, considered eccentric by the rest of the world, but she felt she was no longer a young girl, that she had reached an age when eccentricity was allowable, and she went her own way. But though she let it be thought that her parish duties took her to these lonely places, she herself knew that it was self-indulgence. She wanted to be by herself. At the rectory there was always the fear of a ring at the doorbell, followed by the tap on the door of the drawing-room, or the sound of her father's fretful voice and the footsteps of those who came to call her to him. Nobody could reach her when she was out on Sunbeam, and nobody now had the authority to suggest that to ride out alone was imprudent or unconventional.

In fact, she knocked on the doors of very few of the farms. She was always afraid of hostile looks, was uncertain what she should say to the woman who opened the door. To say nothing of the dismaying sights that she might see inside, for she had encountered with Cousin Richard degradation that she had never dreamed of. Poverty she could understand, but she expected it to be a clean and bare poverty, as presented in the Sunday books she had had as a child. She knew now that it could take hideous, almost animal shape, and so she was afraid of what might lurk inside those little stone houses that crouched on the hillside, cowering for shelter in their thickets of windbattered sycamore. Occasionally she did call at the homes of girls in her Bible class, perhaps making the excuse that she had a book to give them. (While she knew it was expected she should call she could not bring herself to do it unless she was ready armed with a purpose.) But her unease communicated itself and so the smiles and the welcome that she well might have received were lacking.

These homes were in fact all fairly near Ludwardine, up Mutton Dingle for the most part, a well-trodden and accessible lane. If you climbed up to the top of that you moved out beyond the patchwork of little fields on the lower slopes of Wolfpits, and on to the vast uncultivated spaces of the forest where the sheep wandered – and usually nobody else – tiny dots of white among the bracken and heather. There was a network of grassy, sheep-nibbled tracks, and you could ride from end to end of the forest and meet no other human.

As spring advanced, Margaret rode there with Edward beside her. They skirted the edge of steep valleys that bit deep into the tableland, and looked down at the silver ribbon of streams far below, that you could hear if the day was fairly still and the wind was not rushing past your ears. Sometimes they turned off the top of the forest and took tracks that led down through woodland and reached some isolated farmstead where they were welcomed and given tea and oatcake. Jack's Green, the Warren, Smatcher and Upper Harley – Edward knew them all and the histories of the families in them, and introduced her proudly.

They picked primroses in the little hazel wood above the Vron farm one day of warm sun in April. Margaret, lifting her face from the cluster in her hand had spoken about their fragrance – not so much scent of their own as the cool freshness of spring. And then she had quoted 'A primrose by a river's brim a yellow primrose was to him'. She did not see, she said with heat, why this implied stupidity, lack of sensitivity. A yellow primrose was in itself so perfectly beautiful that you needed look no further. Her companion had understood.

As they came back along the Vron hillside the rabbits who had been basking in the sun now about to set behind the Myndd opposite whisked into their burrows so that the steep banks were alive with flitting shapes; you could see the movement but not what made it. They went on through the pine wood where January gales had torn down great swathes. Tree had fallen upon tree and had let in unexpected light. And with the light had come a new life. Before the stillness had been palpable, the trees above and the carpet of needles below had muffled all sound and suppressed life. It had felt a place of death; the trunks of the trees themselves clothed in dead wood, only fungus growing below. Now grass and plants flourished, birds sang.

The Vron farm habitually kept a boar in this wood, running with the breeding sows, but Margaret with Edward beside her was fearless and laughed at the jealous screams in the undergrowth. In May they had made an expedition right up Harley Valley to the source of the stream at Shepherd's Well. Up and down over their heads flew the cuckoo, pursued by demented meadow pipits. The stream had shrunk between its banks and was running soberly now, the black cattle were back on the grazing ground. One lifted its head from the water and looked at them, startled, with dripping jaws before lumbering heavily to the other bank. An old donkey was there with untrimmed hooves so grotesquely long that it had to pick its way with a mincing gait. All these things they pointed out to each other and vowed to remember. It was always a matter for self-congratulation if they saw the dipper, white-bibbed, poised and intent on his stone in the stream, but astonishing how often a fleck of foam could be mistaken for him. He never seemed to look at those who advanced on him, and surely he could not have heard above the swirl of the water, but as you approached on the path he would fly leisurely off, skimming upstream a few inches above the water.

In June in Upper Harley, picking their way carefully along the high banks, through the bracken, they had found the dipper's nest, near a waterfall, and had sat on warm turf, leaning up against a mountain ash to wait for the bird to fly out, while Edward recalled how it had been his ambition as a boy to find the nest and the eggs inside it, and how he had waded fruitlessly up streams, bruising his feet on the stones and tearing his face on the thorns of bushes that swept the water. There were never any words of love spoken, there was no need for them – each was fully aware of the other's feelings, could see them in the other's face.

And then in June sudden and terrible doubts had swept

over Margaret. They had arisen after a sermon from Mr Dugdale who habitually preached at the evening service at Ludwardine. As a man he was not imposing; he had the fussy and over-authoritative manner of the person unsure of himself. But in the pulpit he had stature, even eloquence. Style and elegance might be lacking, but there was feeling. And it seemed that however unprepossessing he might appear in society, he understood human nature and did not hesitate to dissect it and expose all its pitiful futility. All this she recognized and often found his sermons disconcerting, though she remained detached from them.

On that memorable fourth Sunday after Trinity he had preached upon sin, upon light sins that people regarded in themselves with complacency, if not vanity, as rightful possessions that set them apart from the common herd, sins that they hugged to themselves with joy. Most, said Mr Dugdale, staring down sombrely into the rectory pew, would much more easily part with Christ than with these sins. Yet these were the sins that came to possess us and separate us from Christ. 'Men perish with whispering sins, nay with silent sins, sins that never tell the conscience that they are sins, as often as with crying sins. And in hell there shall meet as many men, that never thought what was sin, as that spent all their thoughts in the compassing of sin; as many, who in a slack inconsideration, never cast a thought upon that place, as that by searing their conscience, overcame the sense and fear of the place.' He had a fine speaking voice and he intoned these words carefully, deliberately. (He was quoting from Donne, though he did not tell his congregation, who would not have heard of him and would have cared less, and who in any case were for the most part sitting in a hot Sunday stupor of unwonted quantities of food and waiting for the moment when they could leap to their feet and joyfully bawl out the concluding hymn.)

But Margaret heard, and the doom-laden words pierced the happy haze. It was as if shelter had suddenly been torn away from her and the icy wind of truth was buffeting her. In spite of the warmth of the late afternoon she shivered and cowered, lowering her eyes so that she need not meet Mr

Dugdale's stern face. Her sin had become her whole life, so much a part of herself that she would not know how to prise it away. How could it not be a sin when it was so dear to her? For it had just bleakly rushed over her that it not only mattered to her more than anything on earth, but more than heaven itself. Everything else had become a shadow.

Then followed a terrible week. She did not write the journal. Life, which had always been tranquil and pleasant – at any rate it now seemed so – had suddenly become a void. She had never troubled to think about the purpose of life; she had been content to enunciate the formulae of the Church on Sundays and to repeat them for the benefit of those she taught. But now she saw that they had no meaning for her, since no hope of eternal life was able to console her in her present desolation.

She had never had any sort of spiritual direction from her father; what she had imbibed was a love of decorum and a confidence that had hitherto sustained her, that if one kept within the guidelines (so obvious that there was no need for anyone to indicate them to an adult) one would safely arrive at one's destination when life was over. Now Mr Dugdale had snatched aside this comfortable curtain, and she seemed to stand looking out at a dark chaos where there was not a pinpoint of light.

Of course she had heard him preach before, and probably just as eloquently, but in those days she had been deaf, and blind too to what lay outside the little cage that was her life. She saw now, and marvelled that she had not seen before, that there were issues and complexities she had never dreamed of. Right and wrong were not the easy matters she had so childishly supposed – but who could tell her what they should be? The moral teaching she had received at school and derived from her books had always suggested that what was pleasurable was deeply suspect, so that she felt uneasy if she did not choose the hard way in even trivial things: an upright rather than an easy chair, history rather than fiction; avoiding, when she ordered the meals, the food that she particularly liked. What now seemed so extraordinary was that she had never thought to consider imagination as a form of self-indulgence of the grossest sort.

Her despair seemed to take away all physical energy. At the school she sat in front of her class in a stupor, staring blankly out of the windows (which were high in the walls so that nothing could be seen but sky). There were long silences in which the girls shuffled their feet (a thing absolutely forbidden if Miss Garbett was anywhere near), sometimes actually tittering. At home even the rector peevishly noticed that she was not attending to what he said. She moved slowly, leaden-footed, so much so that Sarah, remarking how she dragged herself up the stairs, asked anxiously if she were ill. She could not even summon the concentration to give the household instructions for the day, so that Dora found herself standing there in the dining room waiting for orders that were never given.

What made it all worse was the rain that week. From her room Margaret could see it sweeping over the Deward opposite, a continuous grey curtain. Down in the kitchen they wondered what she did in her room, hour after hour – even the time that she usually devoted to her father. She was sitting dully at her desk, staring out at the weeping skies, the rain-soaked garden where the rosebushes bore mouldering buds that had never opened.

When on the Saturday she dressed herself to attend the meeting of the Society for the Propagation of the Gospel in Gletton, she had come to an extraordinary decision. She must find among the clergy present someone who could give her guidance. She could never have believed that she would have been brought to this pass. She had always supposed that everybody ought to be able to make his own decision for himself, and had found it incomprehensible that Roman Catholics and the extremer Anglo-Catholics – not only timid women but men too – seemed to require confessors to lean upon. But now she found herself craving authoritative pronouncement of what was right. It must of course be someone remote from Ludwardine, whom preferably she need never see again.

As she pinned her collar and put on her waterproof cloak she rehearsed what she should say to him, and Sarah

176

passing the open door, went down to the kitchen to report that Miss Talbot really did seem to be in a strange fit these days, looking in the mirror and muttering. To which Dora replied that she didn't wonder; this rain and the rector were enough to send anyone out of their minds, and she had now taken to removing the keys from all the doors when she locked up, as she was afraid the old gentleman would go opening them and wander out into the night – if he didn't fall downstairs and break his leg first, which all things considered might be the best thing for him and for everyone, since it would at least keep him safe in bed.

Edward had been at the SPG meeting, and Louise, marshalled by Lady Benbow. She had known they would be, of course, and prayed that she might be able to avoid them. Sitting in the body of the hall she had lowered her head and stared into her lap so that she might not see Edward, sitting on the platform with the other clergy. Afterwards Louise had come over.

'This rain – I think I'll die! It's much worse in the country than ever it is in towns. The Proctors had to give up their croquet party, but we all danced instead. There wasn't much room and Annie Proctor doesn't play very well, but still . . . though I do wish we all lived in London. Don't you think there is much more to do in London? You haven't been to see us for so long. Still, you'll have to come soon, because the school is getting on and Edward says he will have to call a meeting to find a schoolmistress. Do more things happen it Ludwardine than they do in Mairwood? Nothing ever, ever seems to happen there, though Edward says it will be better when the church and the school are ready. But I don't know about that, because now we go to Knulle every Sunday and that makes a bit of a change, and at least I can have a talk with Clara Proctor afterwards and laugh at the sermon. Of course we don't say so to anybody else, but really Mr Liddell is so very funny, his voice goes up and down so and he waves his hands about (once he knocked all his papers all over the floor). If I catch Clara's eye we both nearly die trying to stop laughing. Oh there really isn't anything more awful than wanting to laugh and not being able to; the whole of you nearly bursts. I said "burst" to Lady Benbow once, and she was very shocked. To say it about people, I mean. She has taken up some new people now, you know. The Reedys. He is curate at Cwm Hir. They are so poor you can't think, it must be dreadful to be as poor as that. I think I'd die. And there are three little children. Didn't you see him on the platform? I can never stop looking at his shoes, they're so full of patches, I didn't know anyone could wear shoes like that. Though I don't suppose you could see the patches from where you were sitting. But I think I'd rather have holes in my shoes than Lady Benbow fussing me about them. Because,' said Louise confidentially, 'she does fuss so. Edward doesn't notice. He just brushes it away like a fly, but then he doesn't have to be with her as much as I do. Oh look, there's Beatrice Orde Wilson, she's making such signals to try to catch my eye. You will come over soon, won't you?'

But Margaret, watching while the company jostled out of the hall towards the tea that was to be provided in the schoolrooms, had been giving Louise very little of her attention. She had had of course to attend the meeting as the rector's surrogate, but it had passed like a dream as she had struggled with her own predicament. And, as in a dream, she felt herself floundering helplessly, almost paralysed with indecision. The hall was emptying, in a few minutes everybody would be dispersed. Making a tremendous effort of will she stepped forward. Mr Jenkins of Cascoed was detached from the knot of clergy walking through the door. She touched his black, broadcloth arm.

Chapter 8

SUMMER, 1883

The counsel that Mr Jenkins gave Margaret that day in late June at Cascoed could hardly be said to be very positive or forceful. She had dragged out of him the opinion that there was nothing intrinsically evil in imagination, and that because a thing was enjoyable it did not necessarily follow that it was wrong. But to her these rather lame words were like water in the desert, like miraculous respite from long pain. It was not just the agony of doubt she had endured after hearing Mr Dugdale. Added to that was the extremity of horror at the prospect of baring herself in front of a stranger – she to whom reticence and reserve were a clothing she hardly knew how to remove. So that when Mr Jenkins gave his views and she realized that she had not only survived the interview but had survived it with dignity still intact, she was filled with trembling gratitude and a euphoria that clouded such powers of judgement as she had. His surprise at the question she had put to him seemed to give her predicament a new perspective; clearly she had done nothing which most people would deem wrong. He had spoken of spiritual duties, she determined that she would put more effort into these than ever before – give more time to them, pray with more zeal, show greater tolerance to the weakness of others; she felt she could promise away the world in her thankfulness.

Dr Mortimer had noticed her radiance as she drove back from Cascoed. Sarah and Dora, nearer at hand, and with far keener interest in the vagaries of human behaviour, were at a total loss to account for her change of manner.

'Perhaps it's because Mr Alfred will be back.' Sarah had seen the envelopes that used to lie on the hall table ready for posting; Margaret had had no thought of concealing them, they were nothing that mattered very much to her.

'But we've all of us known that for the last month or more. And she was in that state all of the week before. Well, I don't know. But I don't think anything will come of her and Mr Alfred – not with her.'

'She's not that old,' demurred Sarah.

'She's all set to be single, anyone can see that.'

At the Grove there was also speculation about the outcome of Alfred's return. 'He seems so devoted,' said Mary Mortimer in a moment of confidence to Tiger to whom it was not easy these days to confide anything at all.

'He always was soft about her. But she never noticed.'

'Surely she will now, after all those letters. And she is that much older, she must want to be settled.'

'Why is it that everybody seems to think that every woman wants "to get settled" as you call it? Some people might feel that it is preferable to go through life without the millstone of a husband and children!'

'I think,' said Mary Mortimer, ignoring Tiger's outburst, 'that we should do something to entertain Margaret when Alfred does come. It is so long since she has been here properly. In the old days it was easy, she was to and fro the whole time. But now she would feel she had to be invited before she came.'

'You are matchmaking, Mamma,' said Tiger contemptuously.

But when Alfred arrived it was the first thing he asked about, once the greetings were over. It was five years since they had waved him off on his way to Liverpool, and neither side was prepared for the change that time had made. They found him graver, more silent. For his part he noticed how his parents had aged. Both of them seemed to stoop a little; his father was grey, his mother's face lined, and her cheeks which he remembered as rosy now a network of little red veins. But it was Tiger's appearance that shocked him; five years had turned her from a girl into a sharp-faced, sharp-voiced old maid. In the old days he would have commented now he said nothing. He was shown the improvements in the garden, had given the presents he had brought (they were objects he had bought at Port Said since Upper Burma had seemed to have little to offer). Then, as they waited for tea to be brought he asked about Margaret.

'Oh she's all right, I daresay,' said Tiger. 'You know her father has softening of the brain, don't you?'

'Senile dementia,' said the doctor.

'I didn't know. I mean, I saw from Mother's letters that he didn't do very much, but I never realized . . . and Margaret said nothing. How terrible for her – can he still go about?'

'He takes morning service, if that's what you mean. Though everybody is on edge in case he is going to lose his way in the Prayer Book. He doesn't preach any more, Mr Dugdale does that. But Margaret doesn't seem to notice anything.'

'Doesn't notice!'

'I am reminded of what I went through with Boys Talbot,' said the doctor. 'I tried to convey to him that his wife's mental state was very precarious. I never succeeded. I think I described it then as like wrestling with a hill fog. It is the same now with Margaret.'

'Does it mean that she is with him all the time? I mean, I suppose he has to be looked after.'

'Oh no, she leaves him quite a lot,' said Tiger lightly. 'She's become very independent, quite unlike how you probably remember her. She wanders all over the hills by herself – getting thoughts for her books, I daresay. And she goes over to Mairwood, she's very thick with them there. All those High Church junketings will be just her cup of tea. But if she writes to you you probably know all this.'

'Yes, she seems independent.' Alfred, to the disappointment of his mother and sister, said no more about the content of the letters. 'But I would like to see her. Doesn't she ever come here any more?'

'Well, you'll see her in church,' said Tiger briskly. 'And probably run up against her in the village.'

'We had thought,' interposed her mother, 'that we would ask her in, perhaps to luncheon. It would be very nice to see her properly again.'

Tiger noticed her brother's expression of surprise. 'It's quite different from the days you remember, I daresay. We don't see much of her. I suppose you could say we've grown out of each other.'

But when the planned luncheon came off a few days later it was more like the old days than any of those present would have believed possible. By then Charley and Julius were home for the holidays, and Johnnie from Osborne. By dint of some special pleading Arthur had got leave from his regiment, and there was thus a fuller mustering of Mortimers than there had been for years. Claud, who had severed all connection with the Grove when he had taken himself off from school to become a railway engineer nine years before, had long ago ceased to be considered part of the family circle, and it was many years since Ernest had spent his leave at the Grove.

Henry Mortimer genuinely supposed himself to be a conscientious father (admittedly afflicted with trying sons) and did his best to go through the proper motions when his various children returned home after absence. But twenty-four hours was as long as he could keep up the effort, and by the end of forty-eight his habitual irritability had reasserted itself. So that when Mary Mortimer had proposed to Alfred that they should invite Margaret over, he had shown some reluctance to expose her to the family tensions.

'Don't you think it had better be something when Father isn't there? I mean she never was used to hurly-burly, and now . . .'

Hurly-burly was hardly the expression to describe the fraught and resentful silence usually present at meals at the Grove, but his mother understood. 'I hardly like to ask her over just to tea.'

'Why not have a picnic? Papa wouldn't have to go to that,' said Charley, coming into the room at this moment.

'Yes, a picnic, a cracking good picnic!' said Julius just behind him.

'But would Margaret enjoy such a thing now?' Arthur was doubtful.

'Yes, I think she would.' Mary Mortimer spoke wit

conviction. Charley's schoolboy suggestion would solve many problems and relieve her of all responsibility for a social occasion for which she had no appetite at all. 'It is quite the best sort of thing to recall the old days. And it is so much less formal; I think you would find her more at her ease. Between us Mrs Tilley and I could make up quite a good hamper of provisions, and you could stow it in the governess cart and take it where you will. But I should have it soon, while the weather seems reasonably settled.' (If the rain came then it would all have to be eaten in the dining room, and the habitual constraints and tensions would probably be worse than ever from the inevitable disappointment.)

And so the following morning Alfred himself went over to the rectory with a written invitation. He had barely seen Margaret since he had arrived home, since so many people had crowded round him after church on Sunday that he had been stopped from greeting her with anything more than the most formal bow as she had hurried past. He found her in the dining room with Dora standing before her, intent upon deciding whether the mutton should all be eaten cold that day or a little saved for a shepherd's pie for the kitchen.

'Did she seem, well – loverlike?' Sarah asked eagerly afterwards.

'Not what you'd call. *He* did more. But it would put anybody out, having to speak up in front of another party. Now, my girl, has Mr Rhodes called yet? If he hasn't you'd better ask him for an extra loaf, Miss Talbot was thinking of anchovy toast for a savoury.' Dora observed a code; in the kitchen you could speculate or make observations about what went on in public, but if Miss Talbot was caught at a disadvantage in private then you didn't pass it on.

Not that there really was anything to discuss. Margaret had made the proper enquiries about Alfred's journey and about how he found Ludwardine. He had given her his mother's note (extraordinary formality, but ten years had passed since the days when she regarded the Grove almost as a second home) and had explained what was in it, and that it was tentatively suggested that they should take lunch to the Pool, up above the Forest Inn. As he spoke he noted how whereas Tiger had grown unattractive with the passing of time Margaret was now almost beautiful. He had used to think she was too self-effacing, had wished – while never wanting her to have Tiger's force of manner – that she could have had more confidence in herself. He said something to his mother of the change he had noticed.

'Yes, she is different, we have all remarked on it.'

'Have you any idea why?'

Mary Mortimer guessed something of what was in his mind but what he could never ask. 'I did sometimes wonder if it was Edward Benbow. But I don't think it can be. He is never over in Ludwardine, and though she does go over to Mairwood occasionally it is for the school they are starting there, and for the young girl who lives there and who inexplicably seems to be a great friend. I think . . .' But she said no more.

Luckily for the peace of mind of all the Mortimers the day of the picnic began fine. It was gusty and not particularly warm, but it was good enough, and the rugs, the hampers, the tea-kettle were piled into the governess cart and the cavalcade set off on the road that went west from Ludwardine, up over the forest towards the heart of Wales. Alfred and Arthur had set off earlier to walk there over the hills. It was some five miles by road, uphill all the way. You crossed the bridge over the stream that flowed out of Harley valley, passing the mill and mill farm that stood on either side of it. You looked up at Vron farm with its high-pitched roof and seventeenth century chimney stacks, the pine wood and the Vron hill behind. A little further on was the track that led to the ravine in the hills where the waterfall called Davy Morgan's Washpot poured down (a spot where they had often picnicked in the past). Then round the Myndd hill and Ludweardine was out of sight, and you were on the level for a mile. Lower House Farm was on your left and there would be the ritual remarks about Edwin Williams being a surly old devil (inevitably capped by a further remark that it was this expression that sent Dean Farrar's Eric toppling to perdition). Old Min's cottage was nearly opposite, a blackened, tumbledown hovel, and you might see Old Min, nutcracker jawed, berating her husband as between them they dragged along the donkey (which, let out to cottagers who had none of their own, was their sole source of income). Then came the hamlet of Llanfihangel which consisted of a farm, an inn, and the tiny church hidden by majestic yew trees. Beyond that the road rose steeply, but before the top of the forest was reached one turned off by the Forest Inn on to the Builth road. The Pool was a half mile climb beyond that, a lonely, reedy expanse of dark water surrounded by heathery slopes.

'I can't think why Alfred chose here,' said Tiger, climbing down. 'It gets every wind there is.'

'Don't be cross, Tyg,' Arthur shouted. 'Alfred and I have been collecting wood all the way up, and we're going to have such a fire. You boys, scatter around and get some more, we want a real blaze that'll last all afternoon.'

The rain that Mary Mortimer had feared would overtake the party before it had set out swept over the hills while they were still at lunch, but huddled under the shelter of waterproof sheets that Alfred had rigged up they had laughed and cheered; nor had the rain been able to extinguish the fire, though there had been much horseplay about who should next extricate himself from the mob in the shelter and run to throw on some more wood, and more horseplay about the charred potatoes that had been baked in the ashes and were being thrown around and leaving sooty smears on everybody's hands, and on a lot of faces. Indeed, Julius decided that he might as well black the whole of his face and turned himself into a nigger minstrel, and wanting to see what it looked like tried to do the same to Charley.

The rain stopped as suddenly as it had started; the sound of drops thudding on the macintosh above their heads faded to a light pattering, then silence. The rain on the grass sparkled in brilliant sunlight, and the water in the Pool shone blue. The melée in the shelter disentangled itself and people scattered, some to the pool to wash the plates, others to round up the ponies. Alfred and Margaret were left standing by the fire.

'I have so much enjoyed myself.' She spoke with sincerity. 'It was really like the old times.'

'It has meant a great deal to me, being back here.' He wanted to say more but did not.

'Do you feel homesick all the time you are away?'

'I never knew how bad it would be. You take these things so much for granted when you live here all the time. It is only when you are thousands of miles away that you realize what they mean.'

'I think *I* could realize.'

'Oh I didn't mean you, of course not. I know from the way you write. You know your letters mean so much . . .'

She did know; his own letters chiefly consisted of this sentiment repeated over and over again. 'I like writing about the little things I see; I feel it somehow preserves them – I hate to think of them just vanishing for ever.'

'I was wondering if while I am here . . . we could ride together. I am sure I could borrow a horse from somewhere, and there are so many favourite places in the hills I want to see again.'

It would have of course been impossible to keep the matter of the rides from other members of the family. Alfred did not discuss it with any of them, but they discovered soon enough that he was casting around for the loan of a horse and they talked among themselves.

'I take it Margaret feels no scruples about being out with him alone,' said Mary Mortimer to Tiger.

'I suppose not, if she's going. She's her own mistress now.'

'I admire her for it. I would have thought she would have had all sorts of worries about propriety. And Alfred would not have been the one who could have overruled those easily. So perhaps . . .'

'I don't think it's any good making schemes, Mamma. It's because she is so remote from what you've got in mind that she is willing to go out with him.'

Mary Mortimer said no more, but it occurred to her that the remoteness need not be necessarily permanent.

But Alfred was finding it hard. His father had compared trying to make impact upon Margaret as like being confronted with a glass wall. If Alfred had been as articulate he might have expressed his own feelings likewise. It seemed impossible to make any impression on her. It was not that she was cold, or hostile, or even ill at ease. On the contrary she seemed to enjoy their rides. But the impersonality rebuffed him. Every time he would set out with his mind humming with the sentiments that he would speak out; but always he returned with them unuttered.

Time passed; Arthur had long ago gone back to join his regiment in Ireland. He had shaken his brother's hand on parting and, with a meaning look, had wished his well, and added as an afterthought that he could always come over to join him in Dublin if he got tired of what Ludwardine had to offer; that he would get some spanking good sport there and a selection of pretty girls. Charley and Julius and Johnnie had dispersed to their various educational establishments, and the Mortimer household was down to four. It was now September, mellow and sunny after a stormy August, and the bracken on the hills was tipped with brown.

With September Margaret's own duties were resumed. The school had of course reassembled, and she was down there three times a week to give the scripture lessons, so that there was not so much time for expeditions with Alfred.

'Surely you can make room for one really long one before the evenings get too short,' he said to her one day when they met in the village street, she with books tucked under her arm as she hurried towards the school. 'And before I leave.'

'Are you leaving soon?'

He looked at her, wondering whether there was any expression of regret in her voice – up to now he had not mentioned any parting. 'I shan't be going back until November, but there are visits to fit in before that; I half-promised Arthur, and there is my aunt in London. And I would like to make the round of the forest with you before I go – you know, going out by Black Mixen and coming back down the Saddle.'

'Why yes, if it was a Saturday I could do that.'

'Well then, I tell you what,' said Alfred emboldened. 'Why could we not make the full circle of the hills? This

187

Saturday? Go via Evancob to Paradise valley, then Beggar's Bush down to Cascoed and scramble up through the woods to Black Mixen and home that way.'

'It's a very long way,' said Margaret doubtfully.

'I know. But I'll beg some hard-boiled eggs and a couple of mutton sandwiches from Mrs Tilley and we'll make a whole day of it. It'll be my last sight of the hills, I daresay.'

After this Margaret could not demur. The time fixed, the arrangements made, he still lingered and she looked at him questioningly. Then he shook his head, raised his hat and strode away. She felt a sadness that her rides after this would be solitary again. His companionship had not been the intrusion she had feared, for he had spoken so little. When he rode behind her she was easily able to think that Edward was there, and indeed the delighted exclamations, the spoken recognition of familiar landmarks that she had given without turning her head had been addressed to Edward whom she could see there, scanning the landscape with the same eager pleasure as her own.

When she woke on Saturday it was to find that it was a brilliant day, with the hint of haze on the Deward and the pale sky that meant heat when the sun was properly up. As she leant from the window to feel the cold air on her face, she was astonished at the feeling of melancholy that suffused her. As long as she could remember September was the month when her spirits rose highest. As a child she had wanted to run and leap and shout for the irrational joy of it. Growing up had sobered her behaviour, she concealed her heady elation. But it had still been there, a breathless, fleeting sense that the world was hers, she only had to reach out and take it. Once she had ventured to say something of the sort to Cousin Richard when she was out riding with him, phrasing it decorously, of course, and merely speaking of the excitement of autumn. But he was puzzled. He admitted that he was always surprised at the way the seasons affected people's spirits, but supposed that surely spring would be the one that invigorated, since it was the beginning of life.

And autumn was the dying of the year. He had not said

this, but it was implicit. At the time she had put it behind her. The withering of the leaf, the brown on the hillside, might deceive people into thinking of decay, but to her senses autumn brought life and vigour and hope and promise. And every September, the time when the year hung poised in still calm between summer and autumn, she found herself swung up into this mood of giddy joy.

But not this year. As she stood by the open window she knew that it had gone forever. Of course autumn was the prelude to death, and she marvelled that she could have ever thought otherwise. The hint of frost in the air, the robin's reedy piping, the swallows that twittered on the stable roof below, how could she not have felt saddened by them before?

She spoke of it to Alfred as they took the road to Beggar's Bush a couple of hours later.

'But I thought autumn gave you such high spirits— That's what you wrote to me last year at this time. I've still got the letter.'

'Yes, I've changed. I suppose I'm growing older.' How could he understand? She had thought she had been speaking to Edward.

At Kinnersley church they swung to the right, the harshness of the forest with its dark slopes heavily scored by stony gullies for the moment behind them. They were in farmland now, and they rode between hedgerows comfortably full of blackberries and the glassy red fruit of the honeysuckle. At Evancob they took the field path that was the quickest way to Gletton; only four miles over the hill, but seven or eight if you went by the road down the Ludd valley. There were children looking for mushrooms in the field, they lifted their heads and stared.

'They think we are foreigners,' Alfred said, 'Evancob is as remote a place as you'd find round here, not on the way to anywhere. Here you are, don't get your boots too wet, you'll be in trouble at home if you do. Here's a penny for you if you can find it.'

The path led through a plantation of sweet chestnut and arch to a firm track on the ridge of the hill, and a view of the tree-clad slopes on the Ludd Valley road, and of the out-skirts of Gletton itself in the far distance.

'We could take the long way to Cascoed, through Gletton?'

But Margaret, who had not been expecting *his* voice, shook her head decisively.

'Yes, I expect you're right, we should stay on the hills. It's too tame down there, and there's no knowing who we might not run into. The Orde Wilsons, for one.'

As the lane descended they could see Paradise Farm on the other side of the valley to their left, massy oakwoods pressing in behind it, fields bright with sun sweeping down in front of it. To reach the farm you had to keep to the lane through a shadowy beechwood before you could strike out into the sun of Paradise valley.

'I'm not entirely sure of the way after the farm. We'd better ask there, if we can find anybody.'

Long before they had ever reached it the dogs had seen them and the usual threatening shrieks broke out.

'Caesar and Pompey would have squared them in the old days – I'd probably have had to whip them off. These farm dogs have got precious little fight in them when it comes to a real scrap. I always reckon they don't get fed enough.'

A man was at the door of one of the outbuildings, standing with his eyes shaded, looking down towards them. Margaret puzzled at what it was hanging there in the doorway, something that he had been working at as they approached. Only when she was quite close did her short-sighted eyes recognize it, a sheepskin that he was flaying, rags of flesh still on it, and a head and bloody pile tossed below.

'Good day to you. I'd have tidied up if I'd known there would be a lady passing.' He spoke however with compla-cent satisfaction, and looked down at the shambles with seeming pleasure.

While Alfred asked for directions, Margaret wandered up to the wall of the small garden in front of the farmhouse. Nothing grew there but rank grass through which hens were busily scratching. Nobody had ever thought to plant flowers there; it would have been extravagant, ridiculous, when all one's time was needed for the brutal business of keeping alive. But on the wall a wild rose had taken root and had sent up thriving shoots.

'I think I've got it clear now,' Alfred called. 'We mustn't be misled by the lower path which doesn't go anywhere. The diagonal one, climbing the hill, is the one for us. What have you found there?'

'It was just a wild rose. I thought there was a late flower on it – but it was only what we used to call a robin's pincushion – a canker.'

The leafmould in the wood deadened the sound of their horses' feet. The oaks grew densely and only thin grass thrived in the shade. They emerged into the fields beyond through a gate that was part of a bedstead, and which Alfred had to dismount to heave open.

'That was the one he meant, that he thought we might have difficulty with. Rough sort of johnny – grinned all over his face as he said it. Now we go through to the next farm and then strike off right and we'll get to the road to the Bush.'

The Bush, Beggar's Bush, was a meeting place of four roads on a hilltop. It held a signpost, nothing more. Margaret had often wondered who the beggar had been. Had he died there, under a thorn that had long ago gone the same way as he? She would have spoken of this to Edward, but Alfred she merely asked if they could take the top lane to Cascoed through Ack Wood, and get down to Cascoed valley by the church. (That way at least one would avoid passing Mr Jenkins' rectory.)

'Right you are! I'd always rather be on top of things instead of thrashing around in valley bottoms – though we will have to go down in the end before we go up if you see what I mean. And I tell you what, we'll eat Mrs Tilley's provisions at Twiscob and give the horses a bit of rest before we do the last grand climb – it'll be all of two thousand feet.'

Ack Lane was turf, sometimes with bracken springing from the middle of it. The neglected hedges had grown into trees: hazels and bright-berried mountain ash that cast deep shade and only allowed intermittent glimpses of the wooded hills on the other side of the valley. The lane wandered for a couple of miles, and then they were briefly out in the open before they plunged down the hill in a dark tunnel of trees with six-foot banks on either side of them, and ground, even at the end of the summer, soft with mud. At the bottom they met the road and the stream, which ran culverted below it.

'We used to come here for braveness tests. Arthur and I would make Claud and Ernest creep under the road through that culvert. They had to bend themselves more treble than double and somehow get through like frogs. Not fair really, as there was no question of us doing it, we were far too big. But boys are brutes, and I suppose they had to face worse things at school.'

'Is it terrible, being a boy?' she asked suddenly as they sat eating their lunch half an hour later. She was remembering what Alfred had said about school, but for the moment he did not follow her.

'I mean, our lives are so easy, we are sheltered from everything. We don't have to compete about being brave.'

'I think you're brave.' He thought of her life in the rectory with only the doddering old man as companion and there was tenderness in his voice. He noticed that she frowned a little, and faint-hearted, hastened to a more impersonal topic. 'But no boy worth his salt would want to be anything else – I know Tiger often enough wished she was one.'

She sighed a little, as much for Alfred's slowness and lack of sensibility as for recognition of the deep difference between herself and Tiger. 'And you have to go out into the world and fight your way while we can stay at home.'

' "For men must work and women must weep" – I seem to remember Father saying that to Charley and Julius when Tiger was trying to teach them. I don't know what it comes from.'

They were sitting at the furthest end of the Cascoed valley, where it pushed right into the hills that rose sheer all round, forested for half their slopes and then, though this could not be seen from the valley, heather-covered. Margaret had found a tree-trunk, Alfred sprawled at her feet, and the horses grazed down by the stream.

'This is the place I always think of when I can't sleep in that cursed heat. Looking back down the valley with that shingled spire of the church just poking through the trees. And the stream tinkling away. Water doesn't tinkle in India, it's full of mud and it surges along, or oozes like oil. But now I shall think of you sitting here with me.'

'Do you think we'd better go now?' Margaret rose to her feet. 'There's still the worst part to do.' 'Worst?' This word so lightly said wounded him, though he did not comment.

Pushing up through the woods she felt that the trees seemed to stretch for infinity ahead of them. But turning to look back she could see that they had already climbed so far that the valley where they had rested was only an impossibly remote patch of sunlight, just visible through the tree trunks. Somewhere in the depths of the wood trees were being felled, they could hear the ring of an axe. Otherwise it was totally silent.

'We used to try and frighten the younger ones with stories about a demon of the woods which we called, I don't know why, a wendigo,' remarked Alfred. 'It was surprising how worked up they could get about it. I remember Ernest running screaming to the bottom, all the way we'd come. It served us out; we had to go after him and go back the way we'd come. And it's a long way.'

Margaret, staring at tree trunks all round her and up at the branches that shut out the sky knew much of what Ernest had felt.

The emergence into light and sun and space seemed miraculous. The hill stretched on above them, dark and tussocky with heather, with here and there ribbons of grass where the sheep had moved, but it was a most merciful release. She reached the drovers' track before Alfred did, and turned her horse to look back. Up here the valley was hidden, so steep had been the ascent, and you looked down on to the tops of hills, and beyond them more hills, fold upon fold, curving round the horizon and stretching eastward till they met the sky. It seemed that the whole world lay spread below her; beyond – nothing.

'"And year by year our memory fades from all the circle of the hills."' She was not speaking to Alfred, but he answered her.

'What was that?'

'It's from *In Memoriam*. I learnt a lot of it once. Just to please myself.'

'The circle of the hills – it's right. They do make a circle.'

She hardly heard him. 'Our memory fading – that's what I mind. That no one will remember; oblivion. And the hills will still be there but I will no longer see them, and no one will remember that I once looked at them.'

'But . . .' Then he looked at her intent, gazing face and liked to say no more.

They passed no one on the way down from the moorland to the gate that led into the lane down Mutton Dingle; sometimes a sheep looked up at them with foolish vacancy from the midst of bracken and clumsily blundered out of their path. Once far away they saw a man with a horse and cart beside him, cutting the bracken, and the rasp of the scythe he was using came to them faintly. Only when Alfred held back the gate for her did he speak again.

'You said you had learnt a lot of *In Memoriam* – is there any more that you remember?'

She said it almost to herself.

> I climb the hill; from end to end
>   Of all the landscape underneath,
>   I find no place that does not breathe
> Some gracious memory of my friend;
>
> No gray old grange, or lonely fold,
>   Or low morass and whispering reed,
>   Or simple stile from mead to mead,
> Or sheepwalk up the windy wold;
>
> No hoary knoll of ash and haw
>   That hears the latest linnet trill,
>   Nor quarry trench'd along the hill
> And haunted by the wrangling daw;

Nor runlet tinkling from the rock;
　　Nor pastoral rivulet that swerves
　　To left and right thro' meadowy curves,
That feed the mothers of the flock;

But each has pleased a kindred eye,
　　And each reflects a kindlier day . . .
　　　　Her voice faded.

Looking at her surreptitiously he saw tears on her cheek and hesitated to speak. Nothing was said until they reached the rectory gate.

'I shall be going on Wednesday. Can I come to say goodbye?'

She gave herself a little shake as if pulling herself together. 'I will be free on Tuesday morning.'

'I'll come then,' he promised.

Chapter 9

AUTUMN, 1883

When Margaret had named Tuesday morning to Alfred her mind was not on him; indeed she hardly believed in Tuesday at all – it was irrelevant, lost in the mists of the future that would never arrive. For Monday stretched to the limits of the horizon, Monday being the day which had been fixed for the first official meeting of the managers of the Mairwood parish school. They had to consider the applications for the post of schoolmistress advertised the previous month. They were to meet in the library at Mairwood House.

She walked the three miles to the house. It was a day of mellow warmth with a golden haze on the hills, but her feeling of melancholy persisted. She had chosen to walk so that the pleasure might be spun out, and was annoyed to find herself troubled and uneasy. She wanted nothing more than to be in Edward's presence, playing a mute, acquiescent part; very well, here was just such an occasion, and there would be many others of the same sort. But the feeling that had been so strong as she had looked out over the hills was still with her – life was finite, there was an end to everything, and after that a void.

She was the last of the managers to arrive. It was a small assembly; there were besides herself Edward, Louise, Mrs Howes of the Home Farm (an imaginative gesture this), Mr Reedy the impoverished curate of Cwm Hir – a parish which having no school of its own would help fill the classroom at Mairwood. They were standing by the windows at the end of the library, the conversation appeared to be flagging, and Margaret was greeted with relief.

The meeting was not a long one. There had only been four applications, of which two were clearly hopeless, penned by candidates who seemed to have difficulty in forming the letters. The obvious choice would appear to be a young woman who had been a pupil teacher at Gletton, whom Edweard Benbow had met and could speak of as seemingly very satisfactory, though on the young side. But Mr Reedy felt that he had to speak about the fourth application, an elderly widow from Hereford who had once kept a small dame school in her own kitchen. He was always deeply conscious that his poverty put him at a loss with his social equals, he was resentful of Lady Benbow's tea-parties (organized, he felt certain because she thought his children looked hungry), and he felt the need to assert himself, to show that he did not necessarily bow the knee to patrons. And so he droned on about the merits of Mrs Flannery.

They all accepted the boredom in different ways. Mrs Howes sat very correctly, hands folded, her eyes upon the speaker; Edward with lowered head stared at the memorandum book before him; Margaret fidgeted a little, uneasy that Mr Reedy was making a fool of himself; Louise rolled up little balls of paper and flicked at them with her pencil. One landed before Margaret and Louise arched her eyebrows and made gestures with her fingers that it should be returned. But Edward reached over, took it and resumed his scrutiny of the notes he had pencilled.

'And so,' floundered Mr Reedy, 'I feel that we should give consideration to this worthy woman who after all has had some considerable experience with young children.' He stared round at them defiantly, suddenly suspicious that the silence was in deference to his inferior status, and that an equal would have received the compliment of argument.

'But is she not a dissenter?' asked Mrs Howes calmly.

'A dissenter?' Mr Reedy was totally thrown.

'She says so in the letter. A Wesleyan.'

'A Wesleyan – I confess I did not see that.'

After that it took only a further five minutes to bring the meeting to a close.

'Oh the tedium of it – boring, boring, boring,' said Louise some ten minutes later. The meeting had dispersed, but she had barely waited for the last back to disappear through the door. She yawned and stretched herself and then went to kneel on the windowseat. 'Boredom really hurts, don't you think it does?' She turned to look at Margaret. 'Oh dear, you look disapproving. Do you think I am very bad?'

Margaret could say nothing. The gesture of reproach that Edward had made to Louise had disconcerted her even more painfully than poor Mr Reedy had been disconcerted upon realization of his oversight. She felt that she herself had been publicly humiliated.

'You're looking like Edward does. Sorrowful. I'd much rather people were angry with me. Like that awful time on Good Friday when I played polkas on the organ in the drawing room. I mean it had been so solemn all the week and by Good Friday I felt fidgeted to death. Though I would never had done it if I'd known how he was going to look. What made it worse was that I was making so much noise that of course I never heard him come into the room and I looked round and there he was standing right by me, looking so stern. I was so frightened that I just burst into tears. I cried and cried and couldn't stop and Lady Benbow had to give me sal volatile. I get like that if I cry,' Louise remarked complacently. 'It's useful, it quite frightens people.' She paused, looking up at Margaret almost defiantly. 'You know, I think he is fond of me really – I mean, fonder than he need be if I were only . . . well, just Robert's sister. Only the trouble is that I am so little like Robert and I don't think he altogether realizes.'

'But you are fond of him?'

'Well, I think I am – because it is always pleasant to be liked. But sometimes I do find it difficult. I mean, one can never be sure whether he is laughing or serious. He can joke about things that I would never expect – like hymns, sometimes sermons even – and then suddenly be all serious. You know, I sometimes think that he ought to have had . . .'

'What should he have had?' But she knew she should not ask the question.

'Well, someone more like you.' Louise said this in the tone of one who spoke of a fantastic impossibility. 'But of course you would never want to marry.'

'Would you?' It was a question she had never asked anyone.

Louise stared. 'Of course. I mean, everyone does. I'd like to be the first of everybody at school to marry, that would just show them. Miss Elliot couldn't say anything to a married woman. What I'd like to do is go back married and just sweep in and laugh in all their faces. Just think, I'd be able to chaperon Miss Elliot! And Lady Benbow wouldn't have to chaperon me any more, I'd be my own mistress. It's funny that Lady Benbow must once have had to be chaperoned herself, I can't imagine it, can you?'

'There's a picture of her in the drawing room before she was married.'

'I've never seen it.'

'By the big portrait of Sir Samuel.'

'I can't think which one you mean.'

'With ringlets and a lace bertha.'

'That one! I thought it must be one of Edward's sisters; I didn't like to ask because Lady Benbow goes so weepy when she talks about them. But of course, now I think, they all died when they were little. That was Lady Benbow! Oh well, perhaps I will look like her one day then, and play gooseberry.' She laughed at what was an impossible contingency.

'Oh look, there is Edward. Edward, can you see me in a widow's cap with grey hair?'

He was standing in the door. 'It happens to many women – perhaps you could say most women.'

'Oh well, it won't be for a little while, I daresay.' But Margaret knew that she said this as a child might to conciliate a stupid adult, that she knew better, and it would never happen.

'Miss Talbot, you have not seen the latest progress with the building. It seems hard for you to come all this way to discuss the appointment of a schoolmistress for what must seem to you to be surely a mythical school. So if you have time perhaps you would care to walk over to the site. Louise has seen and heard far too much of it to wish to come, I know.' He smiled gently in her direction. Any annoyance he might have felt at her frivolous behaviour at the meeting had surely vanished.

They walked in silence out of the house, over the gravel, past the entrance to the stables, and down the lane – much rutted now by the passage of wagons – that led in the direction of the church. She had not been there since the day the foundation stone was laid and was amazed by the height the walls had reached.

'I never knew that window arches were made like that – around a wooden structure. Though I suppose there would have to be something to support it, but I had not thought of that.' As always when under the stress of strong feelings she chattered to try to conceal them.

'Yes, the centring. You can see pictures of windows being constructed in just the same way in medieval manuscripts. The mason's craft is a very conservative one.'

As they walked down the drive towards the school, which was being built near the lodge, he spoke of his regret that it was not to be sited by the church. 'I wanted, as you know, to have a tightly knit community of buildings up there, all looking towards the church. But I gave in to expediency – it would add an extra half mile for the children coming from Cwm Hir. An insidious thing, expediency.'

'Oh look, there is Edward. Edward, can you see me in a from the road, the school had already reached the stage of being slated. They picked their way through the mud and peered through unglazed windows into dark, unplastered rooms. He spoke of the care that was being taken over detail, to proper water supply and the latest thing in kitcheners for the schoolmistress's living quarters. But Margaret sensed that he was abstracted. Back on the road he halted.

'Miss Talbot, I wondered whether you would be affronted if I consulted you about a very personal matter?'

His face was troubled. How could she not wish to do anything in her power to help him? She wondered whether her eagerness was evident in the way she spoke.

'It is, as I say, entirely personal, and you may think it very strange that I should speak to you about it. But you have known Louise ever since she came here, and there is no one whose opinion I would better trust.'

Her face burning, she stared at the ground, dreading what might be coming now.

'I would like to ask her to be my wife – but I wonder if I am doing right. I am fourteen years older than she is. I don't think this is too great a disparity, but in some ways she is younger than eighteen, and I suspect she thinks I am unimaginably old. Do you remember Marianne Dashwood who thought Colonel Brandon impossibly aged and infirm because he wore a flannel waistcoat?'

'But she married him,' said Margaret with trembling lips.

'Yes, she married him. And we are to suppose that they were happy. But could I expect to be as successful as Colonel Brandon? She confides a little in you, does she not, though you are not over in Mairwood as often as we should like you to be. Has she said anything to you that might help me to decide?'

'I think . . . that she may be conscious of not being serious enough for you. She said today that she was very different from her brother.'

'Now that is what makes her so endearing,' he said with great warmth. 'This artless recognition of her own character. And she is always so sorry if she feels she is wrong. I remember one occasion – it was Good Friday – when her high spirits broke out for a moment, and she wept heartbreakingly all evening. My mother told me it was because she was so grieved at upsetting me. I feel that if I ask Louise to marry me she may say yes because she dislikes causing displeasure. And obviously I need to know the real truth. So I am asking you now; do you consider that we could be happily matched? Is it fair to Louise? Please do not hesitate to express any doubt you feel; it would be much kinder. But indeed I am putting this to you because I am so confident that you would speak out.'

Margaret raised her eyes. 'I think you will make each other so perfectly happy that . . .', she began, but could say no more, her voice being thick with tears. Then she tried again. 'I think it would be a perfect match.'

He recognized her emotion and was touched by it. It was an indication of Louise's quality that she should have such a devoted and feeling friend. What Edward Benbow never knew of course was that he had just proposed marriage to Louise in the person of Margaret Talbot. And that she had accepted him.

When Alfred called at the rectory next morning Margaret had forgotten all about him. He found her at the bottom of the garden where she had wandered, ostensibly to try to find Atkins the gardener to see about picking the pears, but in reality because she was too fretted and restless to be in the house, or to settle to anything. He noticed her agitation at once and it gave him confidence, even while making it more difficult to find the right words.

'I came to say goodbye . . . but something more as well,' he began, despising his clumsiness.

'Oh yes, of course. Goodbye. And thank you very much for all the expeditions. I enjoyed them.'

Her calm dismissal did not make it easy to proceed, though as yet he was still confident.

'But I hoped it wouldn't be goodbye.'

She looked at him, perplexed. 'Have you decided to stay on a little?'

'What I meant to say was that I hoped you could . . . that you might come to . . . that you might marry me.'

She looked at him with such appalled consternation that he blenched. He tried to phrase it more delicately. 'I am sorry if I startled you, though you must have guessed my feelings all these weeks. Perhaps I should have spoken about them before so that you were more prepared.'

'But I *never* knew,' she said, with indignation it seemed.

'Then I am sorry. But surely, when you are used to the idea, you might think it possible? I will not always be in Upper Burma, I am due for a better posting soon, and though India is perhaps not the place that would be one' first choice it's got its points and together we could b happy. At least I think we could, and I'd certainly do a that's in my power to make you happy.'

'No!' Margaret said almost violently. Then she tried to pull herself together. 'It was very kind of you to think of it. But it really can't be.'

'But why can't it? Is it your father?'

'My father?'

'I mean,' he blundered, 'that you are worried, that you feel you cannot leave him.'

She rushed to grasp at this straw. 'Yes, it would be difficult to leave Papa.' But to follow Edward she knew she would have gone to the Antipodes and would hardly have bothered to say goodbye.

'But could you contemplate – some time perhaps when you are easier in your mind?'

There was a long silence. Margaret remembered how in the past she had been castigated by Tiger for her pusillanimous spirit, her refusal to be frank, her instinct to make vague promises she had no intention of keeping. She braced herself to be strong. 'I am afraid that . . .' She tried to summon the words that would express absolute finality, persuade him that there was no point in saying a syllable more on the subject. 'No,' she said at last. 'No, I never could.'

'But I don't understand,' he burst out. 'On Saturday it was different. You led me to think . . .'

She stared at him in amazement. 'What did I lead you to think?' She could hardly remember that she had spoken a word to him at all.

'You spoke a lot about your feelings.'

'My feelings?'

'Oh not for me. But then I suppose . . .' He supposed, but realized that this could hardly be expressed, that a woman speaking to a man of her feelings must inevitably represent them as impersonal. 'I mean that I felt you would not speak of things so close to you unless you were a little – well, fond of me. And there was the poem,' he rushed on. 'From *In Memoriam*. But you *must* remember. I know I'll remember it forever. About how on the hills there was no place that did not have a memory – of a friend.'

She was scarlet with confusion. 'I am truly sorry if I said

anything that misled you. But I never meant anything by
that.' Indeed she had not realized she had spoken the lines
aloud.

'Then there is someone else?' he said accusingly.

She looked down at the ground. The heat had left her face
now and she felt cold; even shivered. 'No,' she said at last.
'No, there is no one else.'

Alfred went back to the Grove in such a state that even
Tiger was stirred. 'I told you how it'd be – but I'm sorry,' she
said to him as he stormed round the morning room, picking
up books and throwing them down, laying his head for a
moment against the window pane, sitting down and then
leaping to his feet again.

'But on Saturday she was so different, almost close. She
spoke about things that really mattered to her.'

'I've never heard Meg do that in my life; you must have
been dreaming.'

'I wasn't, I tell you. And today she stares at me as
if I've taken leave of my senses when I talk about it.
She says there's no one else – is she really speaking the
truth?'

'There may be someone in her mind, I suppose. She may
be still remembering her cousin. Or she may admire Edward
Benbow from a distance, though he's completely wrapped
up in his own affairs.'

He was balancing restlessly on the fender, shoulders
against the mantelpiece. Now he pushed himself away with
a clatter and came over and stood by her. 'Couldn't you go
and talk to her?'

'Me? Whatever would be the use of that?'

'Oh I don't know, you're better at words than me.
Perhaps I didn't say the right things, perhaps she didn't
understand. I mean,' he said loudly, staring over Tiger's
head out into the garden, 'she *must* like me a bit – look at all
those letters she wrote.'

'Oh writing! You just don't understand Meg. She could
write her soul away – and you were so far off. What did she
say in them?'

'Of course there was nothing personal.'

'Why do you say of course?'

'You know as well as I do that no lady could do that,' said Alfred impatiently. 'But they were so long and so full of everything that was going on here.'

'She wasn't thinking of you at all.'

'What was she thinking about then?'

'I don't know – her literary style, I dare say. I tell you, she's a cold fish, you'll never do any good there.'

'But just go and try,' he begged. 'Please. I can't bear to go back and think that I didn't do everything that was possible.'

And so on the day that Alfred left for his visit to Dublin Tiger went to call on Margaret, a thing that she had not done in years, it always having been understood that while Margaret might run in and out of the Grove as though it were her own home the Mortimers did not come to the rectory – it was a household where the young had no place. As she stood in the drawing room while Sarah went upstairs to summon Miss Talbot, Tiger supposed that the last time she had been in this room was ten years ago almost to the day, when the rector had given the dinner party to welcome his cousins to Ludwardine. A great deal had happened since then; two of those present were now dead, and the rector so nearly dead as made no difference. But the room remained exactly the same; even the position of the chairs; the ornaments on the chimney-piece had not altered by a hair's-breadth, it seemed, and the same albums were laid out on the table near the window.

When Margaret came down she knew instantly why Tiger was there, and Tiger knowing that she knew, did not bother about preliminaries.

'He begged me to come, though I told him it was no good.'

Margaret shook her head dumbly.

'Is it India, or Alfred, or what?'

'I don't know,' said Margaret helplessly.

'Oh don't be so weak, Meg. You must know why you can't marry him – you aren't such a fool as you sometimes try to seem.'

She tried. 'I am sorry if I gave him a wrong impression. It never crossed my mind that . . .'

'Meg – even from you I find that hard to believe. But putting that on one side, now that it *has* crossed your mind, why do you reject it out of hand? You surely want to marry, don't you? I mean, you're the sort that usually does. And Alfred would do very well for you. He is kind and steady and he adores you. Not to mince matters, there's hardly likely to be anybody else.'

'I want neither Alfred nor anybody else.'

'What do you want then?'

'To be left alone.' And Margaret marched out of the room.

'It is quite useless,' Tiger wrote to Alfred in Ireland a day later. 'As I knew it would be. She seems to want eternal spinsterdom – and if it was Edward Benbow she was pining for then she will get it, for his engagement has just been announced to Louise Fleming. Most of the local people think this is a beautiful match, but if you had ever met them you would realize how ludicrously ill-assorted the couple are.'

A few days later she was writing again, and this time solely on the subject of Margaret. 'Poor Meg – and the irony is that it should have happened to her, of all people, for I don't know anybody else in the world who shrinks more from oddity or untoward behaviour. Unless it was the rector himself. But it has brought her face to face with reality at last, in a way that none of us have been able to do.'

For the rector, whose mind that Sunday had been more than usually clouded, had wandered out of the vestry in the sight of all the congregation – wearing no clothes.